HE IS

OTHER

PEOPLE

STORIES

DAVID-JACK FLETCHER

OTHER TITLES BY
DAVID-JACK FLETCHER

The Haunting of Harry Peck

Raven's Creek

The Count

Copyright © 2025 by David-Jack Fletcher

ISBN-13: 978-1-59021-587-6
Cover design by TreeHouse Studio
Interior design by TreeHouse Studio
Edited by Steve Berman

For anyone who's ever been mistreated,

bullied, or made to feel less than.

Hell really is other people.

TABLE OF CONTENTS

Introduction

About the Author

Acknowledgements

INTRODUCTION

The stories in this collection were written over the last few years. Some have been revised and reworked for this most recent publication. Nevertheless, I am proud of them all. After a stint in academia lasting over a decade, which wasted what I consider my youth, my husband encouraged a return to the thing that drove me through much of my childhood.

Horror is an interesting genre—it isn't necessarily jump scares or gore, and it certainly doesn't have to be ghosts or demons. Sometimes none, sometimes all. And that's what I love about the vast abyss of everything that creates nightmares. There is no one-size-fits-all because everyone is scared of different things. More than that, horror is a space for under-represented voices and a place for the marginalised to speak back to the social, cultural, and political forces restraining them.

When I dove back into writing, I wanted to do something with my stories and use the genre to redefine and undermine the pain, frustration, and fears I had as a gay man in a small town. So, horror was the only genre I explored, and I realised that creating nightmares was perhaps the most enjoyable thing I had done for a long time.

The stories selected for this collection represent a range of nightmarish visions, and though they've been categorised into three primary horror sub-genres, they are all connected by an overarching dread of what it means to be human. And let me tell you, it's pretty fucked up. Each story grapples with the notion that, in one way or another, human beings are the monsters. They are the creatures hiding under our beds. They are the things lurking in the closet. Humans are the things we should fear the most. Hence the title of the collection is taken from a famous quote by Jean-Paul Sartre.

Here, you will find the impacts of psychological trauma, black market organ trading, cannibalism, a haunted painting, living darkness, sentient water, demons, and starving worms. Beneath it all—beneath the flesh and the gore and the blood—the stories are about love, loss, grief, insecurity, and hope.

As such, I hope you enjoy this collection.

Or at least, can't sleep afterward.

ESCAPE
TO THE
COUNTRY

Liz clawwed at the cold concrete, the sound of her fingernail snapping drowned by her screams. He'd come for her at night, just as he'd said. Everything he'd promised would happen to her was about to come true. His words rung in her head as he dragged her from her cell, down a long, dark corridor. Liz's eyes searched for an exit, for something to grab. Anything. Her skin began to tear against the concrete as her captor continued to drag her naked body towards her fate.

Liz knew it was pointless, but screamed, anyway, "Help!"

The man laughed and screamed alongside her. "Nobody can help you now, sweetheart." He laughed again.

Liz heard the creaking of an old wooden door, terrified of the darkness beyond. As her body was pulled through the doorway, she held on to the doorframe with all her might. She knew her life depended on it. His grip was tight on her legs as he pulled her away from the doorframe. Despite her best efforts, she let go and found herself thrust into a small metal box.

"No, no, please," Liz begged as the man sealed the lid.

The air was thick and Liz noticed the box had one small hole for air. She peered through it, trying to see something in the darkness. Anything.

The air hole disappeared as the man—or someone—stuffed something through. She grabbed it. *A hose?* Liz blinked, wondering what came next. Was he about to drown her? She heard the sound of gas flowing through the hose and felt it blow against her body. She banged the side of the box, begging for the gas to stop. The air in her lungs was fast filling with something toxic. Liz coughed and retched, scratched and clawed at the metal walls around her. Her body began to feel heavy, her lungs full of toxic gas. Her eyes began to close for what she hoped was not the last time.

The man waited until the girl was unconscious before turning off the gas. The way she carried on in there, anyone watching would have thought the gas was poisonous, rather than regular old sleeping gas. She had a long journey ahead—she could use the rest. Perching himself atop the metal box, the man looked at his watch and waited. They'd be here to pick her up soon, and he could finally be done with this screamer.

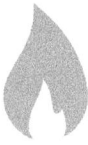

Vacant countryside stretched for miles, the different shades of green and brown blurring together as their red '67 Chevy sped along the ill-kept country road. Tony always drove with the windows down, and John sometimes found it hard to breathe. Despite asking him to slow down, Tony would just smile, wink, and accelerate.

Tony was like that and had been ever since they got

together. He enjoyed teasing everyone, not just John. In the first few months of dating, John had found it exciting and rebellious. Seven years in, though, it sometimes felt malicious. John was a timid man, very shy and not too forthcoming with his feelings. So, when Tony sped up for the fourth time, John sighed and rested his elbow along the car door, placing his chin in his hand. He closed his eyes, restless from the journey so far, and focused on the radio. Tony loved classic rock, though John was never sure of the appeal himself. So, as usual, the radio blared some nonsensical song about solid rock or some sort of watchtower or smoky water. The only song John ever knew from the playlist was *Stairway to Heaven*, even though he couldn't name the guy who sang it. He didn't much care. The song itself reminded him of better days, before what had come to be known as "that night".

Through the drums and the guitar solos, the occasional cow could be heard mooing, and John wondered if they were, in fact, lamenting their foreseeable and untimely deaths in the meat factories nearby. As they drove past another cow, brown with patches of white and a tiny bird sitting on its head, John's stomach churned. Turning round in his seat, he reached back to grab a backpack filled with snacks and refreshments. He didn't think too much about the systematic breeding and slaughtering of cows as he rifled through for food. Placing it between his feet and leaning forward, he pulled out a beef sandwich. The plastic wrapping held the sandwich tight, and juice from the tomato seeped through. It always did, which was why John always wrapped the tomato on its own. This one, well, it was Tony's handiwork.

"This place we're staying," John said over the radio. "Are you sure they're *friendly*?" He pretended to be nonchalant as he chewed through the beef. Inside, his heart was racing.

Friendly. It was one of those terms in the LGBTQI+ world that really meant, "Are they going to kill us for being gay?" Both men looked at each other with knowing glances that recognized a shared history of abuse—physical and sexual—for being gay. John had been through the worst. That night.

"Are they friendly?" Tony echoed, his tone sounding disappointed as he turned the radio down. The guitar solo in some old classic rock song faded away as Tony reached across the gear stick to grasp John's hand.

"I'm sorry, I just—"

"I checked the place out thoroughly," Tony interrupted. "Yelp, Facebook, anywhere there are reviews, okay? I promise you, they're gay-friendly." Tony smiled and tightened his grip on John's hand. "Okay?"

John nodded, reluctant. "You know what they say about country people."

"Country people?" Tony stifled a laugh and adopted a crude hillbilly accent as he continued. "May I remind you that *I'm* a country person?"

John nodded again, gave a half-smile, and looked at his partner. "You don't need to remind me. I'm reminded every time you speak to your brother."

"Do you mean my father?" Tony asked, raising an eyebrow.

"Aren't they the same person?" John's deadpan delivery was uncharacteristic, and Tony laughed as hard as John had ever seen him and wiped a tear from his eye.

"Look," Tony said, serious once more. "I wouldn't bring you out here if I didn't think it was safe. Trust me, I love you."

John looked out the window, taking in the view once more and finishing his sandwich. The words "I love you" meant little to him since "that night". It wasn't that he didn't feel it, it wasn't even that he didn't want to say it back. He just had trouble expressing himself in that way since the attack. Tony said he understood, and he'd continued to confess his love for John several times a day. He never even blinked or looked upset that he hadn't heard it said back for months.

The two continued in silence for a while, save for the rhythm of some song about living on prayers. Gina and Tommy were having a rough time, that's all John could determine from the song. The singer must have been religious if he relied on prayers to get people through financial turmoil. Tony always said John thought too much about the music—*Just feel it,* he'd say. *Feel the music.*

Unlocking his mobile phone, John saw the reception bar empty and a line through the antenna.

No reception. Great. He looked at Tony and asked, "Where is this place, anyway?"

"What's wrong, no Facebook?" Tony smiled. "We're nearly there, don't worry. I purposely wanted to take you somewhere without reception. Give you a break. Give us both time to focus more on each other."

It sounded sweet. Tony was a very thoughtful guy, even if he did spend a lot of time making fun of other people. Deep down, he was a teddy bear and it really showed in moments like this.

John put his phone into his left jeans pocket and sighed again. He hated long trips, which is why he'd never been to Europe. Thirty hours on a plane, no thanks. Even if the pictures of places like Venice and Barcelona looked incredible, he was happy visiting different places in Sydney exploring his hometown. In the safety of daylight, of course.

They'd been driving for five hours—since 6 am—without a rest. John didn't know how Tony could focus on the road for that long without a break. He drove a lot for work, mostly just an hour each way to the office, and John didn't drive at all. He never had a need for a license, growing up and living in Sydney with the local bus route pretty much outside his front door.

John was starting to feel restless, and his body was falling asleep. It must have been obvious as Tony pulled over and turned the engine off.

"What are you doing?" John furrowed his brow.

"Go on. Get out."

John stared at his boyfriend, wondering what was happening. His bottom lip started to tremble. It was perfect, really, dumping him here. He looked around and gulped, knowing they were far from home, far from anywhere, with no signal and no idea where to go to get one. His heart throbbed, and he stared at Tony, wondering if he'd had enough. Finally, enough. Enough of the heartache, enough of the crying and PTSD—he was being abandoned. Tony noticed the lip, grinned, and reached across to caress John's cheek.

"Go stretch, dickhead." The word dickhead was soft and playful. He was a bit rough around the edges and struggled to reign in the foul language. John had learned long ago to appreciate the vulgarity in Tony's demeanour.

"Oh." John breathed a sigh of relief. "I thought—"

"Why would I abandon you?" Tony leaned in and kissed John gently on the lips. "Why would you even *think* that?"

Looking away, John shrugged. "I just… I know I've been difficult since—"

Tony interrupted again. "Hey, I'm not going to leave you. I would *never* do that. Do you trust me?"

Nodding, John leaned in, wrapped his arms around Tony's body, and just hugged him. "I do, I'm sorry."

They both got out of the car, conscious that the side of a country road was perhaps a dangerous place to stretch one's legs. Although, they hadn't passed a car for a few hours. They'd parked overlooking a valley, a giant expanse of trees and mountains, and John spotted a tiny shack somewhere amidst all that nature, smoke rising from a chimney.

"Must be nice, curling up in front of a fire." Tony stood next to John and pulled him in close. The two men stared into the valley, silent, appreciating the absence of people on their phones, traffic, and planes overhead.

"It's going to be a nice weekend," John said. "Fire or no fire."

After a few more minutes of walking and stretching, they returned to the car and continued on their way.

The B&B was larger than the photos. John had expected some sort of log cabin with one room and a front desk situated away from the guest houses. That was not the case. From the outside, it was a large two-storey house made of a mixture of brick and stone, with a large chimney and a small front porch. The Australian flag hung from the portico and flapped in the breeze as the men drove up the gravel driveway towards the house.

A front garden filled with roses, daisies, and garden gnomes added a sense of family to the house. It felt like a nice place to stay, like Mum and Dad would greet you inside with a cup of tea and some homemade biscuits. It was hard to think of the place as a house, and John searched for a more appropriate word.

It was more like a mansion. John counted the windows on both levels, trying to peer through the white curtains, gently moving in harmonic rhythm with the wind.

"How is this possible?" John asked, walking around the car towards Tony, whose own eyes were grappling with the monstrosity before them.

"What do you mean?" Tony wondered, without taking his eyes off the B&B.

"This place, in the middle of nowhere," John said in awe. "Who would build this?"

Tony shrugged, mumbling about old money and lots of larger places around these parts. John accepted that, having remembered seeing a few larger homes situated among the dry, brown farms they'd passed on the way up.

Just as the men started to grab their luggage from the trunk, an older woman emerged from the mansion, her eyes like intense headlights as she beamed at them. Yellowed and veiny.

"Hello!" she called, waving as she descended the porch. "Tony and John, I presume?"

Tony dropped his bag onto the gravel and held out a hand to the old woman. "Tony, " he said, nodding towards John, as he introduced them as partners.

The old woman—Jane, she said—shook their hands without missing a beat. John was surprised at the complete lack of homophobia. He had convinced himself over the years that non-city dwellers were all close-minded bigots. Hell, even city folk were known to be bigoted every now and then. Now that he was confronted with this old woman, smiling and greeting them with open arms, John started to wonder why he had imagined country people that way at all.

"My husband is inside," Jane told them. "But leave your things, please. The least we can do is escort you to your room."

Jane must have been in her seventies, complete with thin, wiry hair and wrinkles that housed wrinkles of their own. Her eye bags could have carried their own luggage. She wore classic cowboy boots and a faded plaid shirt. As John shook her hand, cold and fragile, he felt her paper-thin, soft skin. He could tell she was on blood-thinning medication, the same as his own mother had been. Even so, her grip was strong and caught him off balance. Her eyes, John thought, held secrets. Maybe dangerous ones. He shook it off and took a deep breath, reminding himself that not everyone he would meet would be an enemy.

A man, thick, burly, and rugged with an unkept, faded strawberry beard, appeared in the shadow of the B&B's front door. He, too, smiled wide, displaying missing teeth.

Maybe they really like meeting people. Maybe that's why they got into the B&B business.

John supposed that there was no sense in opening your house to strangers if you didn't like meeting new people. The man walked towards them, arm outstretched a little too soon, and introduced himself as Graham. Gray, for short.

"Nice to meet you." Tony smiled back, again reaching for his bag. It was warming up outside, and Tony was sure these introductions could be done in the comfort of the home.

Jane ushered the men in, again telling them to leave their things. Gray was going to arrange their bags in their room. John kept the backpack with his food and some other items but left the big stuff for Gray. First, Jane just *had* to give them the tour. John was curious, he admitted, as he hadn't quite seen a house this large before. Not without calling it a mansion. Or a castle. The centre of the building was two stories, fading into a single storey on either side as the house expanded, like wings on a brick bird. Majestic. Jane smirked at that comment and put an arm around his waist.

"I like you already," she said.

John looked over at Tony, who just shrugged and gave a quick wink. Affection and John didn't quite go hand in hand, so the love of a strange old woman wasn't sitting well with him. To keep from being rude, he let the old lady continue as she was, ushering them through the house with her arm around his waist.

Each room was as impressive as the next. The main living area was warm and inviting, and the walls were made of thick, light brown, exposed rock. The space housed a fireplace, already lit with an orange glow, though no warmth was emitted. John rolled his eyes at the deer head hanging above the fireplace, antlers jutting into the room like knives. He had to admit, the aesthetics were nice. His sense of morality was at odds with his taste, though.

Jane was talking about original features and pointing things out with calm enthusiasm when John zoned out. This place was a little *too* nice. Tony didn't have the kind of money this place would cost. Not the money and certainly not the care factor. The last few months had been awful for their relationship ever since that night. They hadn't shared so much as a passionate kiss, let alone had sex. Yet here they were, being treated to a weekend away in some clandestine mansion with Jane and Gray.

"This is where you'll be sleeping." Jane pulled John back to the present as she opened the door to their room.

"Wow." Tony exhaled, taking a slow step inside. He looked around in awe at the expansive room. In the centre, a four-poster bed surrounded by luxurious, soft white carpet, and a bearskin rug. Another fireplace on the far wall and an ensuite with one of those freestanding bathtubs. It was such a perfect mix of classic and modern that John, too, felt overwhelmed.

"We certainly are royalty now, aren't we?" John quipped and lay on the bed, stretching his arms like a snow angel.

Tony climbed next to him and cuddled into the space left between John's body and arm.

Jane raised an eyebrow at this—only for a moment—and smiled again. "Make yourselves at home, boys."

Tony realized how exhausted he must be. "Thank you so much."

Standing in the doorway, Jane cleared her throat and announced that Gray would soon be up with their bags. They were welcomed to place their dinner order in the next hour or so for a 7 pm serving time. The menu cards and Wi-Fi password were in the top drawer of the bedside table. The way she spoke was now cold and more formal, almost as if she had been reading a script.

"Thank you," John said and then paused. "Can I ask… are there any other guests here?"

Jane's lips twisted into a smile, but it didn't fill her eyes. "We had a guest check out last night, actually. Lovely little thing." Jane left the room without saying anything else and closed the door behind her.

"Let's see about this Wi-Fi John mumbled, moving away from Tony, who yawned and rolled his eyes. As Jane had promised, the password was hand-written on a folded piece of paper in the top drawer. John reached into his pocket for his phone.

"Hmm," he said, confused when his phone was not in its usual place in his front pocket. Trying the other pocket, John looked at Tony. "Do you know where my phone is?"

Tony shrugged.

"Well, can I use yours? I want to check my email real quick."

Shaking his head with disappointment and letting out a deep sigh, Tony reached for his. Furrowing his brow, he realised his pocket was empty, too. "Maybe it's in my bag." He didn't seem bothered about the missing phones, not that John was surprised.

Tony was odd when it came to technology. He didn't like social media, he didn't even have a Twitter account, and the last time he was tagged in a photo on Instagram was a few years earlier at a New Year's Eve party somewhere along Sydney harbour. The only thing Tony used his phone for was making calls. He didn't even have his email set up. In contrast, John had it all. Facebook, Twitter, Instagram, LinkedIn, BlueSky, Slasher, all of them. He had several messaging apps and took photos daily, saving them all to the cloud. He was Apple's wet dream.

John was just about to head to the door, to trace his steps. Maybe he'd dropped his phone somewhere. Jane or Gray might have found it, even. As he stood to leave the room, Tony grabbed his arm.

"Please," he said, his voice low and soft. "Forget the phone for a minute."

"But…" John started.

Tony pulled him close, until the air between them was thick and hot. "Can't we just…" Tony paused. "Can't we just *be* together for a minute?"

As Jane walked down the hallway, leaving the new guests to fornicate all over the fresh sheets, she tried not to imagine their naked bodies intertwined. The thought disgusted her. It should be man and woman, not man and man. And *certainly* not woman and woman. She shuddered.

For the life of her, she couldn't even think what two women would do together. Before heading down a dark and disturbing abyss, Jane fumbled around in her pocket and pulled out a mobile phone. Clutching it to her chest, Jane smiled, thankful for small mercies. It had been a while since Jane and Gray had so many guests, and their employer was getting impatient.

By now, Gray would have dismantled Tony's car and stored it in the shed with the rest. Any personal belongings would be sorted later for the auction. Now, she needed to figure out where the boys belonged. That Tony, he was handsome. He could do well in the sex trade, though he also came across as quite feisty. The other one, the small one, what was his name? Johnny? He wouldn't survive there—he was too weak. Slap him around, and he'd crumble to pieces on the floor. No, organ harvesting. That's where he belonged. Jane licked her lips as she thought about the money they'd get from that man's kidneys. His bleeding heart was sure to get her and Gray a big fat cheque. It was just a matter of how to take it.

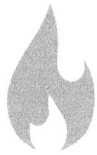

Tony had mentioned a local swimming spot at the rear of the property, so the two men undressed in silence and changed into their board shorts. John hoped it wasn't deep, as he wasn't a strong swimmer. He was the sort that liked to dip his feet at the side of the pool and catch some sun. Tony placed a cigarette and his lighter in his shorts pocket, declaring he was ready to go. Navigating their way out of the house wasn't too difficult. John just followed Tony, who'd somehow mapped the whole place in their short, guided tour. Just as they reached the front door, Gray blocked their exit, shrouding both men in shadow. He seemed twenty years younger than Jane, but John didn't wish to judge. They'd welcomed both men into their establishment, even with the evident homosexuality.

"Judging by your outfits,"—Gray's voice was gruff, and he looked Tony up and down—"you boys are headed for the water hole."

Water hole. John frowned at the phrase, figuring it was part of the local lingo. "Uh, yeah, heading out for a quick dip."

Gray nodded, licking his lips as he took in their nude torsos. His eyes were wide with excitement, though the rest of his face remained neutral, shaded by his Akubra. Tony and John both put their arms around their torsos, using their towels to cover their bodies. It was obvious to both men that Gray was interested in something. Maybe he was on their team, with little choice out here. Being so vulnerable in front of such a big man made John uncomfortable.

Tony cleared his throat, drawing Gray's attention. "If it's

okay," he said firmly, "my boyfriend and I would like to spend some time alone together."

Gray grinned, stepped aside, and ushered them outside. The burly man tipped his hat and whispered, "See you soon, gentlemen."

As Tony and John headed towards the rear of the property, the river came into clear view. It wasn't spectacular or even impressive—at least, not compared to the cathedral of a B&B that stood behind them. The river had no current and did not ebb and flow, yet the water was a cool blue and looked inviting enough. John tried to judge the depth and was satisfied it was shoulder deep, maybe less. Perfect.

Unlike the beaches in Sydney, the river didn't have a shoreline or somewhere to sunbathe. It was surrounded on both sides by dry grass, thistles, and dying or dead tree branches.

Odd. There were no trees by the river. *Where did they come from?*

So far, John was finding it hard to get into the spirit of the weekend. The weekend consisted of a large house, a boring river, and Wi-Fi without any phones. He looked around the property to see what else might be around. Like most country properties, there was a shed with three slide-down garage doors. John imagined it housed a tractor and other farming equipment and decided it wasn't worth exploring.

The river it was, then. He didn't want to seem ungrateful to Tony, but taking him out of the city, his natural habitat? Bringing him here, where there was nothing to do, nothing to see, and no Wi-Fi, just seemed like a strange joke. Still, Tony must have had something planned, so John spread out his towel along what he was calling the riverbank.

He stretched out on his towel, rubbing in some tanning

oil and gazing into the vast emptiness surrounding them. He liked it, felt safe. Felt he could see any dangers coming. Relaxing a little, he watched Tony dip into the water, his head disappearing with a few small bubbles as his breath left his lungs. Popping back up, Tony flicked his hair back before tracing his fingers across the wet mess, pushing it off his face.

"Come in," he said, "it's so beautiful."

He had a choice: refuse and cause more annoyance, risk disrupting their weekend, or do as asked. Conscious that he was often saying no to Tony, John relented with a smile and descended into the water.

Tony waded over, arms extended in a hugging position, and John moved closer so that Tony could embrace him. Tony's body was warm against him, arms wrapped tight around him, and John felt his shoulders relax for the first time in months. Tony's grip softened a little, and John felt his hand move towards his neck.

"You okay?" Tony asked.

John nodded, sheepish.

"Just relax."

His hand crawled further still, and Tony gripped John's hair. At first, it felt like his passion was getting the better of him, and John leaned in for an expectant kiss. But the grip tightened, and Tony—rough, strong, forceful—shoved his head beneath the water.

John fought as hard as he could to escape Tony's grip. He was too strong. Flailing his arms about, thrashing at the water, John struggled for air. He turned his attention to Tony and, curling his hand into a fist, punched his boyfriend in the side again and again. His lungs were almost empty as Tony's grip loosened, and John kicked to the surface, gasping for air, taking oxygen like an addict.

With what lung capacity he had gained, John cried as loud as he could. Bellowing into the sky for help, he somehow knew it wasn't coming. Tony lunged at him, ploughing a fist into the side of his face and cupping the other hand over John's mouth.

"Shut the fuck up," Tony growled through gritted teeth.

Again, Tony pushed John under the water's surface. He kneed the man in the groin, punched his face, and held his body weight over John as he thrashed and fought. His lungs burned, death within his grasp as his eyes struggled to stay open.

A flash of that night. The blood. The sneering laughter. The taste of concrete as his head was pushed into the ground. He couldn't breathe then, either. Could only let it happen.

His body started to convulse, the burn in his lungs now so intense he thought his chest would burst.

And then, black.

Across the property, Gray peered through his binoculars, watching the young man drown, and gave a heavy sigh. Regardless of how fun the unfolding events might have been, he and Jane needed both of them alive. The harvesters weren't ready, and they needed the organs to be as fresh as possible. Shaking his head, he started towards the river, adopting his best worried expression, and broke into a run.

Pulling John out of the river, Gray thrust his body onto the riverbank with a thud. Kneeling beside him, he pressed hard on John's chest, performing CPR. He and Jane had been trained some time ago in cases of incident or injury, though he hadn't carried out this particular task for quite a while. John lay motionless beneath Gray while Tony kneeled on the other side, begging for John's life.

"Please…. God, it was an accident," and some other such things were blubbered through the man's tears.

Gray had to hand it to him, and Tony might have been made of stuff similar to that of his wife and him. He'd have to be mindful of that later.

Gasping, John coughed up water, and Gray moved the young man onto his side. "Take it easy, fella," he said in the calmest, most nurturing tone he could fabricate. "You're going to be okay."

John tried to speak, but the sounds came as muffled chokes. Gray watched Tony's eyes grow wide at the prospect of John pointing the blame his way. He concealed a smile and jumped in before John could say anything.

"You had an accident. Tony saved your life." Gray looked up at Tony, who exhaled with an intensity Gray recognised all too well.

John shook his head as hard as he could, though to Gray and Tony, it was imperceptible. Gray silenced the man by shifting him into a seated position and pushing John's head into his chest. "We should have warned you—it gets slippery out here. I've got you now, son," he said. "Let's get you back to the house."

"We can call an ambulance," Tony added.

Gray stood up, lifting John and carrying him in both arms. "Ain't no need for that. The missus and I can look after him."

Gray and Tony continued in silence towards the property, John lying limp and semi-conscious in Gray's arms. The burly man walked on as if he was carrying nothing at all, and Tony was both impressed and weary.

In John's semi-lucid state, his fear of what Tony had done to him and his fear of the attack several months earlier converged. Despite his best efforts, John recreated the night in question.

He'd been tormented by a group of straight men on his way home from a nightclub a few months before. Despite insisting on their heterosexuality, all four men held John down, tore his clothes from him, and raped him, one by one. John had screamed into the Sydney night air, his cries for help echoing off the cold concrete walls of the alleyway and disappearing.

He'd been found the following afternoon, unconscious and naked, with dried blood and semen across his face, arms, legs, and ass. Most of the blood had come from his torn arsehole, and he had also suffered a concussion from being repeatedly punched in the head as the men raped him. All the testing came back negative for HIV, STDs, and AIDS. The nurse had smiled at him and said how lucky he was. What a fucking joke.

For months, John had felt phantom pain where they'd plunged themselves inside him. He would dream of their faces and the absolute helplessness he had felt as they tormented him with taunts of "faggot", "filthy homo," and other slurs.

For months, John had leaned on Tony for support, comfort, and love. Only to be attacked again. This time, it was from the man who told him daily how much he loved him. It was attempted murder.

He began to stir. He felt intense cold as if he were outside on a snowy mountain. The feeling seeped back to his fingers and toes, making the pain even worse. John sat up, opened his eyes, held his head, and looked around.

"What the fuck?" was all he could say when he looked down at the bathtub full of ice.

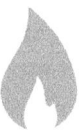

Tony watched as Gray kicked open a door on the second floor of the B&B. He craned his neck to see past the thick, middle-aged man. Tiled walls and floor—a bathroom. As Gray entered the space, Tony saw it contained two metal tables in the centre. Three bathtubs lined one of the walls, and several fridge-freezers lined the other, humming and whirring. Large bathroom cabinets filled the other wall, and a small gap for a window was the only source of natural light.

Before he could ask what in the hell kind of bathroom this was, Gray lowered John into a bathtub and turned on the tap. Tony took a step forward, inching past the doorframe, to watch Gray take bags of ice from a freezer and fill the tub, searching one of the cabinets for something. Pulling out a needle and a small bottle, Gray turned to Tony.

As Tony turned to leave, Jane appeared behind him with a metal rod and jabbed him in the back. A powerful wave of electricity rippled through his body, and Tony fell to his knees. Looking up at Jane, the old lady who had been so welcoming only hours before struck him again with the metal stick.

A cattle prod, Tony thought, as his body gave way to the tiled floor beneath him.

"Keep that one cold and unconscious for now," Tony heard Jane say. Then, leaning over him, she added, "This one is headed to the auction. We have a few hours to get him ready."

Gray mumbled something, and Tony heard the water stop pouring into the tub. Footsteps came closer, and Tony saw Gray's strawberry-grey beard fill his vision. Without a word, the burly man grabbed Tony's arms and dragged him. The electricity had disrupted some of the signals in his body—he was disoriented, couldn't speak, and found it hard to use his muscles.

Jane made small talk as they travelled through the house, Tony's head bumping against each step as they descended to the first floor. He tried to lift his head to avoid the next smack, finding it impossible.

"How much do you think we'll get for him?" Jane asked, looking back at Tony.

Gray grumbled. "He's feisty, which is good. Some of the more hardcore buyers will pay extra for a scratch or two."

Jane nodded and clapped her hands in excitement.

"What…" Tony started to form a sentence and then smacked his head at the next step.

"Give him another one, darlin'," Gray said, and Jane gave Tony another zap with the cattle prod.

The next thing Tony saw was the grey concrete walls of a cell. Metal bars and a heavy chain around his ankle separated him from freedom. Tony pried at the chain, though he knew it was no good. Jane and Gray had said something about an auction; what did that mean?

He moved to the bars at the front of the cell and peered left and right. Cells lined both sides of his immediate vision, though he couldn't see anyone else.

What are these two doing out here? Tony wondered. *What auction?*

Tony remembered something else Jane had said. *We have a*

few hours to get him ready. That meant they were coming back for him at some point. He didn't know for how long he'd been unconscious but hoped it was only minutes. Hoped he had a few hours to find a way out of this dungeon before Jane and Gray came back for him.

Looking around the cell, Tony was disheartened that he could not use anything as a weapon. The chain was deadbolted into the wall; it wouldn't budge even if he tried. He'd need a jackhammer to get free.

Checking his pockets, he was surprised Jane and Gray hadn't searched him—his lighter was still in there. Not that a lighter was his key to freedom. It was something, though. He kept searching, knowing he'd taken nothing to the river but the lighter and one cigarette soaked from the water.

"Great," Tony whispered, exasperated. This had not been his plan for the weekend. All he'd wanted was to rid himself of John once and for all—the needy, ungrateful little prick. Now these country hillbillies had come straight from a B-grade horror movie to fuck it all up. At least if they were harvesting John's organs, as it appeared, the guy was done for. That was one thing working in his favour.

Taking a breath, Tony studied each inch of the cell again. Moving to the bars again, he examined the lock on the door. It looked new. He might have been able to pick it up if he'd had some equipment. All he had was a pair of shorts, a dead cigarette, and a shitty lighter, and he wasn't MacGyver. No quick wit and incomprehensible science was going to save him.

"Fuck you, MacGyver," he muttered and slapped at the metal bars.

His only option was to wait for Jane or Gray to return and unshackle him. For the auction. Throwing the lighter to the ground, Tony sat down, holding the chain in his hands, and cursing John for not dying in Sydney all those months earlier.

John noticed a catheter in his arm, attached to a bag of... something. It was empty now; he guessed it had been dripping through the plastic cord into his veins. He ripped the catheter out and threw it to the floor. John had seen enough true crime documentaries to know the intention here was to steal his organs, so he felt around his abdomen to make sure there were no stitches or evidence of tampering with his kidneys.

His skin remained uncut for now.

He crept out of the bathtub, trying to push aside the remnants of his vivid nightmare and the very real fact that Tony had tried to murder him. It occurred to him that Tony had not brought him here to this bathroom. That had been Gray. He had a vague memory of the older man looking down at him after saving his life.

Did he save me so he could harvest my organs?

As John climbed to the floor, hands and feet slipping against the tub and the tiles, he saw the bathroom in its entirety for the first time. It looked more like a coroner's office, with the cold metallic table and fridge-freezers lining the walls. Looking towards the door and realising he was naked, John went to one of the fridges, not sure what he was looking for. His shorts wouldn't be in there, though there might be something else he could use. He'd been drugged, so there was a good chance he could find something to use against Gray.

All the small bottles in the fridge were labelled—*Thank*

god!—and several syringes were in a nearby drawer. However, John didn't know what any of the labels meant. Rushing back to the tub, he read the label on the drip swimming into his veins.

Propofol.

The word meant nothing to John, but with the fact that it had been used to keep him unconscious, he assumed it was a sleeping agent. He filled as many syringes as he could and then realised he had nothing to keep them in. He was still naked. His body trembled at the cold, and he tried to shake it off. There were more important things to worry about right now.

Rushing to the cabinets on the other side of the room, John searched every drawer, hoping against hope that he'd find some kind of weapon. All he found was bandages, sewing scissors, tape, and surgical tools. A scalpel lay among them.

John grabbed it, gripping it tight, feeling somehow safe with it clasped between his fingers. He was about to leave the room when he saw the surgical tape again. Grabbing it, he taped the six syringes together in a sort of thick makeshift knife and made a stabbing motion to practice. If Gray or Jane came for him, he'd be ready now. And Tony, for that matter.

In the meantime, he needed to get to a phone. Tony had said his phone was in his bag, so he'd have to find his way back to their room and get it. He peered around the doorframe into an empty corridor. John didn't remember this part of the house from the tour, though that didn't mean much. He was hopeless with directions, a quality he was kicking himself for now.

Creeping down the hallway, breaths short and sharp, heart hammering in his chest, John saw a staircase up ahead, and something in his mind flashed. A memory. Tony had commented on the grandiose winding staircase only a few hours earlier. When they'd all felt so safe. When Jane had her hand around his waist—*That's how she got my phone!*

The bedroom had been on the first floor, that much he did remember. Sneaking down the stairs, John's eyes were wide, his heart racing. His grip tightened around the scalpel and the syringe stack he'd fashioned earlier.

As he crept down the stairs, he heard a noise. Voices. Hushed whispers. Had they seen him? Were they planning an attack?

John stopped. Listened.

"…check on the other one," he heard someone say. Gruff, deep.

Gray. Check on who? Me? Where's Tony?

Standing halfway down the staircase, John didn't have anywhere to go. Run back upstairs and he'd probably be heard. Head downstairs, and he'd be seen. All he knew was that the phone was down there, somewhere. And he needed it.

He took another step towards the first floor.

"Going somewhere, son?" A voice from behind him. From the second floor.

John looked towards the voice. Gray stood at the top of the stairs, shotgun in hand, smile on his face. Without thinking, John turned and ran down the stairs, his surroundings blurring around him. Jane appeared at the bottom of the stairs, a handgun pointed at his head. John slammed against her, swiping the scalpel at her face, and pushed her out of the way. The older woman fell to the side. John ran, his heart pounding in his ears.

He heard heavy footsteps behind him, Gray was fast and coming up close. John saw an open door to the left, jumped through, and swung the door behind him. It slowed Gray down, not by much. John found himself in a bedroom, but not the one he needed.

Fuck!

Searching for an exit, he saw a window on the far side of the room. Hurling himself towards it, he jumped, smashing the glass against his naked body. He could smell the blood, could feel the glass tearing at his skin. He didn't stop; he'd suffered worse than that. He landed on a dry patch of grass outside. John got to his feet as Gray jumped out of the window behind him, his boots crunching against the small pieces of glass.

John scanned the area for somewhere to hide. Or some way to escape. The car, where was Tony's car? He saw the garage; one of the sliding doors was mid-way up. That was it, his only option in a sea of dying paddocks and endless hills. Heading for the garage, John heard Gray's boots approaching from behind.

Reaching the garage, John slid underneath the open door, grazing the skin on his bare ass and upper thigh. Ignoring the pain, he turned to see Gray running towards the door. John threw the door down with all of his might and reached for the latch on the interior, locking himself inside.

Gray struggled with the door for a moment before realising it was locked. Banging against the steel, he yelled, "You're trapped now, son. You've got nowhere to go."

John stepped back and checked the other two doors, ensuring the lock mechanisms were in place. In the dim, cold garage, he stood in the fading light, and the pain in his ass and feet began to throb. His eyes strained through the light, searching for something to cover his body. A pair of boots sat by the door. He threw them on, testing their fit. They would do. They had to.

The garage mostly housed remnants of old cars. Car doors

were stacked in one corner, an old engine of some kind hung on the wall. The car in the centre of the garage didn't look old at all. John approached the machine, recognising the red exterior and the leather seats.

Tony's car. The whole thing was a set up.

Gray, or maybe someone else—maybe a third person he'd not seen—had begun deconstructing the car. A door was missing, and the tires had been stripped and stacked against one of the walls. If the engine was still intact, he could put the wheels back on and get out of there. He popped the hood and saw the engine still in place, though other parts were missing. John was no mechanic—there was no way he could put it back together and drive out of here.

Our luggage.

Opening the boot, he saw their luggage still sitting there untouched. He thanked a god he didn't believe in and threw on jeans and a T-shirt. The fabric against his skin was comforting, and somehow, it made him feel like he had a chance of surviving.

Still equipped with the hand-fashioned needle knife and scalpel, John wondered if there was anything else he could defend himself with. Emptying the clothes from one of the luggage bags, he filled it instead with a crowbar, a wrench, some screwdrivers and other items from a mechanics tool kit.

His main concern was on the other side of that garage door, though, and he knew Gray would find a way inside sooner rather than later. Even if it meant shooting the door down. He had to find a way out, to get help somehow. Clutching his bag of assorted weapons, John scanned the garage. He couldn't help but think of old horror movies, the ones where the final girl walks through the killer's maze, discovering all the bodies of her friends—except John wasn't a final girl, this wasn't a horror movie, and he didn't have any friends. Not even Tony. Not after what he'd done.

Pushing the fear deep down in his gut, John treads through the garage, eyes wide, searching. He scuffed his boots on clumps of muddy hay and dried horse shit stuck to the concrete garage floor.

Tony's car wasn't the only one in the garage. The garage was more like an abandoned factory of old car parts, riddled with the stench of rusted metal. As John stepped through, he noticed the glint of a piece of old jewellery. A faded silver locket with a long strand of thin metal attached. He picked up the tattered necklace and opened the locket to reveal a photo. It was hard to distinguish the individual captured within; the image was yellowed and torn, as though it had been removed and replaced a few times. John guessed a young woman, around twenty-five, smiled at him from the damaged photo. Her chestnut hair flowed, captured during a heavy wind. She was happy, he could tell. Next to her was a man of similar age, his arm caressing her shoulder. He was gazing at her through the wind. John could almost hear echoes of their laughter as he stared into the image. He wondered if someone out there was still looking for the couple. Hoped he wouldn't turn into a cold case, too.

Placing the locket around his neck, John took a deep breath and continued searching the garage. Walking past a gutted and rusted '76 Dodge, John wondered how long Jane and Gray had been abducting people.

How could they get away with this for....

Before his thought was fully formed, John slipped on a fresh clump of hay, banging his elbows on something that felt much harder than concrete. Holding back a groan—afraid Gray was on the other side of the door, listening—he let the pain envelop him and breathed through the spikes of hurt throbbing through him. He couldn't let Gray, or anyone else, hear him.

Rubbing his elbows, John sat up and looked at what he'd crashed into. A metal door set in the floor. Wiping away the hay and the dirt, John exposed the door, noting the heavy lock. Unlike the rest of the garage, the metal had a shine to it. New. Or, at least, not old.

He reached into his bag of tricks for the crowbar and pried as hard as he could at the lock. All that budged was a muscle in John's back that he didn't know he had. In frustration, he hammered the crowbar against the lock again and again, screaming and yelling until the metal snapped under his rage.

Fastening his bag around his neck and shoulder, John eyed the door. Lifting the heavy metal, all he could see was a ladder disappearing into the deepest, darkest black hole he had ever seen.

Gray felt the door slam in his face and heard the sliding of metal against metal as the boy locked him outside. He slammed balled fists against the door, knowing his screams to be let in were no good. They had well and truly lost control of this situation, and Gray cussed as he imagined what his employer's reaction would be. The auction was tonight and they hadn't delivered on their end of the bargain.

Even if they captured John, they'd still be short for the auction. He could only hope the others had been more successful than he and Jane had been. Stopping to breathe for a moment, Gray invoked the calming techniques of his favourite YouTube meditation specialist. Her advice—*Listen to your body, take control of your breathing, be at one with the world around you*—flowed through him. He felt the rage dwindling and the chaos around him seeping into the background.

Gray went back to the house, where Jane sat at the kitchen dining table with a pot of tea in hand. He stared at her momentarily, his body tense as he tried to continue his meditation.

Breathe. Breathe.

The pot of tea was fresh, the steam jetting from the spout. *She's sitting around making tea. What the fuck—* He slowed his breathing. Steady. *One, two, three.*

"More of your silly meditation?" Jane asked, pouring herself a cup of camomile. "How's that working out for you?"

"How can you drink tea right now?" Gray yelled at her before he could think to stop himself. Slamming his fist against the timber table, he sat down and breathed hard through his nose.

"He's locked himself in, hasn't he?" Jane said between sips, the steam nestling among her crow's feet and the wrinkles on her face. Gray curled a lip and looked away as Jane continued. "He's going to find the cellar and save his… *boyfriend*." She choked on the word.

Gray smirked at her homophobia. *If only she knew.* "The boyfriend tried to kill him at the water hole," he said and poured himself a cup of tea. The scent of camomile was working its magic, and a wave of calm swept over him. *We'll get it sorted. There's nowhere for the guy to go.*

As he lifted a teacup to his lips, Jane slapped the back of his hand. Her eyes pierced him like wooden stakes. "You don't get a *fucking* drink," she spat as Gray's teacup spilled to the table. "Clean up your mess!"

Rubbing his hand, Gray shot back with a fast smack across the old woman's face. Most women might recoil or run away, but Jane was a country gal—bred tough and not one for taking shit. Before Gray's hand had left her cheek, Jane threw the hot tea on her husband's face and watched with delight as he tore at the burning skin.

"Bitch!" he cried. *One, two... Fuck this!*

"You're lucky I don't rat you out for this mess," Jane said quietly, holding her own cheek. Between them, their faces were red and hot, and neither of them was sure the tea wouldn't scar Gray's ageing face.

Without another word, Gray stood up, a plan in motion. Leaving his wife in the kitchen to think about their encounter, he headed towards the front door. He cursed Jane for throwing hot tea over his face, and then smiled at the memory. She was one impressive lady.

God, I love that woman, he thought as he headed for the garden shed. It lay just beyond the garage, out of sight from visitors, and always locked. He didn't want anyone else getting their hands on his chainsaw.

Darkness surrounded every inch of his body as he climbed down the ladder. As his feet touched the dirt landing, John spun around. Up ahead, a dim light, strung to the walls like in an old mineshaft, revealed a narrow tunnel. Knowing it was the only path, John held his breath and stepped forward.

The lights were strewn on the walls every three feet, giving just enough glow for his eyes to make out a structure ahead. Approaching it, John saw makeshift cells. The tunnel had been dug out to make individual cells, and the walls were lined with metal, the bars on the cages thick and round. There were six in total, stretching into the darkness beyond his vision.

The first cell was empty. John peered through the bars, noting chains bolted to the rear wall. The cell floor was also enforced with metal. These were designed so nobody would ever escape. The second cell was also empty, though it looked like someone had relieved themselves in one of the corners not too long ago; a brown muck spattered across the walls and the floor. As John eyed the scene, the smell of faeces rose to his nostrils, and his stomach lurched. He choked back the compulsion to vomit, managing to gag instead.

"Hello?" a low voice called.

Startled, John froze. He searched the dim passage behind him, though he knew neither Gray nor Jane would have announced themselves.

"Is someone there?" A whisper.

John approached the voice, letting out a small gasp upon seeing Tony chained to the wall by his ankle. He rested against the wall, legs drawn to his chest, terrified eyes peering over his knees.

"John, is that you?" His voice was weak from fear.

John took hold of the bars. "It's me."

"You've got to get me out of here." Tony crawled towards the door.

John took a step back, shaking his head. "I know what you did." His whisper was pained and low, yet seemed to reverberate off the cell walls.

Tony shook his head, begging. "No, no, please, you don't understand."

"You tried to drown me, you fucking psycho! I should leave you here to rot!" John's voice scratched as he yelled, holding back tears.

Tears escaped Tony's eyes, leaving trails in the dirt on his cheeks. He stood up, reaching through the bars for John. "Please, don't leave me here."

"Give me a reason." John shrugged and turned away, heading past Tony's cell into the darkness. The tunnel had to go somewhere.

"You're not me," Tony called after him.

John stopped.

"I did try to kill you," Tony said. "But *you're* not a killer. *You're* not me. If you let me out of here, we can escape together."

His voice carried a desperation John had never heard before. Not even from himself on the night of his attack. He walked back to Tony's cell, looking him over. In the bleakness of the moment, Tony seemed small. His shoulders hunched, tears streaming down his face, ankles shackled.

He wasn't a man in this moment. He was nothing. "Once we get out of here you can turn me in," Tony pleaded. His words almost unintelligible sobs.

"Why did you do it?" John asked. "Why do you want to kill me?"

Tony lifted his head, meeting John's gaze. "Please." Was all he could muster.

Every fibre of John's body screamed at him to walk away, to leave his would-be murderer for dead. But every inch of his conscience told him to save the man who, up until a few hours earlier, he'd been in love with.

Tony was right. John wasn't like him. He wasn't a killer. If he left Tony there, he'd be culpable. Deep down he also knew he wasn't a hero. He wasn't a survivor. If they were going to get out of this, he'd need help. Even if Tony was that help.

"If you try anything, I will kill you," John said, and reached for the crowbar.

The cell door wasn't as strong as the fresh lock he'd hammered through earlier. It was old and a little rusty, and the metal buckled with a lot of strength and pressure. As Tony proclaimed his gratitude and everlasting thanks for his release, John focused on opening the door.

It creaked as it swung on rusted hinges. Tony pointed to his shackles, whispering, "Hurry up", and "We have to get out of here" in panicked tones. John went to work on loosening the captive ankle.

The garage door came open with a spare key. Jane had thrown it at the man as he'd walked off to get his chainsaw, intent on tearing through the door himself.

"Fool," she'd spat and watched the key bounce off his back fat to land in the grass.

She'd watched him scrabble through the grass, looking for the small bit of metal, muttering. He kept one eye on her, his face still burning from the tea, his lips still shaped in a crooked smile.

"Thank you, darling," he'd said to her and tipped his hat.

Their love was that rare sort, where they could violate each other in any way they saw fit, but at the end of the day, they would curl up in bed together and laugh. And kiss. And fuck. Until six months earlier, that was when he'd started thinking for himself a bit more. When he'd first seen the website, holding his breath in case Jane was around. When he'd first slipped his hand down his pants, thinking those shameful thoughts, and watched two naked men touching each other.

He thought about the video—and all the others like it—as he unlocked the garage door and rolled it to the sky. Thought about how when he was young, he'd met a classmate by the river a few times. How they'd laid under the stars, talking about their futures, maybe even a future together.

Enough of that. Gray concentrated on the task at hand, swallowing his guilt, and reminding himself that Jane was the one who'd saved him from that life.

Save from the stripped cars, the garage was empty. No humans. No naked man running around, searching for safety. Disappointed, Gray hoisted the chainsaw with both hands, and got it ready, in case John popped his head up somewhere.

In the silence of the garage, his ears were attuned to any nearby sounds—the mice in the field outside, rats scurrying in the corners of the structure, a bird cawing somewhere above. No heavy breathing, no whispered voices.

He must have gone under.

Making his way to the cellar door, Gray was just about to heave it open when he heard the faint noises of movement. Hands and feet tapping against the ladder just on the other side of the door. Stepping back into the shadows, Gray waited, smirked as the heavy cellar door flung open.

John spilled out into the garage, clutching at clumps of hay and mud as he pulled himself into the room. Another hand followed him, and Gray gave a surprised "Hmph" as Tony came up from below.

As the couple shut the door, John twisted to see the garage door open. "Shit," he hissed. "Gray's opened the door!"

"I sure have," he said, and emerged from the shadows, chainsaw in hand. "Don't you go running again. There ain't nowhere to go."

He stood between them and the exit, their eyes switching between the chainsaw and their freedom. Gray switched on his tool. A present from Jane last year, he loved the electric one. His hands were getting a bit too old to be pulling at strings time and time again.

With the click of a button, the chainsaw whirred to life. John and Tony rushed back, searching for another exit. Gray lunged at the closest man—Tony—who dodged the electric teeth. As John came to help his boyfriend—*Why the fuck is he helping this twat?*—Gray swung again. The teeth chewed at John's arm but only managed to grab at the top layer of skin. He squealed in pain and fell to his back.

"Get out of here!" Tony cried.

He and John exchanged looks for a micro-second and Gray descended onto Tony once more. Over the buzzing and clanking of the chainsaw, the teeth whirring like a hungry dog, Gray didn't hear John's reply. He didn't much care. He saw the young man bolt for the exit, slipping past Gray.

Turning to him, he swung the chainsaw again, the teeth munching on John's shoulder. He was down, and Gray stood over him. Motioning to Tony, he said, "One move from you and his head becomes my bowling ball. Get it?"

Tony nodded once. Something in his eyes was familiar. A glint. A darkness. Jane had it, too. Gray often wondered if he had it, staring at himself in the mirror, studying his eyes.

"What do you want from us?" Tony asked.

Gray smirked. "We just collect. It's the others who want you."

Clutching at his shoulder wound and groaning in pain,

John sat up, staring between Gray and Tony. "Please, let me go."

Tony shot him a look.

"I won't say anything to anyone," John said.

The chainsaw buzzed again, Gray using it to silence the men. They fell quiet, eyes wide, and he could *almost* hear their hearts pounding hard in their chests. Rattling against the ribcages. Keeping the tool on John, he turned his head to Tony.

"What we're gonna do is, you and Johnny here are going down to the cellar. And that's where you're gonna stay until it's collection time," he said. "Now get your skinny—"

John kicked at the older man, in the back of the knee, cutting him off. Off-balance, John rose and ran for the exit, still groaning about his shoulder, and Tony was close behind him.

Getting to his feet, Gray grabbed at Tony's arm. Flesh against flesh, Tony was pulled back as John disappeared outside. Thrusting Tony to the ground with a dull thud, Gray forced himself on top of the young man. His weight alone was enough to keep Tony in place, but he leaned forward and put the chainsaw to the man's throat.

"You wanna be a bowling ball, is that it?" Gray growled.

"Wait." Tony swallowed, his Adam's apple scraping against the chainsaw teeth. "I can help you."

Gray smiled.

"I can," Tony insisted. When Gray raised an eyebrow, he continued. "You saw what I did at the riverbank. I tried to kill John. It wasn't the first time."

"I saw," Gray admitted. "What do you mean it wasn't the first time?"

"A few... months ago..." Tony stuttered as the chainsaw threatened the fine skin around his neck. "I organised with

47

some gang members… to have John taken out. It was supposed to… look like… a bashing. A hate crime."

"And?"

Tony looked down at the teeth, gnashing for his blood. "He survived. This was my plan B. Take him… Take him to the middle… of nowhere. No cameras. No witnesses. Just… an accident.…"

Gray narrowed his eyes, considering Tony's story. He could have been making it up, but his eyes. That darkness lurking inside the colour. *It could be true.*

"We both want the same thing." Tony's voice was sharp and desperate, but Gray recognised honesty when he saw it. "We both want John out of our lives. Let me help you catch him."

Gray curled a lip. "Why would I do that?"

"Because"—Tony shut his eyes and gulped—"you aren't getting any younger. You could use someone like me."

He was right, and they both knew it. Jane might even go for it, and Gray was aroused at the idea of having a young man around he could play with. He pushed that thought away and pressed the chainsaw closer to Tony's throat.

"This ain't a one-time thing," Gray said. "You help us now, you're in this for life. Or.…" He cocked his head to the cellar door. "You end up down there. Again."

Nodding hard, Tony agreed.

Gray shuffled off the young man, ignoring the tingling in his groin at being so close to another man, and held out a hand. "Alright then," he said. "We have work to do."

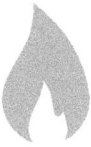

Clasping a hand over his mouth to stifle the pained groans, John listened hard to the conversation in the garage. He'd run, tasting freedom and an end to the nightmare before his conscience—that fucking voice in his head that wouldn't go away—ordered him to go back. He'd dropped his bag somewhere in the garage, had no weapon, but couldn't leave Tony back there to die. Even after what he'd done at the riverbank.

You aren't him.

Pressing himself against the steel shell of the garage, he'd heard Tony confess. The bashing a few months before. He'd planned it. The worst night of his life. The round robin of raping and beating, being left to die in an alley like a piece of trash. All of it. It was all Tony.

Hearing the words, he wanted to believe Tony was making it up. Tony was telling a story to get out of there alive, saying whatever he could to survive. But John knew it was true. It was the way Tony spoke—cold and calculated. He believed him.

Fuck you. John let a tear escape. Just one.

Then began scanning the farm. Their car was no good, the engine taken apart. However, Jane and Gray had to have transport of their own. A car, a truck, a fucking tractor, whatever. He just had to find it.

And a phone. The phones were in the house somewhere, they had to be. As he listened to Tony and Gray finalise their deal, John raced back to the house. *Find a phone, find a car.*

Except it was now three against one. John was outnumbered and literally outgunned. Jane and Gray had shotguns and pistols and chainsaws. John had nothing. Slipping back into the house, he was conscious the wound on his shoulder was spiking with pain, the blood beginning to soak his shirt. If he wasn't careful, it would get infected. He could already feel himself slowing up, despite the adrenaline and the fear propelling him forward.

Sneaking to the second-level stairs, John heard clanking from the kitchen. Jane was busy doing something, though he couldn't fathom what. A thin wooden door separated him from the kitchen, and he swallowed hard as he snuck past to climb the stairs.

One of the stairs creaked under his weight, and John stopped, squeezing his eyes shut. *Please don't hear me. Please don't hear me.*

Nobody came.

He continued upstairs, his eyes peeled for anything he could use as a weapon. He passed a cabinet with crystalware, and decided there was nothing of use there. The crystal would smash; unlike glass, it wouldn't split into shards or shanks.

Making his way to the bathroom where he'd woken in the tub, and closing the door without a sound, John searched the cabinets for bandages and a first aid kit. He took supplies from a cabinet and stood in front of the bathroom mirror to assess the wound. Sliding his shirt off, it slapped to the ground with a wet squish, blood circling the drain. A thick red gushed down his shoulder, and John winced as he took a towel and wiped at the wound.

"We will be ready," Jane said from the other side of the door. Her voice passed the bathroom, growing faint. John stopped and listened. "They've given us a little trouble, but we've got one for organs and one for the sex trade."

What the fuck?

After a pause, she added: "Uh huh." Another pause. "Yes, sir."

She was on the phone.

John finished cleaning himself up, wrapped a bandage around his shoulder, and slipped on his blood-soaked shirt again. Among the supplies was another scalpel. He slipped it into his pocket, and refocused on Jane's conversation. On her phone.

I have to get that phone. Call for help.

Pressing his ear to the bathroom door, he waited until Jane's footsteps disappeared, and then clicked the door open. The hallway was empty, and John peered left and right. He hadn't heard her shuffling down the stairs, which meant she was still on this level. Somewhere close by.

"Uh huh" and "Yes, sir". John wondered who she was speaking to and who was giving the orders, but it didn't matter at that moment. He wouldn't be around long enough to find out—he hoped.

He found Jane pacing back and forth in a bedroom and figured by the wedding photos of her and Gray on the bedstand that it was hers. With a final "Yes, sir", she hung up the phone and threw it across the room.

"Fucking piece of shit *cunt*," she hissed, and breathed deeply to calm down.

Watching from the door, her back to him, John paused for a second. His hands trembled, his body shook, and his mind raced with the knowledge of what he had to do. He thought about the scalpel in his pocket, but he didn't want to hurt the old lady if he could help it. The goal was to get her phone.

He lunged forward, reminding himself she wasn't just an

old lady—she was a fucking monster—and as he tackled Jane to the ground, she spun to face him, her lips forming a scowl.

They hit the carpet, her thin skin tearing against the abrasive fabric, and she cried. John's shoulder throbbed, but he scrambled to get on top of the old woman, unsure where to go from here. As he grabbed at her arms to restrain her, she punched him in the nose, and reached into her pants for something.

White flashed across his eyes as Jane pressed the taser to his next. He fell to the carpet, spasming as electricity surged through his body. She clambered to her knees and leaned over him, her unbrushed teeth and hot breath in his face.

"Gotta love these babies," she said and tasered him again. "Never go anywhere without it."

She tasered one more time, and the last thing he saw before the world went black was Jane's grimace turned into a wide smile.

John heard voices through his haze and the beckoning call of consciousness. His eyes fluttered until his half-awake brain realised who the voices belonged to. Snapping his eyes shut once more, he listened.

"I don't want this piss-ant on our team," Jane spat.

"Come on, darlin'." Gray's voice was deep but soft. "He's worth more to us this way. We can trust him."

"I… I know it's a strange turn of events, but I think this is what I'm meant to do," Tony said. "I've always had this… darkness… inside me. What you're doing here excites me."

Jane scoffed and choked back a laugh. "Excites you?"

John risked opening one eye and scanned the area for Tony. He wanted to see that prick's face. But wherever he was, it was pitch black. Opening the other eye, he squinted through the darkness. His other senses began to awaken, and he felt his body moving. Heard the squeak of an old wheel. Tried to reach up with his left hand, but both hands moved, and he realised his wrists were tied—*Of course*—with a cable tie.

Dim lights came on, and John recognised the tunnel. He was being ushered to one of the cells. With the shallow light assisting his eyes, John looked around and saw he was being transported through the tunnel on a trolley of some kind—pulled by Gray. They'd passed the cells where Tony had been held earlier, heading somewhere else. An unknown place lay at the end of the tunnel.

"The auction is set to start in an hour," Jane said, "so we need to get this done."

"I thought he was going in as an organ donor?" Tony asked.

Gray sniffed, and said, "Plans change."

Tony and Jane were behind—he could tell based on where their voices came from—and John was careful not to stir too much. As his mind continued to wake, thoughts rushed through his mind—*Get out of here. Call the cops. Escape. How? With what? Three against one*—and he felt the panic bubbling to his throat.

Swallowing it back down, John focused. It was three against one, though it was odd to think Jane and Gray would accept Tony into their ranks with such ease. He didn't trust it, and he didn't understand why Tony did. That was something he could work with.

What else?

His mind went hazy again, his head throbbed from the tasing, and John squeezed his eyes shut again until the sensation passed.

The taser.

It was a chance, but as he was thrust through the tunnel towards a fate he didn't understand, but knew he didn't want, there was no other choice. Taking a deep breath, John rolled from the trolley and hit the dirt.

Tony called out, "Fuck, he's awake."

Gray spun around, and Jane pushed past Tony, arms outstretched and grabbing for John as he caterpillared on the ground. He let her get close, let her hands slap him hard on the face. Gray was at his shoulders now, heaving him back to the trolley, Tony standing in the wings, watching on.

A little closer.

He let Gray lift him, let Jane stand over him until he could reach her pants pocket. Slipping his hands inside, he felt the taser, and ripped it free. Before Jane had a chance to react, John pressed the taser firm against her chest.

Squeezed.

She squealed a little as she went down, and John looked up to see the shock on Gray's face. Fumbling to reach John's hands as Tony raced over to help, Gray called to his wife. The taser sparked again, at Gray's hand. He snapped it back, but the shock had worked. John jumped to his feet, unstable on the uneven dirt, and lunged at Gray.

He felt hands on him, pulling his elbows, and John thrust his head backwards fast and hard. Gray recovered and came at John. Smacking into Tony's nose with a dull slap, John felt the hands loosen just as Gray swung at him. Pressing the taser into the old farmer's belly, he squeezed and watched the bolt of electricity surge through the man.

Gray was down.

Jane was down.

Tony was—

"John," Tony said from behind him. "You've done it! We can get out of here now."

John spun to face him, pointing the taser at Tony's face. Breathing hard, stepped forward.

Raising his hands, Tony looked from the taser to his boyfriend. "John… we can go now. You saved us. Look, they've taken us to an exit. I think it leads to the auction site or a pickup location or something. But we're free."

John ignored him. "Why'd you do it?" he asked, choking back tears. In the corner of his eye, he saw Jane stirring, so he tasered her again. Another shock for Gray, too.

"I'm sorry." Tony's eyes betrayed him. The words came out hollow and rehearsed.

"Am I *that* unbearable?" John stepped forward, and Tony retreated, looking nervous. "Why not just break up with me? Why have me…" He swallowed hard on the next word. "… murdered?"

Tony shrugged. After everything he'd done, all he could do was shrug. And John saw the hint of a smirk tugging at the corners of his pretty lips.

"I forgive you." John put the taser down.

Tony's eyebrows arched. "Really?"

John nodded. "You're right, what you said earlier. I'm not you." Pausing, he looked behind him and saw Tony had been truthful about one thing—there was a door there, large wooden, old. It could have been a way out. "Come on, let's go. Untie me."

He motioned for the scalpel in his pocket, and Tony was quick to get his hand in there. John saw a flash behind the eyes—the fleeting thought of using the blade against John instead—but he sliced through the cable ties without a word. John snatched the scalpel back and returned it to his pocket.

Tony was cocky; John knew him well enough to know that. As he walked over to the door, his stride confident, John smiled to himself. *What a fucking moron.*

Reaching for the door handle, Tony gave John a small nod of appreciation—*Part of his manipulation*—and John nodded back.

"Tony?" he said. "One more thing."

As he turned around, John tasered him under the chin. Tony's eyes rolled to the back of his head, and he dropped like a sack of dead meat. John glanced at him before stepping over his body and pushing through the door.

Through the exit.

Liz hated small spaces. She felt the air heating up around her, filling with her own breath and sweat. When she'd first woken, she'd screamed and punched and felt the walls of her cage shrinking in on her.

It was her legs that started first. The nerves scratching under her skin, begging to move. She was squashed into a box, one tiny air hole her only access to the outside world. The knowledge that she was trapped—that her body had no way to move, to scratch herself or stretch, or wipe at her own tears—made her want to move even more.

The screaming didn't help. The sound of her own voice echoing off the metal container, piercing her own ears, reminded her how enclosed she was. How confined. She'd tried to shift her body, to rearrange as her butt lost feeling and the pins and needles in her hands and arms started to hurt.

She couldn't.

All she could do was peer out the tiny hole.

And scream.

After her throat went hoarse and she couldn't scream any more, the cells in her body begged to move, her mind screaming to be set free. Until she stopped. It was as though her mind left her body, floating away to some distant place where she could run and move and had as much oxygen as she needed.

Liz felt herself blinking occasionally, but the connection to her body was mostly severed. So she stayed in that far-away place, where the sky was blue and the trees were a deep green and the grass scratched at her bare feet and the—

"Hello?"

The voice pulled her back, but only a little. Although she didn't want to leave, she couldn't go back to the box.

"Are you awake in there?"

The voice came again. A whisper. A man.

No, no, no, no, no.

The last man she'd met had put her in that box. She was free now, she was in a wide, open field with birds singing and a gentle breeze.

"I'm going to get you out of there."

The sky opened up, darkness swept back in, and Liz blinked. A man stood over her, lifting the metal lid off to free her.

"It's okay, I'm not one of them," he whispered, his eyes darting left and right.

Liz stared at him. Blinked again.

"Are you hurt?" he asked.

"I…" Liz's throat scratched, and she tasted blood. Too much screaming. When she swallowed, it felt like razor blades lined her throat. "I… don't know."

The man extended a hand to her. He was trying to help. *Where did the sky go?* "Where…."

"I don't know where we are." He was speaking fast, those eyes shifting around the place like he expected something. Someone.

That man.

"Quick. Take my hand."

And she did. Her lips trembled as she realised she *could* take his hand. She could move. She was free. "Thank you." Her words were a croak as he pulled her up and out of her cage.

The muscles in her legs were stiff and sore, and she collapsed into the man's arms. He seemed to understand, let her cry into his shoulder for a few moments before dragging her across the room.

"What did they do to you?" he asked.

He was looking down at her body, searching. She remembered she was naked, and moved to cover herself. His eyes weren't full of lust or desire, though. He was concerned, looking for wounds and scars.

"They wanted my organs," he said. "I woke up in their bathtub."

The feeling in her legs started to return in pins and needles, and she pushed away from the man to stand on her own. She wobbled and stumbled, held onto a wall. Felt the cold bricks under her fingers. She wanted to go back to the field, to the tress, to the blue sky.

"I'm John," he said, but he was looking around the room now, not at her.

Still, she covered her breasts with her arms, and turned side on so he couldn't see her groin. Even if he wasn't looking.

He noticed the nudity—*finally*—and took off his shirt. She recoiled, for a moment thinking the worst. But he passed it to her with a sad smile. It was covered in blood, looked wet.

"It's the best I can do." He shrugged. "I'm sorry."

She took the shirt and slipped it on, conscious that her lower half was still exposed. Sizing him up as he walked towards another door at the rear of the room, she thanked him again. "I'm Liz. I... want you to know my name."

He nodded. "I think we can go through this door, but I don't know where it leads."

"Probably to the auction," she said, stretching the shirt down as far as it would go. "They want me for the sex trade."

"Fuck." John scraped fingers through his sweaty hair. "That's not going to happen, okay? We're in this together now, and we aren't going to let anyone hurt the other. Right?"

Liz agreed with a nod and went to him by the door. "It's the way out, but there will be people there waiting to... deliver us."

"I have this." John held up the taser, but he looked less than impressed. "I think the charge on it is a bit low now."

Searching the room for a weapon, Liz looked around for the first time. Just empty crates and a few other metal cages. A garden hose. She remembered what Gray had done to her with that hose, the way he fed it through the air hole. She picked it up, and John inspected it.

"We could use it as a rope, I guess?"

"It's connected to sleeping gas," Liz told him, noticing the hose wasn't connected to anything. "Or, it was, at least."

As John moved to her, felt the hose, and sighed—lost in thought—the door to the cellar burst open. Gray and Jane piled in, a young man behind them. Jane carried a rifle, Gray clicked on his chainsaw.

John and Liz raced to the other door, hoping beyond hope that something better was on the other side. Liz grabbed at the handle and twisted, but felt hands tug at her hair. She was pulled back, slammed to the ground, and John fell beside her.

Blood trickled from his nose, and Jane stood over him, the butt of the rifle covered in dripping red. The young man crouched next to Liz and put a hand around her throat.

"What's this one for?" he asked.

"Sex," Jane spat. "She'll make someone *very* happy, I bet."

Gray came up on them, the chainsaw whirring like an angry lion. As the hand around Liz's throat tightened, the chainsaw lowered—just before her eyes now—and the old man sneered. "Thought you could get away, huh?"

"Please," Liz choked.

John sat up on his elbows and Jane smacked his nose once more with the rifle. He went down with an "Oof" and didn't open his eyes.

It's just me. Again.

"Whaddaya reckon, darlin'?" Gray smiled, his eyes now on his wife. "Put her back in the box?"

The old woman checked her watch and shook her head. "Let's just load 'em up ourselves." Jane gave a short nod to the young man and the hands around Liz's throat squeezed harder. With the chainsaw grumbling in front of her eyes, she could do nothing but squirm against the cold ground, begging.

Begging.

Begging.

Then nothing.

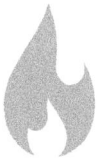

John woke up choking on his own blood. Spitting a mouthful, he looked around. He was outside, a cool breeze flowing around him, crickets clicking in the grass. For all intents and purposes it was a beautiful summer day.

Wait.

The sun was going down, casting an orange glow across the horizon, and stretching the shadows of trees and buildings, and of Gray and Tony.

Standing nearby, John watched as they heaved an unconscious Liz next to him. It was then he realised where he was—in the back of a ute. The stench of metal and grass and dirt filled him as he took in his surroundings.

Still on the farm.

He tried to move, to go to Liz and make sure she was alright, but someone had tied his wrists again. His feet, too, after last time.

"He's awake," Gray said with a wide smile and playful jabs at Tony's ribs to encourage him to join in. "Hello, mate, how'd you sleep?"

John scowled at the old man. "It's not too late to stop this," he said.

Tony laughed and leaned against the side of the ute. "Why would we do that?"

"I saw how you looked at us." John stared at Gray with piercing eyes. "The way you licked your lips when you saw us half naked."

Gray shuffled left and right, scoffed. "I... I did not!"

Nodding, John continued. "You did. I've seen that look before on some of the older guys on Oxford Street. The ones who came out late in life. It's okay, Gray, you don't have to hide it."

He looked around, saw Jane coming across the grass towards them, and lowered his voice. "I ain't a *fucking queer*."

John saw the way Gray paced back and forth, keeping one eye on Jane and one on him. He was right, he knew he was right. If he could get through to him.

"What are you standing 'round for?" Jane snapped, the rifle still in one arm, and a phone clipped to her belt. "We have to go."

He wasn't sure if Tony saw it or not, the fleeting glance between Gray and Jane. He didn't much care—Tony wasn't his problem anymore. He even smiled when the old man punched him in the side of the head, and Jane lifted the rifle to his face.

"… the fuck?" Tony asked, shocked.

"You *really* thought we'd just take you on, like a goddam apprentice?" Gray laughed.

"I thought—"

Jane shook her head. "Young people today."

With the rifle still trained on him, Tony lifted his hands in the air. Gray threw some cable ties at him and told him to do himself up. "Tight."

"Now, get in," Jane ordered, cocking her head to the ute.

Tony hesitated, and she stepped towards him. Just once. He climbed into the ute, still perplexed, and shuffled to the other side of Liz, who was beginning to stir.

"Come on," Jane said to Gray, "strap 'em in. We're going to be late."

Gray nodded and reached beside the ute for something. John told him he didn't have to do this; it wasn't too late; he could still live his truth. Gray ignored him and lifted up a black tarpaulin. He spread it over the three passengers and strapped it to the sides, thrusting them into blackness again.

It was tight above them, and John struggled to move, the thick plastic scratching against his face and arms.

Liz stirred again and her eyes fluttered open. "No, no, no!"

"It's okay, Liz," John whispered, as the ute began to move. The engine blustered to life with a choke. "We're in the ute."

"How is that *okay?*" Tony snapped. "We're going to be sold into the fucking sex trade."

"Fuck off, Tony," John said, his voice seething with rage. "You can fucking die for all I care." All he could think was how much he hated Tony, how much he hated the people who'd beaten and raped him, how much he hated Jane and Gray. How much he hated himself for letting those things happen, for waking up in a bath of ice with nothing but—

A scalpel.

As Tony mumbled a reply, and Liz repeated, "No no no no no," John searched his pocket. The blade of the scalpel poked at his fingertips, and the pain sent joy surging through him.

"Tony," John interrupted his boyfriend—*Ex-boyfriend*—as he continued to mumble about mistakes and blah blah blah. "Shut the fuck up."

He did.

"Liz, I'm going to get us out of here."

The ute rocked as it travelled to the auction, an unknown destination. With all his might, John hoped that he and Liz would never make it there.

"Oh my god." She breathed hard, and smiled.

"What is it?" Tony asked, trying to see past Liz's body.

They both ignored him. Liz gave John a "What's happening?" look, but he said nothing. Just used the scalpel to cut through his restraints. His wrists came apart as the cable tie snapped, and he went to work on Liz's.

He felt the ute slow down, then stop. Their eyes widened, and John's heart clenched. *Are we there?*

The ute turned and he and Liz rolled a little towards Tony, who was still trying to see what they were doing. He caught a glimpse of the scalpel and his breath caught. "You're going to set me free, right?"

"You're lucky I don't slit your throat right now," John spat. "After what you did to me. *Twice.*"

Liz's restraints came free, and she rubbed at her wrists. "You tried to strangle me, you prick."

"My feet are still tied," John said. "If I can shuffle around, you can cut me free."

Nodding, she added: "Then we should be able to jump out onto the road."

It was a weak plan, there was no doubt between them. However, it was all they had. Without saying anything else, John began shuffling around so his feet were by Liz's face. He felt her working on the bonds when the ute stopped again.

"Another corner?" Tony asked, swallowing hard.

The throb of the engine stopped.

"Fuck," he said.

Liz worked faster, and John felt his ankles part as the cable tie split. "When they come for us," she said, "I'll be ready."

John looked down to see her holding the scalpel tight, and nodded. "Me too."

"Guys, please," Tony begged. "I can help."

"Shut up," John whispered, listening to the ute doors click open, and then slam.

Footsteps.

"Get ready," he said to Liz.

After a few moments, the tarp came off, and John pounced, unsure who he was attacking. He felt the beard and the belly, and knew it was Gray. The man stumbled backward, and John scratched at his eyes, frenzied. He saw Liz behind him, swiping at Jane with the scalpel, and Tony shuffling from the back of the ute. He raced away, towards a road in the distance.

John shouldered Gray hard, pain spiking in his wound, and watched him fall to the concrete. Liz swiped again, and Jane dodged, the rifle in her hands. She wasn't using it—*She needs us alive.* He tackled the old woman to the ground, grabbed her weapon, and smacked her in the mouth with it.

Her head fell to the side, and John stood. He grabbed Liz at the wrist and hissed, "Come on!"

Exposed brick balustrades offset the white exterior, and the front porch stretched several metres wide, with glass doors lining either side.

John and Liz ran across the paved driveway, decorated in a herringbone pattern. He let go of Liz's hand to grip the rifle, the pain in his shoulder throbbing hard. "Keep going," he said, heaving through a breath, and ran as fast as he could.

She didn't reply.

He looked back, searching the faded twilight for her. "Liz?" he whispered hard, spinning around.

A few metres back, Gray and Jane had her, and carried her, kicking and screaming towards the mansion. A ringing in his head screamed at him to go. He was free and clear, he could make it out of there. Liz…. Well, she wasn't his problem.

Stop it.

It was the fear, he knew it was. He couldn't listen to it, not this time. Not now, knowing what would happen to her in that place.

As she disappeared from view, John squeezed his grip around the rifle, took a deep breath, and headed to the mansion.

Tony raced through the dying light, his feet moving too fast for his body. He stumbled and tripped, rolling down a grassy hill, leaves and twigs scratching at his face. With his hands bound, his attempts to grab at passing trees failed. When he hit the bottom of the hill, his face slamming hard into the thick dirt, he felt consciousness abandoning him.

"Woah, you right fella?" a deep voice came from somewhere nearby.

Tony breathed into the dirt and mustered his strength. "Help," he said.

A bearded man with a scar down his right cheek crouched in front of Tony's face. Swinging a single-barrel shotgun over his shoulder by a strap, he leaned in to look at Tony and pouted.

"Help me," Tony repeated.

"Hmm." The man sniffed while grabbing a handful of Tony's hair to lift his face. "Which one are you?"

"Huh?"

"The arse or the organs?"

Tony breathed hard. "What?"

Sighing, the man dropped Tony's head back to the ground. "Are you for the sex trade or for organ donation?"

"Please help me. I've got money. If you… get me out of here…"

The man laughed and scratched at his scar. "Come on, son," he said, slapping Tony's back. "Your arse is worth far more than anything else you've got." He grabbed Tony's butt and felt him up. "Mmmmm, trust me... You'll sell."

Hoisting Tony to his feet, he shot a look that made Tony recoil. "You don't have to—"

"Up to the house with ya. I reckon I know who'll bid on you, and if I bring you in, I get a cut of the profits." He licked at his lips and winked at Tony, pushing him up the hill.

Back to the mansion.

After climbing the hill, they made their way across the patterned driveway, and Tony saw Liz being carried inside the mansion. Kicking and screaming. He wanted to feel bad for her, but in that moment he only cared about himself.

The driveway was filled with cars. Bentleys, Mercedes, Jaguars. Looking at the licence plates of each, he noticed they came from all over the country—Queensland, Victoria, a bunch of rental cars, too.

He felt a hand in his back, pushing him to the front door, and he stepped up the front porch steps, searching for a way out. For a way to fight back. As they entered the mansion, the man guided Tony away from what appeared to be a cocktail party. He saw a glimpse of masquerade masks, tuxedos, ball gowns.

What the hell is this place?

Moving into a separate room, decorated with deer heads and World War I paintings, he was forced into a seat, restrained at the armrests. His feet were tied to the front chair legs. The man was silent throughout, and left without another word.

Alone in the room, Tony strained at his bonds and looked around the room. A row of cages lined the walls, just big enough for a person if they were on their hands and knees. His chest tightened at the prospect, and he hoped John would return for him. Despite everything he'd done, he had to believe

John would save him. He was a good person. He would come for him.

"Ah, there you are," Jane interrupted his thoughts. "Let's get you cleaned up." She made her way to him, carrying a bag in one hand, and a hairbrush in the other.

"What are you doing?" Tony asked as she began combing his hair.

"Our guests tonight will want a good look at you." Jane switched the hairbrush for a make-up kit. She began wiping at his face with a damp cloth, humming the tune to "We Gotta Get out of this Place".

"Why are you doing this?" Tony asked. "I can still help you."

Jane stopped humming and smirked. "Let me ask you something: How can you stand being a filthy faggot?"

Tony scoffed and narrowed his eyes. "Fuck you, lady."

"It's not normal." She shrugged. "At least the guys who are going to buy you have money. What do you have?" She looked at him again and scowled. "*You ain't got shit.*"

Tony smiled. "You know your husband is gay, right?"

Jane slapped him hard and fast, the sting settling into his cheek a second later. "Tsk. Fuck." She inspected his cheek. "I'll have to cover that with blush."

Tony struggled at his bonds for a moment before realising it was just no good. His only hope was John, and he doubted he'd ever see him again. The irony wasn't lost on him; he wished he could go back in time and make a different decision.

"Why'd you want to kill him, anyway?" Jane asked, as she powdered a brush and applied make-up to his face and neck.

"It's complicated."

"Money?"

He shook his head.

"Stay still. He cheat on you?"

Another shake.

"What then?" Jane sized up his face and switched the make-up for a damp towel and began wiping his chest and arms and torso.

Tony relented to her question. "I wanted him to need me. And he didn't."

Jane scoffed and mumbled something.

"I have this… thing… inside me," he said, and paused. "He wasn't the first, you know. None of them really needed me. I couldn't deal with that…. That shame."

"Wow," Jane said as she reached Tony's belly button. "You're a fuckin' psycho."

They shared a look, a brief smile, and Jane untied the drawstring on Tony's board shorts.

His eyes widened. "What are you doing?"

Jane raised an eyebrow. "You won't need these where you're going. And I have to clean the…." She cocked her head towards his groin. "The, uh, area of interest."

He closed his eyes and let Jane do what needed to be done. He felt her breath on his crotch and her fingers lifting his member to scrub the sweat and grime away. Neither spoke. He was surprised at how gentle she was.

"Alright," she said, breaking the silence, and dropping his flaccid dick. "I'll get Gray to help move you into the cage."

She disappeared, despite Tony's pleading, and returned a moment later with Gray, who paused at the door upon seeing Tony's naked body. His cock out in the open like that. Tony saw the older man swallow and look away. Then look back, taking in Tony's whole form.

Jane watched her husband for a moment and cleared her throat. "We have work to do."

Gray sprung to action, headed to Tony, and pulled out a knife. When Tony gasped, Gray offered, "It's just for the cables. But Jane here is gonna get her gun. You try anything, you will die."

Tony nodded, and darted his eyes to Jane to confirm she did, in fact, have a gun. A pistol. Black and metallic.

Gray cut him loose and ushered him to one of the cages. As Tony bent down in front of him, he heard Gray stifle a satisfied moan and wondered how a man could live his whole life in the closet like that. He climbed into the cage, facing the wall.

"You won't be alone for long," Jane said. "There are plenty of others joining you."

The cage door slammed shut, and Jane and Gray left him once more. Switched the lights off, descending him into darkness. He stayed there alone for some time, his body aching from being on his hands and knees in the hard metal box for so long.

A door opened somewhere behind him, a stream of light caught his attention. From the corner of his eye, he saw a line of women—like him, all naked—being led into the room in single file. He couldn't see who was leading them, but none of the women seemed to fight or protest as they were forced into the metal cages.

Except one.

Tony smiled, recognising the voice of the "Fuck you!" and the "Get your fucking hands off me!"

Liz.

"I won't go in that tiny cage!" Liz's voice, defiant and strong, carried an undertone of something else. Not fear exactly. He couldn't tell.

He twisted his neck as far as he could, to see behind

him, and caught a glimpse of Liz being pushed around to the cage next to his. She grabbed at the bars, resisted as much as anyone could, but whoever it was that had her punched her in the kidneys. She recoiled with an "Oomph", and was thrust into the cage.

When the door slammed shut, and Liz noticed who was next to her, Tony saw she'd had a similar experience to him. The clean-up, the make-up, someone had done her hair, so it was wavy, and she wore thick layer of red lipstick.

"Are you okay?" Tony asked.

Liz spat at him. "Fuck you."

He knew he deserved that, knew she had every right to hate him. Didn't care. This was bigger than either of them. This was about survival. He leaned close to the metal bars of his cage to whisper, "Where's John?"

He could leave in one of the cars. There were plenty to choose from. A deep blue Jaguar appealed to him as he passed it, holding his breath, on his way to the side of the mansion. Put his thoughts of abandonment out of his mind. Again.

He imagined a rear entrance would be a way he could sneak into the mansion unseen. Grab Liz, get the hell out of there. Report this whole thing to the cops.

The rifle in his hands felt heavy, but he didn't know if it was loaded or not. He didn't even know how to use the thing. Still, he felt stronger with it. Holding it forward, pointing it in front of him, he made his way to the backyard, conscious that he'd passed several surveillance cameras. Someone would be coming for him, and he'd be ready.

As he entered the yard, he stepped onto a pergola stretching at least ten metres from the roofline. Warm yellow lights strewn through the wooden beams. Flourishes of green climb the back walls of the house, and a magnificent dinner table—eight metres long—set with plates and cutlery and wine bottles.

Whoever was hosting knew how to make an event.

He was alone in the yard, though, and peered through a set of large sliding doors with tinted glass, so he could only see shapes and shadows of the people inside. He snuck past, looking for another way in. Somewhere not so crowded.

But first, the shed.

A small garden shed at the rear of the property caught his eye. Everything else seemed so grand and elegant, but this little shed way off in the distance of the yard was dark and forgotten.

He made his way to it, found it unlocked, and went inside. "Huh," he muttered.

Just a garden shed. Some tools—shovels, spades, pitchforks—and some plants. Fertiliser. Garden hose. The hose reminded him of Liz, renewing his energy for the mission. Among the tools and the plants, John saw a glint of silver.

Moving to it, he smiled. "Now *this*, I can use." He grabbed the object and held it up before him. The machete was sharp and looked newish. Between the rifle and the machete, he felt powerful. Like he'd never experienced before. He knew it was a false sense of security, he didn't know how to use either weapon. Still, it might scare off potential attackers.

With the machete in one hand and the rifle in the other, he left the shed and marched back to the mansion, his head swirling with hatred.

For the people who'd attacked him, beaten him, raped him.

For Tony—*that fucking cunt*—who was in that mansion probably waiting to be rescued.

Because part of him still wanted Tony to be okay.

Hatred for every single one of those people up there in that mansion, waiting for an auction to buy actual people and organs and who knew what else.

A hidden door somewhere wasn't going to cut it. He was sick of hiding. Sick of running around in the shadows, avoiding things. Scared of confrontation. Scared to tell people how he felt. What he wanted.

Fuck that.

With the sliding doors in reach, the tinted shadows and silhouettes of the people inside—laughing, drinking, and waiting to buy a person—he grabbed the door handle and pulled it open.

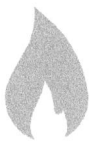

The cages were lined in the middle of the room, a display of weeping women. Tony's cage was dead centre, John saw him first as he burst into the room. The crowd stopped, their masquerade masks tilting with curiosity as they took in the rifle and the machete.

"Nobody *fucking* move." John pointed the rifle into the crowd, the hushed questions and comments disappearing into silence.

Someone stepped forward. A man in a deep-blue suit, a matching mask bejewelled with diamonds. Hands raised, a glass of champagne in one, an hors d'oeuvre in the other, dripping in pink sauce.

"Let these people go," John ordered.

The man smiled, flashing white teeth. "Ah," he said, striding forward. "The escapee, I take it."

"This your party?" John asked, feeling the rage seeping through his skin.

The man bowed. "Indeed."

"Party's over. I said *let them go*," John shouted.

A few of the guests shuffled forward, and John swiped the machete fast so they'd move back. He heard the "Oh dear" and the "He's lively", and small giggles from somewhere in the back.

"I can't do that," the man said, motioning towards the cages. "We're in the middle of an auction."

The crowd was unsettled again, and John spied Gray and Jane somewhere among them. He was outnumbered, his hands shaking, his heart pumping fast, fast, fast. The room felt small, so small, as the man walked to him, sipping champagne like John wasn't even there. Like he wasn't scared, like this was just a sick fucking game.

"Don't come any closer." John's voice trembled. He was out of his depth, he should have run, he should have found help.

The man stopped, sipping again, and popping the hors d'oeuvre into his mouth. Chewing slow. His eyes dead and cold through the mask.

"You think that gun and your little knife scare me?" he asked, swallowing. "I could have you killed where you stand."

John's eyes darted around, scanning for snipers and whatever else. He knew he was losing it, giving in to the fear, but he pushed through it. Stood his ground. Someone rushed at him from the side and John spun, instinct taking over.

BANG.

He felt the recoil from the rifle in his shoulder, grimaced at the pain, and watched the person fly backwards through the air. Blood gushed from the body, splatting against John's face, against the glass sliding doors, against the masquerade masks of the onlookers.

And the room erupted into screams.

John stared down at the body, the unknown person he'd murdered. Felt coldness closing in as his fingertips went numb. The screaming around him faded for a moment, until he felt arms around his midsection, pulling him back to the present.

People ducked and ran and screamed, and someone had John around the waist. He thrust backwards with the rifle, its barrel still smoking, and felt the thud as the butt connected. The hands loosened, and John made his way for the cages.

Liz watched him, her eyes wide and pleading, and the other women watched, too. Some jeered and cried, another laughed and cooed—*Kill the fuckers!*

Liz screamed, "Behind you!"

John spun, saw the man who'd been so confident only moments before. A handgun drawn, he squeezed the trigger. He missed, the bullet zipping past John. Someone behind him fell to the ground with a surprised groan.

He reached Liz's cage, squeezed the trigger in the hopes the rifle was still loaded. The lock came apart just after the bang, and Liz scrambled from her prison. He heard Tony calling for help. Didn't even consider letting him go. The man shot again, and John felt the skin in his thigh tear open. He collapsed to the ground as the man shot again, walking closer.

"You've ruined my party!" he screamed.

Liz jumped on him, wrestled for the gun, pushing him into the crowd of people still fleeing for safety. John got to his feet, the wound in his leg oozing crimson liquid. He aimed the rifle at another cage, squeezed the trigger again. Nothing. *Fuck.*

Turning the rifle around, he bashed the lock hard a few times until it came apart. The woman climbed free, and John gave her the rifle. "Set the others free and get out of here," he told her. "But… leave the guy there. He's a killer."

The woman nodded and got to work.

John turned, searching for Liz. He found her still wrestling with the man, the gun firing into the crowd every few seconds. The screams and chaos around them was thinning out as people made for the exits, and John stepped over an injured man who bled from his neck.

Stepped towards the man, the host.

As Liz struggled with the gun in his hand, kneeing at the man's groin, Gray came to his aid. John raced over, brandishing the machete, and the older man stopped. The blood boiled under John's skin, the fear of his attack turning to a white-hot rage. As he raced to Liz, all he could see was that night in the alley. Earlier at the river. The bathtub. The injustice. The cruelty.

And he swung.

Liz crawled back, away from the blade. Gray whispered, "Fuck", and John looked down at what he'd done. The man's head rolled to the side, a gush of red pouring to the floors like spilled merlot. His eyes blinked once, and the head rolled to John's feet.

Lifting the machete, dripping with blood, John stared at Gray. The older man moved back as John's blood-drenched face began to smile.

Liz grabbed the man's gun and stood next to John. "Thank you for coming back."

The words dissipated into nothing, the sound of his own heart thumping taking over. All John could feel was his blood rushing through his body. His heart pounding at his chest. He stepped towards Gray, his hands no longer shaking, and the older man ran.

Sprinting after him, John was vaguely aware that Liz was behind him, following him. They raced through the mansion, and Gray began to climb a winding marble staircase. Black carpet lined the middle of each step, Gray's shoes leaving a bloodied print as he went.

Jane stood at the top of the stairs, calling to her husband. She aimed a shotgun at John and fired. He didn't bother trying to dodge, he was blind to reason and fear. He had a mission.

Kill kill kill.

She fired again, ducking under the solid railing as Liz shot back. John heard her curse, but the meaning of it didn't register. He just kept going, his eyes on Gray's back.

For an older man with a bit of weight around the belly, he moved fast. John was faster, even with his thigh burning with pain. Gray was strong, though, and both men knew if it came to a fist fight, the older man would win in seconds.

Knowing this, John took the stairs two at a time, swiping at Gray's back with the machete. The blade connected and the older man growled. Kept going. John swiped again, the blade sunk deeper, and Gray fell.

Jane shot again, the wall next to him and Liz exploding into shards of plaster. Liz pushed at the older man's back, stepped over him, and raced to the top of the stairs. Jane was reloading, that much John was aware of as he climbed onto Gray's back and pulled out the machete.

Leaning in close to his ear, John whispered, "Shall we see how much your organs are worth?" And he stabbed.

Liz bounded to the top of the stairs, ignoring the jiggle of her naked breasts as she went. It was just one more reason to hate the fucking bitch who did this to her. She expected the depravity of men, for them to gawk and poke and stare, and relish in the fetishising of the naked female form. But from another woman?

Fucking old bitch.

She remembered how nice and inviting she'd been when Liz first arrived, all tired and strung out from the eight-hour drive. How she and Gray had made her feel so welcome, how they'd lied to her and stolen her stuff and—

Jane shot again, but Liz pushed the barrel up and felt plaster drop into her hair. Lunging into the older woman, Liz elbowed her in the chest and wrestled the shotgun from her. Jane stumbled back, into a wall, and Liz fiddled with the weapon, turning it to hold it properly.

Rushing at Liz, Jane scratched her in the face, sending her backward, but she countered with a blow to the ribs. Jane recoiled, still grabbing at the shotgun. Liz slapped her hands out of the way and, with the shotgun butt in one hand and the barrel in the other, she smacked Jane in the nose and watched the old woman fall down.

"Please," Jane begged, coughing through the blood leaking from her nose. "We can talk about this."

Liz laughed, and she was surprised at how genuine it was. The words sounding like an actual joke. After everything, Jane thought there was room to speak. To chat. To work through their actions.

"You don't know what it's like. We don't have a choice."

Liz aimed the shotgun at Jane's face and shrugged. "Neither do I."

The woman's head exploded like papier mâché, bits of bone and brain and cartilage splatting to the walls and the floor.

Liz looked down at the mess, her face dropped. It hadn't felt good. It hadn't even felt bad.

In one moment, the old woman had existed. In the next, she didn't. Her head was a pool of red and white and pink mush on the floor. Nothing more, nothing less. Liz looked up from the dead woman to the stairs. To John and Gray.

She stepped forward, her bare foot squishing in the mess of Jane's brain matter, and she slipped for a moment. Grabbing the staircase railing, she steadied herself, and stood at the top of the stairs.

Without knowing John, she felt she knew him. He was good. He was a friend. He'd come back for her, saved her. Twice. She could trust him. Even if the scene before her indicated otherwise.

The flesh came apart like stewed apple, and John dug his hands into Gray's lower back, searching for his prize. Even as he felt the organ at his fingertips, he didn't fully grasp what he was doing. The rage had taken over, pushing his sense of rationality and morality to the edges of his consciousness.

Gray was still alive, squirming beneath him, and

somewhere inside John he thought this power—this intense sense of being in control—must have been what his attackers felt. And Gray must have felt the way he had. Helpless. Alone. Praying for death.

Pulling a kidney from Gray's back, the calcified thing sharp and degraded, covered in slick red, John held it to the man's face. Gray breathed in waves, just as John had all those months earlier. John forced the man to open his eyes, to stare at his own kidney.

"Is this what you wanted?" John spat through gritted teeth. "You want a *fucking* kidney? Mine aren't for sale."

He pushed it into the man's mouth, felt the resistance as weak as it was, and pushed harder until his fingers scraped against Gray's teeth. In that moment, he wasn't John. He wasn't even human. He was the monster he'd spent so much time fearing.

The realisation struck him like a lightning bolt, and he stopped. Crawled away from the older man and rested on the step beside him. He caught movement in his peripherals and turned his head to see Liz at the top of the stairs.

She just watched him, looking between him and Gray. Her eyes were empty, and held no judgement. Just sadness. For what she knew John had become in that moment. And as they stared at each other, with Gray choking and moaning between them, they both understood there was no going back.

There was no undoing what they'd seen. What they'd been through. What they'd done. And in that moment, neither cared.

"Let's go," John said, peering down at Gray. "We should go."

Liz sighed, wrapping her arms around her body once more. She descended the stairs, and stopped at Gray, whose weak fingers clutched at her ankle.

"Ple… ase…." He choked. "Kill me…."

Shaking him off her, Liz ignored him, and kept walking. A few steps later, she turned back to John, and motioned for him to come with her.

"I'm n-not…" John stuttered. "I'm not a monster."

Liz nodded. "We did what needed to be done."

John took the machete from Gray's back, stood, and the two descended the stairs together, taking in the remnants of chaos around them. Most of the masked guests had disappeared, driven off into the night. Some had been shot or injured while fleeing, and unmoving bodies were scattered around the place—knives in their backs, throats slashed, other injuries John couldn't identify—some had been stripped to their underwear. John took that as a sign the naked women now had clothing, and were fleeing to their homes, or to the police.

The host, headless and growing cold, lay near the row of opened cages. Bending, Liz rolled him to his stomach and forced the suit jacket from him. Wrapping it around herself, she looked at John and smiled.

"What?" he asked.

She pulled out a set of car keys, and he smiled back. "Let's get the fuck out of here."

"John…" Came a quiet voice. "John…."

Creasing his eyebrows in confusion, John twisted to face the sound. Tony. He'd forgotten about that prick, and smiled at the man, still caged and trembling like a scared child.

"Please," Tony said. "Let me out?"

Liz scoffed, and pulled the jacket tight around her, car keys dangling from her hand. "Ignore him. Let's go," she said.

Walking to the cage, John licked blood from his lips, and

stared into Tony's eyes. "You know what I remember the most about that night?"

Tony shook his head, breathing short and sharp, his eyes pleading.

"As I laid in that alley, blood and cum oozing from my asshole, the bones in my arms shattered, ribs broken… I remember thinking how strange it was that you told me to go out that night. Alone. And I remember thinking, 'If only Tony was here, he could have saved me.'"

"It was a mistake, I—"

John laughed, hollow and exhausted. "A mistake, sure. Just like the riverbank." He gripped one of the metal bars on Tony's cage.

"I'm so sorry, I love you…"

John sniffed and bit his lower lip. Tasted blood and couldn't tell whose it was. "The funny thing is, I used to believe you when you said that."

Tony reached out to touch John's fingers, and he pulled away. As Tony stared into him, begging for his release, John took a step back, and sucked in a deep breath.

"I'll get you out of there. I'll set you free."

"I knew you would." Tony sighed. "You're a good person, you aren't like me. Thank you, thank you."

John nodded. Tony repeated "Thank you" again and again while John stabbed the machete through the bars as quick as he could.

John watched the blade slice through Tony's lying fucking face and down his neck. He watched his ex-boyfriend's body go limp. When he finally pulled the machete free, part of John was glad he'd never have to listen to Tony's bullshit again. Another part of him was grateful he'd never have to listen to that awful music of his. Most of all, he was just glad this nightmare was over.

He'd deal with the consequences tomorrow. Right now, he and Liz needed to go. She half-smiled as he approached her, and they headed for the front door. The host's car was one of several still parked out the front. Liz pressed the button on the key, and a set of orange lights flashed in the night. The blue Jaguar.

Climbing into the passenger seat, John positioned the machete between his legs, the blade facing away from him. The engine started, and they drove into the night, leaving the mansion to grow smaller in the rearview.

John leaned back in his chair, rested his eyes, and realised he couldn't feel safe anywhere. Not in the city, not in the country. Nowhere. After driving in silence, he said, "It's true what they say. Hell is other people."

Sighing, and wiping exhaustion from her eyes, Liz nodded. "You can say that again."

"Should we go to the cops?"

Liz took a deep breath. "Not local ones. Who knows how many people around here were in on it? With those masks, they could have been anyone."

"What do we do, then?"

"For the moment," Liz said, "we drive." She switched on the radio, then searched for a station, jumping at how loud the speakers were. Music came through the static and John frowned at the lyrics to "It's My Life."

Liz switched it off and looked at John. "I hate this song."

"Me too." John smiled as he closed his eyes.

PART I

SUSPENSE

PL8ES

"All I see is death."

I stared at the small woman scratching words into her notepad. Notes about me. About my thoughts. I waited for her to finish writing, willing the pad to flip out of her lap so I could see.

When she realised I'd stopped talking, she peered up at me over her square glasses. Blue eyes. Cold. So cold.

"The death of the little boy?" she asked in a monotonous voice. This was just business for her. She didn't care. Why would she? She'd never taken a life. She didn't understand the gravity of squeezing your hands around someone's fate, watching it fade.

"There were others," I whispered. "So many others."

She cleared her throat and put down the notepad. Giving me her attention.

About time.

"And you feel…" She let the sentence hang, hoping I'd fill the silence. I didn't. "Shame? Guilt?"

I nodded. "All those words, I feel them all."

She was squeamish, this one. She'd never get by in Iraq or Afghanistan. Hell, she'd never make it through the mall without a fucking shopping list. This is what I fought for, though. Freedom. The freedom to be weak. Weakness was something I'd never been able to afford.

Now she was frowning, turning her face upside down to feign compassion. I recognised the expression. On her, it seemed like a mask. With the money she was getting for my mental health issues, the least she could do was pretend to give a shit.

"How's the medication working for you?" she asked. "Are you sleeping better?"

I didn't tell her I wasn't taking the pills. Or that they turned me into a fucking zombie. Instead, I laughed. "Hell, doc, I'm the only one who's *not* sleeping."

She tilted her head. A dog with curiosity.

"Look around." I walked to the window of the fifth-storey office. Peered through the winter fog at the people crossing the street, sipping their pumpkin-spiced lattes, waving goodbye to their friends.

Ants. All of them, ants.

I could be a sniper aiming at them through my scope. They'd have no idea. They wouldn't notice if I wiped out a city block.

"What do you see down there?" the psychologist asked, poising the pen for more notes.

"Everyone is asleep, doc." I grimaced. "It's no wonder the terrorists are winning."

I heard the pen rushing across the page. She was like an

author, inspired by my misery. Just another ant.

We talked a bit more about my sleeping patterns and the tossing and turning night after night. The voices were gone for the most part. But I was always jittery. Anything could set me off, take me right back to Iraq. And all she wanted to know was how I slept.

The session went on, me droning about my CO's face, bloodied and half gone after an insurgent had given him two barrels' worth of hatred. Davies, his name was. He'd spoken his last words to me. The last thing he'd ever said. The message.

Someone will contact you.

I left that part out. She wouldn't understand.

"Any job prospects this week?" I could tell that the psychologist had been working her way down a list. Every week it was the same. Sleep, work, friends—all the safe topics. Nobody wanted to talk about the real stuff. The children burned alive in a gutter. Their parents kneeling, with guns in the backs of their heads, soldiers shouting to shut the fuck up. Those same people coming back as war heroes, planted across the front page like symbols of what we all ought to strive for.

"The bureaucrats still won't pay out a pension." I held up my right hand. "Even with the obvious injuries."

She nodded again, then frowned. The eyes were still cold.

"I thought about driving."

"Deliveries?" she queried.

"Something like that." I smirked. "Those driving services. Like a taxi, but not. Get a few night shifts, take my mind away from trying to sleep."

The psychologist scrawled something else, traces of a smile appearing in the corners of her lips. Dimples. I hadn't noticed them before. Men everywhere probably thought they were cute.

Having convinced her my PTSD was under control and my meds were still staving off the voices, I left her and her dimples to write up more notes on my case. She would be reporting back to the bureaucrats that the end of my military career was still valid. Dishonourable discharge. After everything I'd done. Maybe because of it. Whatever.

By the time I got home, avoiding puddles from the non-stop drizzle, I'd been contacted by an old dog I'd served with. That's what we called ourselves—The Dog Squad. Nipping at the heels of terrorists and biting when we had the say so. An old dog, Tanner, rang me.

Someone will contact you.

He ran a driving service and said he had work for me—as much as I wanted. It couldn't be a coincidence—this was fate. I put the thought into the universe, and it came back with an answer.

Tanner, of all people? Fate was a twisted mistress. We had history. Too much to yap on about. The bottom line was that he owed me. Even after giving me a job, he'd always owe me, and he knew it.

Tanner gave me a time and location in the middle of the city. My first drive was tonight. "Remember to be friendly," he'd said, "and for Pete's sake, smile."

I ground my teeth on the bus ride over, breathing fog onto the windows. The winter air didn't understand the laws of physics, drifting through the metal and glass of the bus and sinking into every fibre of my body.

As the bus rolled along—ants fumbling with their mobiles and talking among each other—I wondered how to make chit-chat with people whose lives were so small they couldn't even imagine pointing a gun at someone. Let alone pulling the trigger. What would I talk about? Based on the news cycle blaring through my headphones, it'd be today's Western-washed topics. The weather was turning cold, football season was about to start, and some local thug got done for dealing drugs to kids.

At least those kids were alive, not burned to ash in an anonymous grave in the Middle East. I thought about ringing up the news station and blowing the lid on the whole thing. The next segment changed my mind. Celebrity gossip took the primetime spot at seven pm. It reminded me of the uselessness of war.

Of everything.

I saw Tanner down the alley, shivering in the cold. I stashed my headphones into my pocket and offered a slight nod. The Dog Squad greeting. Tanner waved at me as I approached, a full five fingers high in the air and a mass of white teeth flashing at me. He'd changed. Maybe for the better.

"Good to see you, brother." We clasped ice-cold hands, and he pulled me in for a quick hug. Slapped my back with his open palm like I'd swallowed my tongue. "Your face looks a lot better."

"Thanks for the job." I ignored the critique.

He took me into the garage and showed me around. The old dog had done well for himself. He had a fleet of seven cars, polished and sparkling under industrial lighting, each stamped with the company name on both sides. It would have cost a small fortune.

"How'd you do all this?" I asked, impressed.

"When they refused to give me my military pension,"—his words were angry—"I hit my mum up for a loan. Started with one car, worked myself to the bone 'til I paid every cent back. It's taken a few years, but man, I'm living the dream."

The system had failed him, too, yet he'd found a way.

Maybe his meds were better than mine. Maybe he was taking his. Or maybe he'd be like me if he didn't have any family. I'd have asked my mom for a loan, too, except she'd walked off a bridge one night in the middle of winter, straight into the harbour. She'd been my only relative.

Never did get that suicide note.

Tanner threw me a set of keys, jolting me back to the present. Gave me a gas card and a phone. Showed me the ropes, so to speak, and it felt like a noose. I breathed through it and paid attention. When someone wanted a ride, they'd ping the number on the work phone. All I had to do was click *Accept*, and the job was mine.

Tanner leaned through the window to tell me, "Don't take jobs that are too far away." I might have winced from his stale cigarette breath. "Cost of gas versus time it takes to get there won't be worth it. We want to maximise profits."

I nodded. Tanner the businessman. Who would have thought the guy who'd spit-shined my boots would build an empire and give me a job? My sense of pride had been buried a long time ago, though. I had no issue taking this guy's money. Like I said, he owed me.

Each car had a starting spot in the city. The drivers would be spread out. Move across one city block each hour, on the hour. Maximise our visibility, don't give the appearance of sitting in the same spot all night. People needed to think we were busy.

My first hour was spent outside a kebab shop, drooling at the smell of meat wafting into the street. A few people glanced at the car, took a step forward. Glanced at me. Stepped back. Maybe the burn scars on my face put them off. Maybe it was my eyes.

The clock ticked over. The first hour was up. I shifted the

car into drive and headed to my next spot. The phone pinged as I ran a red light. Someone was just around the corner. I tapped "Accept" and headed over, practicing my smile as Tanner had suggested.

A guy. Cute. Long brown hair, hazel eyes. Looked like he worked out. He climbed into the back, a silver locket dangling across his chest. I'm not a pervert, so I looked away. Cleared my throat to say, "Hello".

"Hi there." He beat me to it. Snuggled into a winter jacket. A long grey thing with buttons all the way down and a sharp collar folded up around his neck.

"Evening." I tried my friendliest voice. Sounded forced. "Where you headed?"

He gave me the address and I punched it into my GPS, conscious that he could see the scarred fingers on my hand.

I drove in silence, looking at him in the rearview. Aside from the psychologist, he was the only person I'd been alone with in years. He busied himself on his phone, thumbing the screen as he typed a message. A girlfriend, I guessed. Maybe a boyfriend, who could tell? Telling them about the freak he'd jumped into a car with.

"Sorry about that," he said with a smile, slipping his phone into a small, red, leather shoulder bag with long straps. It was ugly.

"About what?"

"You must have thought I was pretty rude, texting like that. I hate that." The man looked at my reflection in the rearview. "Love the one you're with, isn't that the old saying?"

I stared at the median strip. "Indeed."

"Emile." He placed a gentle hand on my shoulder. Squeezed. "Lovely to meet you."

I introduced myself, trying to loosen my body from all the

tension I'd been carrying. The sessions with the psychologist always made me tense. Emile worked the night shift, like me. He loved the night air, the frost on the telegraph poles, and the way the puddles—as black as midnight—could still reflect a face. He loved the eerie quietness that followed him towards the office.

"There's something spooky about it." He giggled, and I felt a tingle in my heart. "Don't you just love it?"

He was charming, more than I'd ever been. Customer service was his game, always chatting to someone about insurance or something. The way he said insurance was strange. A hushed word among a stream of noise. I blinked the thought away. I was losing interest in the conversation when Emile bit his lip and said, "I feel like everyone is asleep."

My eyes shifted in the mirror, focusing on him as he fiddled with the locket around his neck.

Clicked it open.

Clicked it shut.

Opened it again. Stared at something inside.

"What do you mean?" I asked, my voice as quiet as the night was dark.

Emile looked at me. I couldn't read the expression on his face, half-hidden in shadow. "You know what I mean."

I pulled up outside his office building, the streetlamps humming nearby. The city was dead at this time of night. Safe for a clandestine meeting. I turned around as Emile tapped his card on the reader to pay and said a pleasant goodnight.

"Hope to see you again." He waved through the window and walked inside.

As his form was enveloped by the yellow lighting of the building's lobby, I watched to see if Emile turned around. He'd started to give me a message but hadn't finished.

Everyone is asleep.

He waited at the elevator, thumbing his phone once more. Telling someone he'd made contact. Given me the message. The "Up" arrow glowed white, and Emile walked into the elevator. He didn't look back.

I took a deep breath, running my burned and scarred fingers through my hair. Had he been flirting? Hard to tell. With this monster of a face, I doubted it.

It couldn't be coincidence that of all the people in the city, I'd picked him up. Of all the taxis, Ubers, and other cars, he'd landed in mine.

Emile, who talked about everyone being asleep on the same day I'd said that to the psychologist.

Emile, who conveniently worked night shift and lived around the corner from my dedicated position on the street.

Emile, who I'd met on my first shift.

Emile.

A car pulled up in front of me. A Bentley. Not new, though still in good condition. Probably expensive. The windows were tinted the same black as the car. I looked around. No other cars in the area.

This was it, the last half of the message.

The only people awake had found each other in a city afflicted by sleep and dreams. Someone was looking for me.

The engine kept running, releasing smog into the city's cool night air. The exhaust pipe vibrated under the strain of the engine. Someone was in the car, why weren't they getting out?

Are they waiting for me? I squinted through my windshield, hoping to catch a glimpse of the person inside the Bentley. A shadow, some movement. Anything.

A light came on in the cabin. I saw the silhouette of a

figure—too broad-shouldered to be a woman, at least in his experience. The guy was holding something, shaking it in his hands, and throwing it to the footwell on the car's passenger side.

The Bentley tore away from the curb in the next instant, screeching up the street without indicating. The licence plate read F11 WM3.

Follow Me.

This was it. The mission CO Davies told me about. I spun the wheel, shifted the car into drive, and followed the Bentley.

I tailed the car for ten minutes, conscious that Tanner wouldn't be happy about the petrol I was wasting. The driver raced through the streets like he knew someone was in tow. I kept my distance, just as my training had taught me. It was second nature now. Stay back, and when the car turns a corner, wait a few seconds before following. Lots of people make the mistake of turning their lights off or not blinking for the turns. People notice that kind of thing. Any training manual will tell you to act as normal as possible.

So that's what I did.

After the Bentley turned, I waited at the lights until I couldn't see it anymore.

Stay back.

A hundred metres between us. I waited until it was two. I turned, ignoring the ping of another potential customer. Wiped the fog from the inside of my windshield and turned the heat on. Wisps of thick fog drifted up from the sewer below, like ghosts on the prowl. Waiting for someone to rattle. This winter was going to be cold.

The Bentley pulled up, a woman got out, headed into the wintry night. I hadn't seen her silhouette earlier. Where'd she come from? The driver's window slid down, a mass of hot breath escaping into the night air. He flicked a cigarette into the street, threw a matchbox after it. The window went up. The Bentley disappeared down the street.

It was the kind of obscure thing the Dog Squad might have done back in the day. Do something nobody would blink at. Except those in the know.

A message.

I pulled up next to the matchbox, letting the engine ride on idle as I picked it up. Empty. I flipped it over. The picture on the back was code. A luxury hotel, right in the middle of the city only a few blocks away. It's slogan: "With beds so comfortable you won't *want* to sleep."

Sleep.

It had to be a message; the mission was revealing itself. I looked around for the woman. Whoever she was, she was long gone. It didn't matter. I had what I needed.

I drove to the hotel. It was not what I would call luxury— more like a roach motel. It didn't look anything like the picture. I checked the address to make sure I hadn't made a mistake. The lone car parked across the street changed my mind. The licence plate read 1N5 1D3.

Inside.

The Dandelion Motel looked out of place for the middle of the city. An old, four-storey building, maybe from the 1950s, swallowed on one side by the shadows of a fresh high rise. Long, rectangular windows facing the street, a graffitied sign above the door. The motel was right next to an alley, the dumpster overflowing with dirty towels, empty beer bottles, used condoms. Needles dripping the last of whatever drug had been in them. A rusty fire escape led to the second storey. I saw a bleak yellow light emanating from a window up there. No shadows. Maybe someone had left it on.

I leaned into one of the windows, rubbed a circle to see inside. A dim lamp in reception washed a glare across the wall of keys behind it. Not a soul in sight. I tried the door. It swung open with a creak, and I entered the motel.

"Hello?" I called into the pale light. Shadows crept up the walls, taking odd shapes. I twisted around to scan reception. A bronze and rusted service bell gave a low chime as I pressed it. A rainbow flag hung limp on the back wall. I resisted a smile, didn't have it in me. Nobody was going to love me now, not with the burdens I carried.

"Anyone here?" I called again.

This had to be part of the mission. I couldn't fathom how the grimy motel still had customers. I doubted even the hookers would lie here, not even a whore on her deathbed. Yet the Dandelion still manufactured matchboxes and advertised as a luxury hotel. It didn't add up.

"Sorry, sir, I didn't hear the bell." An old man appeared out of the shadows. I hadn't heard him come in, couldn't see where he came from.

"I need somewhere to *sleep*." I emphasised sleep, saying it slowly, drawing out the syllable. I flashed the matchbox.

The old man took a step back as he took in my burned form. He took a second to compose himself and nodded. Then he reached for something under the reception desk—a thick green book. He flipped it to an empty page.

"How many h-hours?" He licked the tip of a pen and poised above the page.

"What?"

The old man looked behind me, searching. "Where is he?"

"Who?"

He searched the room again, peering into the darkness. "Never mind." He cleared his throat and said he was going to assume I'd be here all night. He threw me a room key, avoiding my gaze, and mumbled the room number.

"It's upstairs." He pointed in the general direction I was expected to travel.

I headed to the room, turning the key over in my hands. Travelling the hallway, I heard subdued moans, groans, and the occasional thump. Wood against plaster. The place left a bad taste in my mouth. I hoped I'd receive the next message once I got to my room.

The room hadn't been cleaned for a long time. Mould on the curtains. Mould on the carpet. Damp. Dank. A beam of red filtered through the curtains from a nearby traffic light. Red, like the sun sinking over sandy hills. The night sky illuminating the fire. I could smell the bodies again, and pinched my nose. Tried to shake the memory, my chest heaving. Thunder rumbled in the heavens outside.

The light switched over, covering the room in a dull green glow. Green, like my parents' farm. My breathing settled. Now wasn't the time for flashbacks. I needed to focus on the mission.

A desk in the corner. It seemed out of place, given that rooms were rented by the hour. I opened a desk drawer, found a Bible. Flipped through the pages. Threw the Christian dogma over my back to see if anything else was inside the drawer. I remembered the licence plate.

Inside.

There was something in here. I swallowed my growing frustration and looked around. Bedside tables. A notepad and pen by the phone. A card with the reception number. The bedside tables didn't have drawers. I went to the wardrobe across the room. It was an old stand-alone thing planted in a dark corner.

Traffic lights changed again. The room went red. I hated that colour. The stench of charred bodies filled the room. Thunder rumbled again, lightning struck. My eyes started to ache, my heart burned. I wished for green. Got rain padding against the windows instead.

The wardrobe was empty. The whole room was empty. I slammed my fists against the wardrobe doors. I rubbed my eyes—my vision was starting to blur.

There has to be something. The old man—

The old man. The way he'd looked at me. Avoided my eyes. He'd asked where "he" was. Who was *he*? He knew something.

Green again.

I composed myself as best I could. Made my way to the door, ignoring the squeaking bed and the muffled groans of pleasure from the next room—*Fuck me, Daddy!* My eyes didn't ache so much now, though the smell remained.

The stairs creaked as I descended to reception once more. The old man looked at me. Looked away.

What's he hiding?

"Where is he?" I asked over the pounding rain. "That's what you asked me before."

He held up a hand, stepped away from the desk. "I didn't mean to—"

"Who is *he*?" I raised my voice. Felt the anger in my hands. "Is it Emile? Is that who you're talking about?"

The old man shook his head and started to say something. I leaned over the desk and grabbed his shirt.

"What's Emile got to do with all this?" I spat.

I pulled the old man towards me and saw a tear escaping his eye. I paid no attention to his fear. He should be scared.

"I-I don't know an E-Emile," he stuttered, turning his face from me. "Please d-d-don't hurt m-m-me."

My heart was in my throat, and the rage bubbled through my skin. Seeping out of the burns on my face. The storm outside matched my anger, the motel windows shaking in the fierce winds.

I raised my fist to the old man and barked at him to tell me what he knew. He shrunk before me and cried that he knew nothing about anything and didn't know Emile, and he was sorry for any misunderstanding.

"Misunderstanding, huh?" I screamed, and slammed the matchbox onto the reception desk. "What's this then?"

The old man swallowed hard. Shook his head again. He was holding something back. I'd broken stronger men than him in my time. I'd break him, too. I climbed over the desk, pushed the old man into the wall of keys. Ignored the metal clanging against his back, and the rainbow flag floating to the floor. Wedged my forearm under his neck.

"Don't lie to me, old man," I said through gritted teeth.

"I s-s-swear," he choked.

I threw the old man over the desk and watched him fall to the floor with a pained cry. As I climbed the desk and lunged towards him, he got to his feet and held his left arm. His old bones were frail.

He ran from the motel, disappearing into the storm. I ran after him, caught the old man as he turned into the alley. I lunged, tackled him to the road. He screamed and begged for help, even though we both knew at this hour, and with the raging storm, nobody would hear a thing.

"Tell me what I need to know." I banged his head into the tarmac, pressing into his skull until I saw blood mix with the puddles beneath him.

"Help!" he cried.

I slammed his head into the tarmac again. The old man

would break soon enough. He would tell me what I needed to know. About the mission. About Emile. About everything. I slammed again and again, telling him it could all end if he would just give me the information I needed.

The old man stopped crying. Blood framed his head like a halo. My eyes ached from the colour. I stood up, angry at myself for going too hard. He lay in the puddle of his own blood, unmoving.

Huffing and panting, I poked at him with a foot. No response. I stepped back, shaking, wiping rain from my face. Wondered where I'd gone wrong. The mission had led me here. The codes, the Bentley, the matchbox, the licence plates. Emile, Tanner, my psychologist. They'd all led me here tonight. The message in the plate—*Inside*—had meant something.

Lightning struck somewhere in the distance, the crack drawing me from my thoughts. I went back to the car, held the steering wheel with my shaking hands. The storm pounded at my windows as I turned the key in the ignition. Water and blood dripped into the carpet.

The phone pinged. A new customer. Before I turned away from the kerb, I picked up the phone. Five missed calls from Tanner. I hit redial. He had some explaining to do.

"Hey, man," he answered quick. Too quick.

"What's going on?" My breaths were still heavy. I tried to calm down, to stop shaking.

"Where have you been?" Tanner sounded worried.

"I've been at the motel," I answered. "The Dandelion."

"Why?"

I didn't answer.

"Are you okay, you don't sound good." Tanner's voice was soft. He really had changed.

"We need to talk," I said, and hung up.

Swerving onto the road, I headed back to the garage—back to see Tanner and figure out what was going on.

He greeted me at the door, another wave. I nodded back, but my eyes betrayed me. Tanner knew me well enough to see I was angry. His brow was furrowed in concern when I stepped out of the car and slammed the door.

"What's wrong?" he asked. He saw my bloody fists, caught the look on my face. Took a step back. People were always doing that to me.

"You need to tell me what's going on." I tried to hold back the rage.

Tanner shrugged and stepped forward, putting a hand on my arm. I shook him off. "I don't know what you mean." His voice was low, comforting, and genuine. He motioned towards his office. "Sit down, man, tell me what happened."

"The mission," I whispered, and looked around. "What's the mission?"

Tanner looked at me, curious. Looked at my hands again. Said something about calling someone, walked to his office. I followed him, stood in the doorway. White walls. Plain, bare. An oak desk, black chairs. Simple. Laptop closed on the desk. He saw me eyeing the laptop as he dialled a number. Smiled at me.

"Put the phone down," I said, rubbing my hands.

Tanner put the phone on the desk and pressed the red "hung up" button. I didn't catch the number he was calling, but it was probably 000.

I sat down in one of the black chairs and ran my fingers through my wet hair. Tanner sat on the other side of the desk. Clasped his hands together in full view. He knew that was important. He didn't want to make me any more jittery.

"There is no mission," Tanner said. His quiet voice echoed

against the white walls. Echoed in my ears. He was lying to my face.

I looked away. I rubbed my temples; my eyes ached again. A voice called out in the back of my brain. One of the many I'd been holding back. Tanner kept talking, but I couldn't hear him. His lips moved, his face expressed concern and worry. All I heard was the ringing in my ears. The voice screaming in my brain. The psychologist always told me to breathe through it, like breathing was a magical fucking cure for every pang of anxiety. I couldn't breathe this time. I couldn't wish it away. Didn't want to. Instead, I listened.

Lies, it screamed over and over. *Lies, lies, lies.*

That's when I saw the drops of sweat sliding down Tanner's face. Sweat on a night like this, with a storm and a frost that sank into the bones? He wasn't sweating from the heat. He was sweating because he knew something. He put me in that car. He put me on that corner. He sent Emile to me.

I stood up, cutting Tanner off from whatever bullshit he was spouting.

"Out of respect for what we went through over there,"— my words were slow, purposeful—"I will ask you one more time."

Tanner got to his feet, looked defensive.

"What's the mission?" I pressed.

At the first sign of Tanner shaking his head, I raced around the desk to him. He reached into the desk drawer and pulled out a Glock 17. I swiped his arm to the side and planted my burned hand around his throat. Grabbed the gun from him.

"The mission!" I yelled at him.

Do it, do it, do it, the voice chanted.

"I don't know."

My finger squeezed the trigger. I watched his forehead

split open and the white walls splash with red and pink and shards of skull. I let go of Tanner's throat and he fell to the ground with a thud. The mess of blood and brain matter slid down the wall. I watched it, fighting the memories banging at the door.

My friend. Dead.

Liar. The voice reminded me.

The gun felt heavy in my hand, the barrel smoking with guilt and pleasure at its last kill. I searched the desk, throwing papers and photos of his family to the ground. Rummaged through files on his laptop. Browser history was mostly business sites, e-conferences on building your empire. One site buried in the previous week's history caught my attention. A car site. Bentley. What was Tanner doing looking at Bentleys?

Looking down at my friend one last time, I stared into his eyes, left open in the wake of the bullet's speed. Green. Not calming, not like my parents' farm. Empty.

I tucked the gun into my belt and walked back to my car, ignoring the pain in my eyes. It was spreading to my head now, a dull ache that throbbed with each step. I had to find that Bentley.

Sitting behind the wheel, I put the car in reverse and stopped when I saw the licence plate of another of Tanner's fleet: 7H3 M15N.

I studied the plate. 7H3. *THE.* M15N. *MIS'N.* The mis'n. The missing?

The Mission.

Nothing so far had been coincidence; this wasn't either. It couldn't be. I stopped the car and walked to 7H3's driver's door. I tried the handle. It was locked. Part of me felt that time was running out. Too much time had been wasted with the old man and now with Tanner. I didn't know what was waiting for me or how much time I had left. I just felt in my bones that I didn't have long.

With that thought rushing through me, I smashed the driver's window and unlocked the car. Right there on the front passenger seat. A phone. The same issue as the one Tanner had given me. That couldn't be a coincidence, either. I reached for the phone, checked the notifications. A few customers waiting to be picked up. I scrolled through the list of locations, sensing I would know what I was looking for when I found it. All close by. Nothing jumped out at me. I took the phone and got back in my car, shrugging off remnants of guilt about Tanner.

The Bentley. Find the Bentley. The voice knew what I had to do. The voice was my only friend now.

The digital display in the car read 3:33 am. The storm had retreated some time in the previous fifteen minutes. The roads were still drenched, water cascading down drains. Rushing to get away from me as I sped through the city streets, hunting. The night sky had started to clear with the inevitability of daylight. A dusk glow struggled to breach the cloud line as the sun began its slow ascent.

I couldn't rely on finding the Bentley without another message—the city was just too big. It could be hidden in an alley, underground parking garage, or at someone's house. As I sped through the city streets, conscious that people— *No, ants*—were waking up and heading to work, I searched every licence plate I could see. Most were random letters and numbers. I searched until the clock struck 4:00 am and the phone pinged. The location was familiar.

Emile's building.

I tapped "Accept". Placing the phone into the centre console, I looked back at the road before me. A car approached from behind. The licence plate's message was clear but confused me: L0C K3T.

Locket.

Emile had a locket. He'd twisted it in his hands, clicked it open and shut. What had he been looking at when he opened it? Had that been the mission all along? Emile's locket. As fate had it, I was on my way to him now.

Turning into the street, I saw Emile waiting by a streetlamp, taking comfort and mild warmth from the dim light. Slowing down to a traffic light, my eyes ached again at the red glow. The car slowed to a stop, the brake lights of the car in front illuminating the licence plate. The message sunk into my aching eyes: K1L H1M.

Kill Hin.

I swallowed. He'd been nice to me. I didn't want to hurt him. In another life we could have dated, he was that sort of guy, I could tell. Maybe I could take the locket and let him go. The thought had just formed when the car beeped its horn, revved. *Kill Him* beeped again. Emphasising the message. I knew what I had to do.

Emile had to die.

The orders raced through my mind. The messages I'd received throughout the night. The matchbox, the motel, the licence plates. Despite the reason for the orders remaining unknown, I gathered it had something to do with the locket. Following orders was always a leap of faith. It was a leap I'd taken many times before. And I'd leap again.

Emile recognised my face. Hard not to. He waved me down with twinkling fingers and a smile. Climbed into the back of the car with a heavy sigh and a tired "Hello". I mumbled a response as he settled into the seat. Strapped in. Grabbed his locket. His ugly red bad was nowhere in sight.

He tried to make small talk, though I could tell he wasn't

in it. He'd had a hard shift with whatever he did in there. Insurance, was it? Reached for his phone, announced he was checking some missed calls from his mother. With that thought in my mind, I pressed the lock button on my door. All the doors clamped with a subtle click. Emile didn't blink. Hadn't noticed. Too busy texting.

The Dandelion Motel looked the same in the early morning as it did late at night. The only real difference was the dead body in the alleyway. Except as I pulled up to the motel, the alley was clear. No dead old man, no blood. No police tape. He was just gone.

Someone is watching over us, the voice in my head said.

Emile looked up from his phone, sensing we weren't where we were supposed to be. He peered out the window, eyes filling with fear.

"What are we doing here?" he asked, trying to stay casual.

I turned in my seat, reached for the gun in my belt and held it in front of him. Emile's eyes fell onto the Glock, and he screamed.

"Stop screaming," I said. Calm. Quiet. "Give me your phone." He handed me the phone, keeping his eyes on the gun.

I heard him begging, but the voice in my head was louder. Reassuring me. Telling me I was only following orders. It had to be done. I was doing a good job.

"Please," he said, clutching the locket. "You don't have to do this."

"I think we both know I do." I shrugged, shaking off the stench of dead children. Tried not to imagine Emile in that gutter, along with the rest of them.

I got out of the car, keeping the gun pointed at Emile as I did so, and ordered him out of the car. He complied and obeyed my instruction to move to the alley—in silence. The sun started peering over the high rises, casting an orange-yellow light into the alley.

Like fire.

The stench returned, my nostrils burning at the memory. Emile walked, his back facing me, just as the children had. Walking to their deaths. Crying, pleading, not understanding what was happening. Why they had to die.

You're doing the right thing, the voice said. It had said the same thing then, too.

I didn't want a long, drawn-out scene in the alley. I just wanted to get it done and go home. Emile obeyed the order to get to his knees. I didn't know why I bothered with that tired demand. Just seemed appropriate in the moment. He fell to his knees, begging for me to reconsider. Offered money. Offered sex. I didn't care about either anymore. I cared about my orders.

I raised the weapon. Took a breath. This was the leap of faith. No turning back. As I aimed the Glock at the back of his head, I heard the sound of glass bottles rolling against the tarmac. A whack on the side of my head sent fireworks through my vision.

"Run, man!" a voice shouted from behind me.

I spun to see a vagrant, holding an empty beer bottle. Threw it at my feet. Emile took the distraction, ran to the fire escape. Clawed up the stairs. Desperate screams for help. The vagrant tried to tell me I didn't have to hurt anyone. They were his last words. The recoil was smooth on the weapon, I barely felt it as I pulled the trigger and buried two bullets in his chest.

Halfway up the fire escape, Emile screamed again. I raced after him, stepping around broken bottles and shards of glass. He didn't stop when I shot in his direction. I admired his spirit. But orders were orders. I climbed the rusty metallic stairs, calling his name.

He climbed fast, but with my training, I caught him at the landing of the third storey. Grabbed at his coat and spun him around, before grabbing the locket.

He screamed for help. "Please, why are you doing this?" He begged for a reason. Tears rolled down his cheeks as he repeated the question a thousand times.

"I like you Emile, you see behind the scars," I said regretfully. "But I have my orders."

I took aim, raising the gun to his temple. As I moved to squeeze the trigger, Emile thrust forward, pushing me over the railing of the fire escape. Falling backward, I clutched the locket in my fist, knowing I had one last task before I completed the mission. I aimed again. The gun went off.

I missed. Emile watched me fall back to the earth, leaned over the railing to take in the glory of his victory, and I saw the whisper of a relieved smile form on his lips.

I fired again.

Emile lost his balance. He followed me over the railing.

I landed on my back with a thud, heard a crack. Felt a splinter of pain in the back of my head. Emile landed next to me, eyes dilated. Lifeless. The voice in my head told me I'd done a good job. Told me not to worry about the life I'd taken.

Just another ant.

I tried to sit up. Choked down some blood instead. The splinter in my head throbbed and I moved my fingers around to the back of my head.

Wet with blood.

I'd landed on a broken bottle, the sharp edges lodged in my head. Gripping the glass, I pulled at the shank and let the stream of blood pool around me. As the sun rose into the sky, clearing the storm from the night before, I fought to stay conscious. Clung to the locket, hoping it was worth the life I'd taken.

The locket slipped from my grip as the morning frost dug into my fingers. Crawled into my body. Ushered in sleep. Finally.

Police tape hung limp across the alley, detectives kneeling over the three bodies. The gun had been seized already, the ownership traced. They'd soon find Tanner and put two and two together. They'd write the story everyone was expecting to read. Ex-soldier, mentally unbalanced from serving in the war. People would feel sorry for him, start pointing the finger at the broken medical system. Nobody would ask too many questions. Just as planned. His psychologist stood just beyond the police barrier, huddled beneath an umbrella as she spoke with detectives. Her business card had been found in his pants pocket. A local reporter fixed her make-up before addressing the camera.

And so it began.

Davies watched the scene from an old Bentley across the street, fumbling with the locket. He clicked it open and smiled. The computer chip was intact. He removed the chip, pocketed it, and discarded the locket out the window.

He dialled the only number in his phone and waited. Someone answered but didn't speak. Protocol.

"Packaged received. Asset terminated," Davies said, and hung up.

He looked back at his old friend for a moment, before

driving from the scene. His guilt was forgotten by the time he reached the traffic lights at the end of the street. Red like fire. He smiled at the phantom smell the colour invoked.

There was no time for guilt. There was too much to do.

TICKETS TO PARADISE

It's all about the pitch," Sally said, shifting the car into park. "Once you reel them in, the sale is pretty much done."

Jeremy nodded, fiddling with the corners of his papers. He peered out the car window, towards the house. Well, it was more of a mansion or a country manor. He didn't know what houses that big were called these days. All he knew was two things: he didn't have one, and he wanted one.

Staring through the dirty glass window of Sally's inherited 1978 Buick, Jeremy repeated her words in his mind. Just reel them in, that's it. Get them on that hook. Easy peasy. He knew it was easy. Hell, he'd trained her all those years ago, he didn't need her, or anyone else, telling him how easy it was. He glanced at Sally, busy checking her hair in the rearview mirror and touching up eye make-up.

"Don't you think it's sexist they make you wear all that gunk on your face?" Jeremy asked.

Sally smiled and wiped lipstick from the corner of her

mouth with a pinkie. "They don't make me wear it. I'm practicing." She thought for a moment, using the same pinkie to wipe at her eyeliner. "Isn't it sexist to assume women are still *told* to wear make-up?"

Jeremy supposed it was and looked out the window again. "You stole it, didn't you?"

Thin red lips spread into a smile. "That's not all I stole. I'm getting ready for the big day."

Again, Jeremy looked out the window and took a deep breath.

"I know you don't want to do this anymore, since you got the new job. But it's just this once. For me. And we'll never have to sell anything ever again." Sally followed his line of vision to the manor. Two cement blocks, stylised like lion heads, framed the metal gates. In the centre of the gates, a "H", half the lettering on each gate.

"I don't know…." Jeremy let the sentence hang in the air.

"What's the new job, anyway? You never told me."

"Cleaning. Over at HQ, a few nights a week."

Sally nodded. "Nice work if you can get it. Your name came up in the lottery, huh? Good job, Jer." She kept her eyes on the cement lion heads. "But, since it's just a few nights a week, you need this as much as I do."

Jeremy paused for a moment, considering the truth in her words. He reached for the door handle, ignoring the rusty creak as he pulled. He was used to it by now. His stomach knotted as he climbed out of the Buick, and he chewed his lower lip. The door clinked shut behind him, and Jeremy clutched Paradise Co. papers tight to his chest.

One last time.

The gate to the mansion was ajar, and Jeremy gulped as he manoeuvred through the space. Hedges lined a white gravel driveway, the manor perched on a slight rise.

Approaching what he was fast defining as a country estate, Jeremy practiced his pitch. Sally was counting on him to make this sale. The last family had weaselled out at the last minute, and she hadn't spoken to him for a few days. Until last night, when she'd broken her silence to tell him about the Heatherbraes.

"They're the elite of the elite. If we can get *them*, we'll be set for life." Her voice had that electric shock energy that vibrated through his core, and he couldn't say no. Especially not when she'd told him how influential they were. If he could sell tickets to Paradise to the Heatherbraes, the rest would follow.

Now, with the double-wide front doors staring at him, his fist raised to knock, he wasn't sure this was the right thing to do. Not everyone was interested in Paradise, but he reminded himself that they had requested the appointment. They had invited him to their home.

You're halfway there, Jer. They've had a bite, you just need to get them on the hook for good.

He knocked on the thick wooden doors, then saw to his right a camera shifting to his position. He waved and smiled, assuming a timid posture—arms at his side, head slightly bowed, feet together.

"My husband will be there in a moment." A man's voice— one of the Mr Heatherbraes—came from a speaker. Jeremy searched for the source but couldn't find it. He gave a meek thumbs up to the camera in the hopes that Mr Heatherbrae was still watching him.

A small chill ran down his spine at the thought of him gazing at his pixelated image on a monitor somewhere, and he swallowed hard, shifting the Paradise papers back to his chest.

What do I really know about these people? He'd heard a story—gossip, really—about a Paradise salesman disappearing a while back. *It's just me and Sally here. These people could do anything to us, who would know?*

The door opened wide and a man wearing an airy white shirt greeted him with open arms. "Welcome to our home," he said, and engulfed Jeremy in a hug.

Clearing his throat, and sensing he was quite tense, Jeremy let out a slow breath to relax. He felt the Paradise papers scrunch a little. "Thank you… for seeing me, Mr—"

"Pish tosh"—the man flicked his hand in the air—"call me Kevin."

Friendliness was part of the salesman role, Jeremy reminded himself, and he made a mental note to use the man's first name. It was in the salesman's handbook, anyway.

"Please, come in," Kevin said, ushering Jeremy through the doors and into a marble lobby.

"Thanks." Jeremy made a conscious effort to be seen looking at the house. "You have a beautiful home."

Words like "home" were in the handbook, too.

Jeremy was guided to what he equated to a living room, though the sheer size of it could fit two of his studio apartments, and then some. Kevin plopped on a lounge, and Jeremy did the same, sitting on the edge, as the handbook insisted. *Never make yourself too at home.*

The other Mr Heatherbrae joined them a moment later, a light blue robe flowing behind him, carrying a bottle of wine and a cheeseboard. "We just love company," he said, flashing his white teeth. Jeremy was taken aback at how inviting and kind these people seemed. His prior experience with what Paradise Co. called the "Top 1%" had been quite the opposite.

Placing the cheeseboard on a glass coffee table, Mr

Heatherbrae displayed the wine to Jeremy, label first. He nodded, gracious.

"This is my husband, Bryan," Kevin said, and Jeremy introduced himself to Bryan by way of a courteous bow. Bryan winked and glided from the room. Jeremy watched him go, assuming he'd be back with the wine glasses.

"Help yourself to some cheese"—Kevin pointed to the cheeseboard, palm up—"guests eat first."

"I shouldn't." Rule #28 in the handbook: refuse politely and relent at the second invitation.

"I insist," Kevin said.

Jeremy relented, as he was supposed to do, and cut into a block of cheese. He didn't recognise the type, he was used to days old slices with a hint of mould. Nonetheless, he placed it onto a cracker and bit into it—halfway, as per the handbook instructions. Never, ever, appear greedy. Not to the Top 1%.

As Jeremy chewed, Kevin watched his jaw go up and down, up and down, mashing the cheese into pulp, until Bryan returned with three wine glasses.

"We had this imported from Chile," he said, pronouncing it chill-ay. "It's a fabulous drop, only one hundred bottles ever made."

Jeremy swallowed his cheese and cracker. "Oh, wonderful." He remembered the vocabulary he was allowed to use in these areas. "Wonderful", "fabulous"—which had just been taken, no repeats—and "marvellous". Other words like "excellent" and "great" were too… Top 5%… and were out of the question when dealing with potential Paradise ticket holders.

Pointing a long, thin finger at the papers in Jeremy's hand, Bryan asked, "Is that for us?"

"Oh yes." Jeremy smiled, as Bryan poured the wine.

He had practiced this smile for some time in the mirror

and had it down to a fine art. Don't part the lips too much—
nobody likes to see too many yellowed, middle-class teeth—
and ensure you smile with your eyes. That was the tricky part,
because it was about eyebrow placement, as well as the width
of the eye. If your eyes are too wide, you look desperate. If they
are too narrow, you look like a creep.

The Top 1% cannot be made to feel threatened. Salesmen
must be their best friends at all times. How else would Paradise
Co. get their money?

His smile worked, seeing both the Heatherbraes relax into
the lounge and start flipping through the papers.

"I'm not going to sit here and pitch you," Jeremy said,
taking a sip of wine. "When it comes to Paradise, people have
either made up their mind, or they haven't. I find that when
families like yourselves make an appointment with me, there's
usually a reason. So"—another sip, not too confident, the
handbook said to relax at their pace—"what concerns do you
have that I can help with?"

The Heatherbraes looked at each other, then back to
Jeremy.

"We are so glad to hear you say that," Kevin said with a
slight shake of his head. "We *can't stand* the pitch. We know
what we want, and as you said, that's why you're here."

Jeremy bowed his head a little, indicating with perfection
that he was their humble servant. The Top 1% must feel
empowered at all times.

"It's just," Bryan said, "we have friends who went to
Paradise. It's been over a year and they haven't come back. We
haven't even heard from them."

"I'm not surprised." Jeremy motioned to the papers he
held. "If you view the literature, which I'm assuming you have
done already, you'll see that nobody—and I mean *nobody*—

comes back from Paradise."

Kevin raised an eyebrow. "Never?"

Jeremy shrugged. "Why would you want to? It is paradise, after all." The couple frowned and Jeremy flipped through pages in his mental handbook so as not to lose them from the hook. "Paradise is essentially a new home. It offers each ticket holder a stress-free, unique environment, where you can do anything you want, at any time."

"How do we get there?" Bryan asked, flicking through the Paradise Co. papers.

"It's a simple trip in our teleportation machine—"

"Like the ones at the airports?"

"They should rename those, shouldn't they? Since the last plane flew, what, thirty years ago? But yes, just like those ones, only slightly more advanced. You see, Paradise is located in the Canis Minor constellation, on Luyten's Star. I've been there myself"—he swallowed the lie—"all sales personnel are inducted there. Each ticket holder receives their own luxury living quarters. Everyone in the Top 1%, such as yourselves, also have unlimited restrictions across the surrounding environments. With the proper safety equipment, of course. I have to say, it's just"—Jeremy put a hand to his heart and released a slow, deep breath—"breathtaking."

Bryan straightened his back a little. "Gosh, Kev, that sounds nice, doesn't it?"

Kevin nodded. "And what about our kids? What about school and entertainment for them?"

Jeremy waved a hand and took another sip of wine. Just a small one, because you cannot—simply *cannot*—finish your glass before your host. "The kids will have so much to do there, and they will be among the luckiest children in the galaxy. How old are they?"

Rule #3, show interest in the children, but not too much. Just enough so the hosts don't suspect you of grooming. Which, of course, Paradise Co. does not endorse.

This was the moment. When potentials like these two started talking about their children's needs, the decision was all but made. Jeremy relaxed a bit more and set his wine glass on the coffee table. He sensed he was due to leave soon, as the couple began chatting about Katy and David, their children of six and seven.

Jeremy zoned out for a moment, as he often did when children were mentioned. He hated the grubby little things, even when they were dressed up in Top 1% garments. Torturous little—

"I don't know," Bryan said, gulping from his own glass. "Surely people would come back to visit friends and relatives."

Jeremy stifled a sigh and flashed his perfect smile once more. "Any time you want to come back, you can. There are absolutely no restrictions on that. The teleportation device is free to use at any time. All I can say is that, if your friends have not returned, it's simply because their life on Luyten's Star is just too…perfect."

The couple shared another look and Kevin squeezed his husband's hand. Jeremy smiled at the sentiment. A genuine smile, which caught him off guard for a second.

"It's just…" Kevin said, "… we've seen people at their house. Living there."

Jeremy nodded. "Of course, I apologise for any confusion there. We employ several thousand people as caretakers for our clients' homes. Maintain the gardens, keep things clean and tidy, that sort of thing. In the event that ticket holders do return, we at Paradise Co. would like their abode to be just as they left it. It's also for insurance purposes, to maintain the entire estate in the case of a future sale."

Bryan smiled at that. "That's nice, isn't it, honey?"

Kevin relented with a nod, and low, "Hmmm."

"We just ask that you sign a declaration," Jeremy said, "signing your assets over to Paradise Co. for the duration of your visit. Just a small legality so our staff are protected as they care for your home. You essentially choose one person as an authority to act on your behalf."

This was the final hurdle. Some of the Top 1% didn't like that idea, while others loved it. Jeremy could usually tell, but this couple were a little difficult to read.

"I'll tell you what," Jeremy said, reaching into his pants pocket and pulling out a small piece of cardboard. "I don't normally do this, but I like you two. Take my card. This has my personal number on it. If you need to chat more, please let me know."

Bryan took the card and inspected it with a smile. Flashed those white teeth again. "Please, let me pack this cheese up for you, for the road. We don't want you to go hungry."

Jeremy considered his offer for a moment. The handbook said to be courteous. Be their best friend. Refuse the offer, then relent. He waved a hand to indicate he couldn't possibly take their generous offer, but Bryan pushed the cheese plate towards him. Jeremy thanked him and made small talk with Kevin about the stars they'd see from their bed, and the adventures they'd have on Luyten's Star.

When Bryan returned, he carried a small container. Jeremy took it and thanked them for their time—and for the cheese. He didn't want them to know, but they'd just given him dinner for two days with that gift.

Returning to the car, he saw Sally leaning back in the driver's seat, a frog-shaped mask over her eyes. Jeremy opened the door, ignoring the rusted creak, and slid into the passenger seat.

"They going?" Sally asked without removing the mask.

"They're undecided, but I'm confident. I gave them the work number." Jeremy frowned and fumbled with the container of cheese. "They were nice…. I don't think we should do this to them." He paused. "The thing about Parad—"

Sally lifted the frog mask and glared at Jeremy. "They're Top 1%, Jer. They can't be *nice*. They live up there in a fucking castle and we share a studio apartment with four other people. If they were *nice*, they'd do something about the state of poverty on this planet."

"I know, but—"

"No buts. This is *our chance*. I want those tickets, you hear me?"

Jeremy nodded and wondered if he should tell her the truth, his stomach lurching at the prospect. "Okay, Sal. I hear you."

She switched on the ignition, shifted her grandfather's old Buick into drive, and let a stream of thick black smoke choke out of the exhaust pipe before heading back to their studio apartment.

Jeremy tried to ignore the Paradise Co. billboards along the interstate, tried to look past the advertising on bus stations and shopfront windows. It was everywhere, the corporate message that Sally had bought into.

Come to Paradise. It's all you've ever wanted.

If only she knew the truth. About Paradise. About it all.

"What do you think?" Bryan asked as he slipped into bed next to Kevin.

Kevin turned on his side to face Bryan, who cuddled in, pressing his face into Kevin's chest. Wrapped his arms around Bryan, gently kissing his forehead. "Honestly? I've conquered everything on this planet. We're the top of the Top 1%, for god's sake. I want to conquer something else. Paradise might be it."

Bryan let out a small sigh. "It's always about conquering something. Can't we just be happy with what we have?"

"I am happy." Kevin kissed Bryan's forehead again. "I love you and the kids."

"But?" Bryan lifted his face to stare into Kevin's eyes.

Kevin sighed. "I need this," he said. "I just… I need… something."

"And you can't find that here on Earth?" Bryan turned away. "With me?"

"Don't even go there." Kevin wrapped his arms tighter. "I want us to do this together. All of us."

Bryan gazed again into Kevin's eyes, sizing up his need to see this place. Paradise. On the other side of the galaxy or somewhere. "Okay," he whispered. "Let's do it."

Checking the time—9:25 pm—Kevin rolled over, grabbed his phone, and reached for the salesman's business card. "Thank you, gorgeous man. I'll text Jeremy now and we can tell the kids tomorrow."

Among the snoring and farting of his housemates, two of whom shared a bed with him, Jeremy stared at the ceiling. He wanted to tell Sally the truth, tell her what he'd seen at Paradise Co. headquarters. She wouldn't believe him. Maybe the Heatherbraes would believe him, and he could take it all back. Stop them from going.

They haven't even signed up yet.

The work phone he shared with Sally beeped from the nightstand, shining a dim light through the darkness. Jeremy climbed over his housemate—he couldn't tell who it was who'd slept with him tonight, he didn't care—and picked up the phone. Text message.

Unknown number.

He swiped to unlock the phone and tapped the Messages app.

Jeremy, it's Kevin and Bryan Heatherbrae here. We hope you enjoyed the cheese and crackers. We're ready to go to Paradise. Call us tomorrow if you can.

Sighing, Jeremy put his phone down, and resumed staring at the ceiling. Even if he deleted the message, they'd call again, and there was no guarantee Sally wouldn't pick up. He was well and truly fucked now.

After a few hours of staring at mould on the ceiling and water stains growing by the minute, Jeremy got out of bed. He was careful not to step on whoever it was sleeping on a mattress on the floor, and felt around for his clothes. Slipping into his shirt and pants—the only clothes he had—Jeremy made his way to the front door. Stepping outside was the only way to get some personal space, the irony of which was not lost on him.

Gently closing the door behind him, Jeremy looked up to the stars. Maybe Paradise was within his grasp. Maybe Sally was right, this was their chance. But the Heatherbraes had been so nice.

"You're one o' them Paradise pricks, aren't ya?" A voice came from the darkness.

Jeremy looked around and spotted an old man squatting over a man-made hole. He averted his eyes, hoping the deed would be done sooner rather than later. "Yeah."

Daring to look back, he saw the old man wiping his behind with some tree bark. "Thought so." The guy pulled up his pants. They were torn at the seams, held up by a feeble drawstring. "That place for real or what?"

Jeremy straightened. "Excuse me?"

"I heard nobody ain't never come back." He assessed his waste and spat into the hole. "Must be good up there."

"Better than living like this." Jeremy wiped at his nose as the stench drifted over.

The old man laughed a high-pitched sound, a bird flew from a nearby tree. "You too good to be shittin' in a hole with the rest of us, huh?"

Jeremy chewed his lower lip. "I guess not." He stepped closer to the hole and reached for some tree bark. "I kind of have to go now, if you don't mind."

The old man spread his arms and moved to the side, ushering Jeremy forward. "By all means, your throne awaits."

As the old man disappeared into the night, Jeremy pulled his pants to his ankles and squatted. *This is the last time I do this*, he thought, his own stench stinging at his eyes.

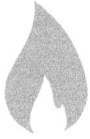

He woke up to Sally spraying him with the household deodoriser. Two sprays each day for each of the six house members meant one can would last six weeks. He'd just had his daily dose of lemon fresh and coughed through the particles lingering above his face.

"I saw the message," Sally said. "From our boy Kevin."

Jeremy sat up, noticing the other house mates had all dispersed for the day. For a moment he tried to remember what they all did for work but couldn't. He and Sally were really the only ones to speak to each other. The others just shared the rent and ate the food.

"I guess we have to go see them," Jeremy said.

Sally shook her head. "No need. I chatted to the lovely couple this morning. They're meeting us at HQ." She chucked the deodoriser into a draw on the other side of the room and turned to face Jeremy. "This is it. We're getting out of here. I'm finally going to get to Paradise."

Jeremy nodded, his stomach falling again. He could tell her now. He could still stop it. He could—

Sally held up a fresh new blazer and crease-free business pants. "I grabbed one of these, too."

Jeremy scrunched his face. "What's that for?"

Patting down her new outfit, Sally said, "It's a flight attendant outfit, what does it look like?" She pointed to the wings on the lapel and the Paradise Co. logo—clouds, of course. "I have to look the part when we greet them."

A silence penetrated the room and Jeremy avoided Sally's

eyes. He hated to think where she got that uniform from, and whether she'd had to hurt anyone. The temptation of reaching Paradise was changing his friend. "Sally, I have to tell you something…"

"Later, Jer, we have things to do. I don't want to be late for Paradise." She began to strip—Jeremy rolled over to avoid seeing her naked flesh—and pulled on her flight attendant uniform. "Those rich fucks won't see me coming." Her smile was the widest he'd ever seen.

"We don't have to…."

"Jer, aren't you excited?" Sally asked.

Meeting her gaze, he opened his mouth. The words were right there. The truth. The awful, horrible truth. He just couldn't say it.

"Jer?" Sally probed. "I wonder what it's like up there."

"Let's go," he said, and got out of bed.

Paradise Co. HQ was a few blocks away. There were only two buildings in their dilapidated neighbourhood that didn't need to be torn down and rebuilt. Paradise Co. HQ and Marty's Bar. Paradise HQ was the only place to work, if they'd hire you, and the bar was the only shop that was still up and running. The only place to spend what little money they had—Jeremy had spent his fair share there and didn't regret it one bit.

Walking through the streets, they both stepped over man-made toilets, holding their breath as they did so. Paradise Co. HQ had promised to gentrify the neighbourhood, bringing jobs and wealth, but the government had increased taxes and the cost of living to the point where ninety-five per cent of salaries disappeared before anyone received their pay slips. People didn't have enough to pay bills—electricity, water, any of it. Those who could afford to move away did so, those who couldn't ended up like Jeremy and Sally.

Except the Top 1%.

Jeremy didn't understand it. He didn't care to. All that mattered was that he was part of the bottom 95%. Going to Paradise was all most in the neighbourhood wanted, and Jeremy had been no exception. Sally, though, she wanted it more than anybody.

As they continued towards HQ, Jeremy thought about telling her the truth. He could tap her on the shoulder or grab her wrist or yell and scream at her to stop walking. He could talk to her, show her that Paradise—

"We can't afford to screw this up." Sally broke his train of thought. "We get inside, thanks to your fresh new cleaner's key card, and we take their spots."

"What about the kids? The people on Luyten's Star will be expecting a family of four. Two *male* parents, by the way."

Sally sneered. "We take the kids with us, force them to say what we want. It's not that hard to get people to do what you need them to, Jer."

"And the fact that you're a woman?" Jeremy asked.

"People make mistakes all the time. I'll say it's a typo. You're Kevin and my name is… Breanne."

Jeremy cocked an eyebrow.

"I'll say it with an accent, so it sounds like it could have been Bryan. Bryan, Breanne, Bryan Breanne. They sound kinda similar."

Tell her.

"Sally, you know how I've been cleaning?" Jeremy asked, avoiding her eyes again.

She nodded, grimacing at her lapels and smoothing her blazer.

"Well, it's helped me realise some things about Paradise."

She gripped his arm tight and butted in. "Oh, Jer, I can't wait. Don't tell me. Don't spoil anything for me. I want to see it for myself. I heard you can watch entire galaxies being born"—hands pressed to her heart, she smiled—"and you can float through stardust. Oh, Jer, we deserve this."

With each step towards Paradise Co. HQ, Jeremy felt his stomach knotting again.

Tell her. Stop this.

They kept going.

The building appeared, just up the street, and Jeremy swallowed bile that rose in his throat. The closer they got to HQ, the further away his words. The further the truth. Sally bounded up the street, pulling Jeremy by his shirt sleeve, until the entrance to HQ was before them.

Sally asked, "Where's the cleaner's entrance?"

"Round back."

"Well let's go." Sally tugged at his sleeve again. "We need to get inside and go meet the Heatherbraes."

The Heatherbraes. Those poor kids.

They reached the back entrance and Jeremy swiped his key card to unlock a black, metal door. Jeremy pulled at the handle, and they breached the building's entrance. Sally zipped past him, despite not knowing where she was going.

"Wow," she said, eyes wide. "This place is so shiny."

Jeremy gulped.

"This is what Paradise will be like, right?" Sally looked at him. "Can you believe all our potentials think we've been there? Saps."

"Well, that's part of rule number one," Jeremy said, feeling heavy in the shoulders. More bile was on the way. "Lie, lie, lie."

"You mean"—she cleared her throat—"build trust and rapport with your potential ticket holder. If they sense you have not been to Paradise, any potential sale is unlikely."

Jeremy eyed Sally and frowned. "That's what I said. Lie, lie, lie." He motioned down a hallway. "Come on. It's this way."

He led Sally down a hallway, to the main reception lobby, where they would meet the Heatherbraes and their children. Katy and David. Pushing through a door, Sally paused for a moment to take in the building. Marble floors, polished so they could see their reflections. Gold railings at a staircase on the far side of the lobby. Thick balustrades stretching to the high ceilings.

"Are you sure *this* isn't Paradise?" Sally asked.

Jeremy was about to respond—to reign in her excitement so passersby wouldn't know they shouldn't be there—when he saw the receptionist glaring at them, sizing up his clothing. Sally fit right in with her fresh new flight attendant uniform. But Jeremy wore the same old garbage he'd been wearing for the past decade. He'd only just gotten the cleaning job, so a uniform was still on mail order. Paradise Co. might have been the only company to work for, but it didn't mean they were *good* to work for. The receptionist sneered at him, and Jeremy turned away, his cheeks flushing.

A few Paradise Co. employees went about their business, ignoring them as Sally searched the lobby for the Heatherbraes. It was still early, though, and not many people were about.

A set of automatic double glass doors at the front of the building opened, ushering in two small children, a boy and a girl, followed by Bryan and Kevin. Jeremy stopped breathing, he began to turn away, he tried to pull Sally away, but she saw them and knew. He didn't know how, but she knew it was them.

She rushed to greet them, and Kevin raised a hand in the air to wave to Jeremy. Bryan gathered the children, one holding each of his hands, and he nodded his recognition.

Jeremy walked over, several steps behind Sally.

"Hello," she said, extending a hand to them. "I'm Sally, your flight attendant today. I work with Jeremy here. We spoke on the phone earlier." Jeremy caught up and flashed a smile. The perfection was absent today, but neither Kevin nor Bryan saw the fear in his eyes. "We've just got some preliminaries to do, and then we'll get you on your way."

"We're going today?" Bryan asked.

Kevin glanced sideways at his husband and mumbled, "I arranged it all with Sally this morning."

Bryan narrowed his eyes but said nothing.

"We're having one of our caretakers prepare your belongings. Although, in Paradise, you will have unlimited access to new items. As part of the Top 1%, you've earned it." Sally flashed her own perfect smile.

Swallowing hard, Jeremy gazed towards a hallway, stretching into shadow past the balustrade and the staircase. A sign hanging from the ceiling pointed to the hallway, stating "Departures".

"Ah, yes," Sally said, following his eyes. "No time like the present. We should all move to the departure lounge." She ushered the family forward, tussling Katy's hair as the girl walked past her.

"Daddy," Katy said, pressing an index finger into her cheek, "do we have a departure time?"

Wow, the kid sounds like she's mid-thirties. Jeremy thought with a frown. The education those kids received was second-to-none, pursuing advanced robotics and linguistics by the age of four. *When I was four, I was sucking—*

"You sure do, little angel," Sally answered quickly, eyeing Bryan and Kevin. "Our system is soooooo advanced that people can come and go from Paradise as they please. Just show up, and"—Sally clicked her fingers—"poof! You're there. Right, Jer?"

He found himself in the hallway, a few steps behind the family—the group led by Sally—his stomach thrashing inside him. Begging his mouth to speak. He raised a hand. Extended a finger to Kevin's shoulder. It trembled.

"Jer?" Sally asked without turning around.

"Uh…" He dropped his hand and thrust it into his pocket. "After the initial set up, sure. The dispersion patterns are coded to the individual. Once we get into the room, we'll take a handprint, which will map your body's biometrics and send it to the other side. It also acts as a consent form. Once that's done, you can zip back and forth as you like."

Katy frowned, her eyes darting left to right. Her brother, David, considered Jeremy's words. "Hmmm," he said. "Does it rely on a—"

"Quickly now." Sally cut the kid off and took his small hand. The end of the hallway was in sight, a green door shimmering in the near distance.

As Jeremy looked upon the door, it began to pulsate. His eyes grew blurry and his hands, still firm in his pockets, shook. "You know," he said, the words spilling from him, "we sometimes find that, uh, we find that… well, some families… they like to…."

"Jer, take a breath." Sally faced him now, her hand on the door handle. A bronze thing, shining at him.

"I just, um…" Jeremy tried again. "You can do this tomorrow. Have more time to consider your options."

Kevin and Bryan exchanged a glance as Sally opened the door. It creaked on its hinge, exposing a bright room. "We could take an extra day or two to say goodbye to our friends," Bryan said.

Before Kevin could answer, Sally guided the children into the departure room. Bryan followed, reaching for Katy and David's shoulders. Drawing them into him, they looked around. The room was sparse—not a lounge in the classic sense, with seats and departure times. Just a machine extending from the ground in the middle of the room, a small panel sitting on top. A small closet on the left, and a fire extinguisher fastened to the wall. At the far side of the room, another door: the gate to Paradise.

"Here we are," Sally said. Flashed that smile again.

Jeremy vomited in his mouth and swallowed it.

"If you put your left hand on the panel here, it'll collect your biometrics."

One by one, the family placed their left hands on the panel, watching with excitement as the machine calculated body mass, DNA coding, genetic build, and other measurements none of them were aware was needed.

"Now, you'll need to elect an official caretaker. We have, as I mentioned before, some already on your property collecting personal items. However, we do require a name to sign your assets to while you're away," Sally said matter-of-factly.

"Ah, yes, Jeremy mentioned that," Kevin said, flashing a look towards Jeremy. "Well, Jeremy, what do you say? It's just for while we're away. We trust you to look after our things."

Jeremy nodded and approached the biometric scanner. A handprint later and he'd inherited their wealth. His body trembled at the sudden fortune and his impending sense of doom.

"Don't get too comfortable there." Bryan winked. "We'll likely be back quite often to see our loved ones."

"Of course, I..." Jeremy straightened and ignored the dread writhing under his skin. His new-found wealth didn't feel real. None of this felt real, like he would wake up in the apartment any moment.

As they continued to scan themselves, Sally eyed Jeremy. Her eyes were wide. Wild. She stepped away from the family, reached for the fire extinguisher.

With the knowledge of Sally's next move, Jeremy opened his mouth. "There's someth—" Before he could finish, bile rose to his mouth. His flesh broke into goosebumps, his heart stopped, and he felt the blood drain from his face. *I need to warn them.* Stumbling backward, his sight disappearing for a moment, he hit the floor. *Don't, Sal, don't.*

Kevin turned to face him, offered a hand to steady him. "You okay, there?"

"Behind... you," Jeremy stuttered.

As Kevin turned, his face contorting, Sally smashed the fire extinguisher into his head. Kevin plummeted to the ground with a heavy thud, and Bryan spun around. Sally launched at the man as the children fled to the corners of the room, tears streaming down their faces.

Jeremy clambered over Kevin's body, a pool of blood spewing to the floor. He stood and reached for Sally—he couldn't do this. These were nice people. These were a family. Something he had never had, and always wanted.

"Sally, please," Jeremy begged. He grabbed at the fire extinguisher, but Sally was too fast. Bryan cowered, an arm raised above his face, as Sally brought the metal canister down.

"Don't wimp out now, Jer. We're taking their tickets." She smashed Bryan again and again, ignoring his pleas and splattering the walls in thick, red blood. Flecks of skin and bone scattered through the air. She kept going, a frenzy of rage and hatred and jealousy. "They're our fucking tickets!" she screamed over and over, ignoring the screams of Katy and

David, their high-pitched wailing as they begged for their fathers' lives.

Jeremy wrapped his arms around Sally's waist and pulled her away from Bryan, who lay splayed across the floor. Unmoving.

"Please Sally," Jeremy said through gritted teeth. "It's not what you think."

"Bryan!" Kevin's shrill cry came from behind them.

Sally pushed away from Jeremy's weak grip and stormed to Kevin. He was on his feet, holding the side of his head where he'd been attacked. Blood drizzled through the spaces between his fingers, and he stumbled forward. Jeremy crawled to Bryan's side, inspecting his neck for a pulse. It was weak, but there.

Rushing to Kevin, the children cried into their father's waist, hugging his legs. They cried and pleaded, shouting for Bryan and Kevin and Paradise.

Sally gripped Katy by the hair and pulled. Kevin flailed to stop her, and she swiped his hand away. "Get into the departure room!" With Katy's hair streaming through Sally's gripped fingers, she prized open the door to the departure room.

"Sally, wait!" Jeremy called from Bryan's side.

"Shut the fuck up, Jer. We could have done this together. We deserve this!" Sally glared at him as she thrust the girl into the room. Heading back for David, Sally grabbed at the boy.

"No, you don't understand!" Jeremy tried again. He watched as Sally pummelled Kevin in the face. His feeble hands tried to stave off the attack, but Sally's initial attack had done too much damage.

"Daddy!" David cried, hiding behind Kevin as he fell to his knees. "Please, lady, stop!"

Sally laughed. It didn't sound human. Horrible sounds

from the depths of her dark soul came from her mouth. She grabbed the boy hard and dragged him, kicking and screaming, to the departure room. Paradise was within her grip now. As the children begged for their fathers, Sally cackled harder.

"Sally, wait!" Jeremy got to his feet. "They're all still alive. We can stop. We don't have to do this."

She ignored him, slamming the door shut with her and the children in the room. Jeremy watched her through a small glass window in the door. She searched the room for a control switch—there was only one button, and she pressed it.

A bright light began to form in the centre of the room, and Sally gathered up the children close to her. She smiled—a real, genuine smile. She was on her way to Paradise. Jeremy stepped away, wiping at tears, and was plunged downward.

"She can't… take… my kids." Kevin had dragged himself to the departure door and pulled Jeremy down.

"Please," Jeremy said. "It's too late."

Kevin wiped blood from his eyes and gripped Jeremy by the shirt collar. "Why did you do this to us?"

Jeremy shook his head, unable to speak. He didn't know anymore. He didn't want this to be happening. He squeezed his eyes shut and wished to wake up. Wished he was somewhere else. Some*one* else.

He saw the light grow brighter inside the room, and Kevin raced to the door on unsteady feet. Pulling the door open, he stumbled to his family, standing in the bright light.

"It's too late," Sally said to him. "It's happening."

Jeremy shook his head and shut the door, sealing Sally and the others inside. "Sal…."

The light grew brighter still.

The children began to scream first. Not from the trauma of Sally's attack. Not from the fear of being abducted. Watching through the glass window, Jeremy saw why they screamed.

As the light grew brighter and brighter, its white glow turned darker and darker, until a deep red shone through the room. Inside the red light, the family. Their skin, bubbling and popping in the intense heat. Sally tried to move, but the muscles in her legs were melting into a mass of pinkish-yellow goop. She screamed and begged until her vocal cords were liquefied, the gelatinous fluid sliding down her body with melted olive skin. Sally fell to what had once been her knees, tipping to her side like a melted wax figurine, her mouth twisted in pain. Jeremy watched her teeth—like pearls—fall to the ground before bubbling into a white mess with the rest of her.

He forced himself to watch, fighting the urge to look away or run or do anything else. He couldn't move. Katy and David melted to the concrete floor as pink and yellow and red goop, and Jeremy saw an eyeball floating in the soupy flesh before it burst like popcorn in a microwave.

Finally, the screams vanished, all at once. As the red light continued to beam from the ceiling, the family and Sally were a mess of liquefied gunk. Jeremy felt something churn in his stomach and spewed onto the glass. It erupted like magma, tinted red by the glowing light in the room beyond.

Wiping at the glass, his vomit dripping down the door, the red light disappeared. He twisted the door handle and entered the room, feeling the remnants of the intense heat singe the hairs on his arms.

"It's not what you think, Sal," Jeremy whispered. "I tried to tell you."

He looked down at the remains of the family. The children. Nothing survived—they were just a puddle of coagulating bodily fluids. Taking a deep breath, Jeremy walked to the small closet and pulled out a cleaning bucket and a mop.

Time to get to work.

Jeremy filled the bucket with soap, letting the suds bubble and foam. He wheeled the bucket back to the departure room and slapped the wet mop against the floor. As the goop of the Heatherbraes and Sally mixed into the soapy water, Jeremy realised he was rich. They'd signed their wealth to him. He was now part of the Top 1%.

I'll never have to do this again.

Despite the immense wealth, Jeremy was unable to smile. He wanted to, but without Sally, what good was it? He had nobody to share it with. Tears seeped from his eyes at the thought.

"Where…?" A small voice came from the other side of the room. Bryan Heatherbrae coughed and choked on a pool of blood in his mouth. His eyes scanned the area for his family. "My kids…."

As Bryan continued to choke and gurgle to death, Jeremy let out a low whistle as he mopped the family into nothingness. Rule #14 in the handbook, he reminded himself, stated all Top 1% should be comforted with a ditty if you sense a decrease in mood.

Jeremy dabbed at his wet eyes and sniffled, mourning Sally the best he knew how. "It's okay, Mr Heatherbrae," he whispered over the final gurgle, "they're in Paradise now."

FAMILY
FEAST

Marcus took a deep breath, holding it for just a second too long before letting his breath fog the windshield. A bouquet of flowers on the passenger seat soaked up the carbon dioxide. He thought he saw the edges of the leaves curl a little. He shook his head, urging his mind to steer clear of the usual paranoid anxiety. He didn't know if it was a date or not, and the flowers might have been too much.

More than that, his last date had not ended the way he'd hoped. Death seemed to follow him, with his entire family gone now, but his date had vanished, too. Turned up a week later, squashed to bits in a garbage truck. It didn't help that his apartment was on its route. It also didn't help that his date had run out of the apartment screaming a few hours earlier. Or that—

Rubbing a circle in the window with a closed fist, Marcus looked towards the house. That's what Dave had called it—a *house*. From his seat in the run-down Ford Fiesta, it looked more like something from a fairy tale. He was surprised, though it did make sense. The car Dave drove, the clothes he wore. The expensive cologne. That *sweet, sweet* cologne made him want to do all sorts of inappropriate things.

They'd spoken at work, exchanging polite nods at the water cooler and talking in vague terms about their weekends. He'd watched Dave at the café below the office. Seen him devouring a peach once. The memory still pleased him.

Shifting back to the present, Marcus grabbed the bouquet and sniffed, ignoring the water dripping from his eyes. The allergies would be worth it when Dave embraced him. He slammed the car door, made his way up the drive, each side lined with palm trees.

As he approached the front double door, surrounded by thick glass windows on both sides, a shadow ran past. Just a silhouette. Impossible to know who it was. Dave hadn't said anything about others coming along—the invite had just been for him.

Oh god, what if it's a work function?

There were no other cars on the street. He ditched the flowers behind a palm, anyway, and knocked on the front door, slicking his hair back with a moist finger.

"Marcus." Dave opened the door, racing towards Marcus, arms in the air. He held a butcher knife, swinging it through the air.

Marcus ducked. Fell to his back. The blade dripped in blood. He screamed and raised his arms over his face.

"Oh my." Dave laughed. "I am so sorry. I've just been preparing things for tonight."

He lowered the knife, wiped the blood on his apron, and helped Marcus to his feet. Embraced him with strong, firm arms. Wrapped tight around him. He felt Dave's heartbeat through his chest. Fast and heavy. Nerves, maybe. Marcus didn't want it to end.

"You didn't bring any wine?" Dave smirked. Marcus blinked, unable to find words, and Dave patted his shoulder. "I'm teasing you, we own a vineyard. Come in. My family are *dying* to meet you."

"Family?" Marcus gulped. "Is that who I saw before?"

Dave nodded, guiding Marcus through the first-floor lobby with a hand around his waist. His fingers were cold, yet comfortable. Inviting. If there was any doubt this was a date, those fears were gone.

Marcus let himself be guided, trying not to comment on the glamour of the parlour and the library as Dave moved him to the dining room. Dave made small talk and rubbed Marcus's back up and down.

Up and down.

"So"—Marcus focused on breathing—"what's for dinner?"

"You'll see." Dave stood behind Marcus now, his breath hot on the man's neck. Marcus wished it was more than breath. He wanted those lips. He'd wanted them for so long now. His heart throbbed at the idea Dave wanted it, too.

"Come on," Dave continued. "Come meet the family."

Marcus nodded as Dave pushed through a wooden door, revealing a ten-seater dining table. Mahogany chairs, velvet table runner. Chandelier above, shining down on him like angels from Heaven. The light had a heat to it, but Marcus was too overwhelmed by the size of the room to care.

"My family are downstairs." Dave cocked his head behind him. To the basement door. As he removed the apron, he continued, "Wait here while I check on them. My parents have some mobility issues."

"Sure." Marcus smiled. "What do I call them? Mr and Mrs, or…"

"Gwen and Bob." Dave disappeared, whistling a tune Marcus didn't know.

In the silence of the dining room, Marcus realised there were no smells. No meat, no fragrant herbs or spices. Yet, Dave had been chopping something. The knife was drenched in blood. Was the house so big that the kitchen was a distance away?

With this in mind, he pushed through another door at the far end of the dining room. The kitchen. Commercial ovens, a gigantic island bar, built-in coffee machine. But no food. Marcus scratched his head. A light from the oven drew his attention. It was switched to "High", but was empty. He kneeled in front of it, sizing up whether he'd fit inside. After a few minutes or so, he figured he'd have to be chopped into at least three pieces, even with the size of the things. If his flesh were to be cooked properly, his torso and upper body would need the whole oven to itself. That would get the juices flowing. A bit of olive oil over the skin to crisp up, maybe some rosemary and garlic. It depended on the fat content of the body.

"Marcus?" Dave snapped him back to reality.

He spun to see Dave smiling at him, a small crease in his forehead. "What are you doing?"

"I thought…" He motioned around the kitchen. "Where's the food?"

"We're going to have to eat in the basement." Dave ignored him. "My parents can't get up the stairs this evening. Is that okay?"

Marcus nodded, but said, "I can come back another time if that's better."

"I wouldn't dream of it." Dave took Marcus's hand and pulled him close. "Now you're here, I don't want to let you go."

"You don't?"

Dave's mouth touched his own. Marcus's knees went weak. He collapsed into Dave's arms, hoping the moment wasn't a daydream. Another one. Dave came up for air, wiped his lips and smiled. "I've had my eye on you for some time," he whispered.

Marcus raised his eyebrows. He knew there were people that enjoyed bigger men. Chubby chasers, they were called. Or bear chasers, depending. But his luck on social media had been less than impressive, and Marcus was in year three of a drought. And it was starting to show in the way he carried himself. Dave was fit and slim and muscular, so his admission came as a shock.

You never can tell, he thought and smiled, deciding to dive straight in and not ask too many questions.

"So"—Dave dragged Marcus back through the dining room—"you're okay to eat in the basement?"

"Sure." Marcus kept smiling from their kiss. "Whatever you want."

Dave stopped at the top of the basement stairs. Gazed into the dim light below. Marcus prompted him to start the descent, and Dave turned to face him.

"I should tell you…" His voice was low. Soft. "My parents are not well. They insisted I bring you home before they… Well, they insisted they meet the special man in my life. Please don't react when you see them."

Marcus eyed Dave, then followed his gaze into the basement.

"What's left of them, that is," Dave mumbled, and started down the stairs, still holding Marcus by the hand.

The last time Marcus had been in a basement, things had been looking worse than bleak.

The rope.

The fire.

The bodies.

Fingers pushing through skin, tearing through it like a shower curtain.

He pushed the memories to the periphery and focused on the present. Just because he'd lost control last time he was in a basement, it didn't mean he would this time.

Besides, that was five years ago. He took a deep breath, taking comfort in Dave's fingers clasped around his own.

The stairs trembled under his weight. Another sign from the universe that he needed to join a gym. Or eat less. Neither option seemed feasible as he continued into the darkness. The walls, made of old greying wood, smelled damp. Marcus sneezed and kept walking, feeling the warmth of Dave's hand pulling him further into the dark.

A bleak light emanated from somewhere in the basement and as the light grew, so too did the voices. These ones weren't in his own head, for a change. Hitting the cold cement of the basement floor, Marcus turned his head to see a light hanging from the ceiling. No light shade over the single bulb, which swung a little, though he didn't know why. The table underneath was adorned with silver cutlery and porcelain plates. Four people sat around it, bickering among themselves. He'd expected the basement to be living quarters, given the parents' mobility issues. But it was just a regular old basement.

"Shut up, shut up, here he is," a woman hissed, noticing Marcus staring.

He wasn't supposed to. Dave had asked him not to do it. But the faces before him needed to be understood. Dave's mother—he guessed it was the mother, Gwen—had deep scars down both sides of her face. As though the skin had been shredded off and the wounds never healed. Purple-brown lesions like stripes up and down her cheeks. Gwen's nose looked melted, as though made of wax, and she licked her cracked lips with a discoloured tongue.

A man opposite her followed the woman's gaze, settling on Marcus with a smile. Yellow teeth flashed under the light, casting a shadow across the dining table. The older man had red patches of skin littering his neck and forearms. Through the man's white singlet, Marcus saw the outlines of a ribcage. The man was thin—too thin. His shoulders jutted out the sides like knives and his neck looked to be propped up by nothing but sheer willpower. A drip-line attached to his right elbow, connected to a slim metal pole behind him, numbers flashing on a small monitor. Feeding him a translucent liquid.

"Everyone," Dave said, guiding Marcus to the table, and pulling out a chair for him. "This is Marcus. Our guest for this evening."

Marcus nodded with a polite smile and combed his hair with his fingers. Four sets of eyes took him in, and his mouth went dry. He hated that. Moisture on the tongue was as natural as anything ever had been. Yet it felt encrusted by sawdust as Dave's family judged him in silence.

"Hi." He gave a small wave and rested his elbows on the table.

Dave's family smiled back, though their eyes were looking at his body. His mother traced a wrinkled finger along her lower lip at the sight of his belly. Marcus couldn't tell if it was sexual or something more sinister. Ignoring her, he turned to the two younger people at the table, assuming they were siblings. Unlike the parents, their appearance was less intimidating. Twins, Marcus assumed, based on the remarkable similarities in their facial features.

"I'm Marcus," he held a hand to the girl—maybe sixteen years old—who caressed his fingers. She gazed at his features through eyes hidden behind thick mascara. Two dots surrounded by yellowed eyeballs, encased in midnight.

Marcus let her explore his fingers, the gentle touch reminiscent of that night five years ago. Though back then, he'd been the one in awe. He'd been so hungry.

"Leave him be," the boy said, and slapped her hand away from Marcus. "I'm Luke. That's Natalie. She doesn't say much." Despite their similar appearance, Luke wore no make-up and he was more muscular. Maybe a footballer.

Stringy.

"It's nice to meet you both." Marcus tucked his hand under the table and glanced at Dave, sitting at the head of the table on the other end. He was busying himself with a bottle of wine, twisting the cap and filling glasses. He filled Luke and Natalie's, too. Maybe they were older than they looked. Dark red liquid splashed through the glasses, the heavy odour of merlot wafting across the table towards Marcus. He placed a hand over the top of his glass, indicating he didn't want any.

In unison, the family twisted their heads towards him, expressionless. Dave, too, moved his eyes between the glass and Marcus's face. His lips tightened, just a little, and Marcus lifted his hand.

"Maybe just a drop." He smiled and swallowed. His throat was dry, the nerves and the awkward feeling in his bones getting the better of him.

It wasn't just the family's odd behaviour—the staring and the quiet fascination with his belly. It was him, too. His own memories of the basement, what had happened down there. What it made him want to do to these people. Even if Dave's parents looked half-dead already.

Dave raised his glass and tilted it forwards in a traditional toast. Without a word, the family followed suit, and they drank together in silence. Marcus did the same, noting the wine had a strange flavour. It wasn't the red liquid he was used to drinking.

"Something wrong?" Dave's father asked, that same, yellow-toothed smile on his lips.

Marcus shook his head and scraped his tongue against his top teeth. "Delicious."

It occurred to Marcus then that, as with the kitchen upstairs, there were no visible signs of cooking. No smell of meat, cooked or otherwise, no sizzling or steam. Just them. Sitting around the table, staring at him.

"So," Marcus said, "what's for dinner?"

Natalie giggled and the others shot her a look.

"I'll just go upstairs and get it prepared," Dave said, and rushed to the basement stairs. He winked at Marcus on his way past and squeezed his shoulder.

The basement door clicked shut behind Dave, and Marcus shifted in his chair. Dave's parents—*Gwen and Bob*—began a quiet chatter among themselves, as though Marcus wasn't even there. Laughing at jokes he hadn't heard, and fussing over where the salt and pepper should go. In the centre of the table, or off to the left.

Mundane conversation bored Marcus and he found himself drifting. Thinking over the events so far. A flash behind the windows at the front of the house. Someone was moving fast, but there'd been no sign. Everyone was in the basement.

The basement. He closed his eyes as the memories flooded back.

Blood. So much blood. The screams, the begging. He'd

never been the same after that. Had sworn he'd never enter a basement again. But here he was, and without so much as a mild objection.

You want to be here.

His heart hammered in his chest, blood pulsed to his ears. He did want to be here. That's what frightened him so much. Not that he'd found himself here, but that he was enjoying it.

The table conversation sounded far away, like he was listening from metres under water. The voices just murmurs under the beating against his ribcage.

"Marcus." A voice broke him free. "Are you okay?"

It was Bob. Flashing his grin again. His words were kind, but the way he said them was not. His tone was darker than Marcus expected.

"Just nervous, I guess."

Gwen wiped at her face, the skin all but tearing open, and smiled. "Meeting the family is a huge step in a relationship."

Relationship? What has Dave told them?

Marcus nodded and picked up his wine glass again. "Sure is," he said, and gulped. As the wine gushed into his mouth, Dave's father put his own glass down and moved his chair backward.

Except it wasn't a chair, not like the rest. A squeaking wheel gave it away. The circular motion of the man's arms. He moved towards Marcus with a slow, but determined pace, pushing his wheelchair through the basement.

"I'm Bob," he held out a hand, despite being two feet away.

Marcus leaned forwards and shook it, trying not to look at the bloodied stumps where the man's legs used to be. It wasn't the amputations that bothered Marcus—he'd seen plenty before—it was the rough and messy chopping, and how the bandages were soaked through. Whatever had happened to

Bob was recent.

He couldn't help himself and Marcus looked down at the sawed-off legs. The wet bandages, ripe for the sucking. The smell of blood, thick with iron and sugar, caught him, and Marcus sniffed. It filled him with deep satisfaction, goosebumps travelling down his arms and the nape of his neck. It was nothing short of orgasmic.

Bob watched him and took his hand back. Marcus steadied himself and cleared his throat. Hoping his moment of weakness hadn't been noticed.

"It's okay to ask," Bob said, wheeling himself back to his place at the table.

"Ask what?" The stench of Bob's blood lingered in his nostrils, and he gripped the armrests on his chair. To hold his desires in place.

"What happened to my legs." Bob's horrible yellow teeth shone once more. Marcus wanted to taste them.

Natalie snickered under her breath. "A disagreement, right Dad?"

Luke smacked the back of her head and she lowered her gaze to the empty plate in front of her. Marcus ignored the comment, still reeling from the sensations rushing through him. He couldn't fight it anymore. It was too much.

The basement.

The smell.

The blood.

The *hunger*.

Desire and need washed through him, and before he could register his body moving, he was up. He was confident he could take out the parents before Luke and his footballer arms could do anything about it. Natalie wouldn't be an issue. He could push her down and stamp on her head if need be.

He moved to step towards Bob, the squeaking wheelchair grating on his nerves.

Dave came back, rushing down the stairs like a beacon of hope.

Thank god. Marcus took a slow deep breath and turned to see Dave empty-handed. *Where's the food?*

"So." Dave smiled. "What's the verdict?"

Marcus looked back at the family, unsure what Dave's question meant. Bob and Gwen winked. Just once. And Marcus felt something prick his neck.

"What the…?" His question faded away with the light.

"Hush now," Dave whispered in his ear, helping him to the cement floor. "You'll make a fine meal."

He woke with something in his mouth, stretching his jaw and scratching against his teeth. Marcus tried to push the object with his tongue, but started to choke. His hands were bound behind his back, the rope tight around his wrists cutting the circulation. He felt strange and wondered if the wine had been dosed with something.

No, the rest of the family had also been drinking.

"He's awake," Bob said.

Marcus was upside down. It took him a few seconds to realise that Bob and the others weren't the wrong way round—it was he who was dangling from the ceiling by his legs. The room came into focus and Marcus saw the family sitting around him. He'd been stripped naked and hoisted above the table.

"What the hell is going on?" he shouted, conscious that his hairy belly and thick legs were on display. Let alone his manhood, hanging flaccid in front of Gwen's waiting mouth. In his fear and confusion, a little bit of pee dripped out.

"I have to confess." Dave held up an electric instrument and caressed its silver casing. "We're going to eat you. You weren't my first choice, believe me, but we're getting desperate."

Natalie and Luke laughed, holding hands above the table. Bob and Gwen just smirked. They seemed tired. Weak. Perhaps unable to do much more. Until they fed.

"Wait," Marcus begged. He strained at the rope around his wrists, tried to make his bones smaller somehow, to squeeze free. "Please, just wait."

Dave approached Marcus, dropped the instrument to his side. Reached forwards and pulled Marcus towards him. Helpless, Marcus grimaced at the touch as Dave pressed his face against his stomach. Smelled at the hair and the skin. Sucking in the scent of Marcus's body.

"It is a shame," Dave mumbled. "I really, *really* liked you."

"Then why?" Marcus held back tears, determined this family would not see him cry.

"We have to eat." Dave shrugged. "Look at my parents. How weak they are."

He spun Marcus around to face them. The injuries on Gwen's face made more sense now. The size and shape, like strips had been sliced from her. They matched the width of the machine Dave held.

"We've tried everything." Dave held a hand to his head. The regret seemed genuine. The torment real. Marcus could see the man felt he was out of options. "Homeless people are too thin. Stringy. Not enough nutrients. They taste… dead. We tried murderers, ex-cons, rapists. Priests. All the worst of humanity, but...."

"But they aren't enough." It was Gwen. Stroking the wounds on her face. "We even tried auto-cannibalism. As you can see."

In his chest, Marcus's heart ached for them. He understood the desire. The craving. He understood how awful it was to need to prey on the ones you loved. But that wouldn't help him now. These people—this family—wanted to devour him. Dave's choice in men made sense now. Going for the plumpier in the crowd. It was just a ploy, a ruse, a way to get him and his family well fed.

Struggling against his bonds, the rope began to loosen. Just a little. He needed more time. Had to keep them talking. "Why humans?" he asked, the words coming out slow and mumbled.

Dave began to speak, but the blood was rushing to Marcus's head. He tried to blink away the dizziness, but his eyes were falling closed. The chairs below were a thick oak. Hard and heavy. If he could get free, get his feet back on the ground, he could break a chair and use a leg as a weapon. But his hands were numbing now. The rope not loose enough.

"It'll be painful, I'm not going to lie." Marcus tuned in to Dave describing his impending skinning.

Dave held the machine to Marcus's eye level. "It's called a Dermatome. Typically used for skin grafts, but in this case... Well, you get the idea." A low buzzing filtered through the basement as Dave switched on the machine. It vibrated in his hands like an electric razor.

"Please," Marcus begged, but knew it was pointless.

The machine touched his shoulder, the metal cold against him. Dave pushed the Dermatome along Marcus's skin and a thin strip of flesh lifted with ease. Marcus screamed as the machine chugged along, tearing away the top layer of skin.

"I know," Dave said. "It hurts. I know. But it has to be done." He held the skin strip for Marcus and the family to see. Natalie and Luke licked their lips, eyes wide, ignoring the pained groans from the man hanging from the ceiling.

As Dave handed the strip to his sister, his dizzying brain told him it was just bacon. A nice, juicy, fatty strip of bacon.

With the blood gushing through his body towards his head, and now to the site of his wound, Marcus fought to stay awake. That machine was the key. It was powerful. Did as it was told. If he manoeuvred himself at the right time, it could slice his hands free.

The buzzing came again, this time slicing through his upper thigh. Dave held Marcus's arm to steady himself. To make sure he cut straight. Marcus struggled against Dave's grip and the unrelenting machine. The family sat, watching. Waiting. Cooing in anticipation.

Marcus knew if he didn't try now, he never would. He used all his energy—what little remained—to push away from Dave. He swung, a human pendulum, and Dave smiled. Readied the machine for Marcus's return. He twisted himself as best he could, until his hands were facing the machine. The buzzing choked for a moment as the rope was sucked into its grip.

Just long enough to weaken the rope. Marcus snapped free and as the twins sprung to action, he grabbed at the Dermatome. Snatched it from Dave's surprised hand. Luke leaped across the table towards Marcus, who slashed with the machine at the young man's face. A shred of skin fell to the table, splatting on an empty plate.

"Stay the fuck away from me!" Marcus warned. He was outnumbered, hanging upside down, with no escape. His plan had been just to get his hands free. He had nothing after that. Now it was here and he saw how pathetic he must have looked.

But as Luke clawed his way back to Marcus, swinging punches in rage, Marcus grabbed the young man's arm. Pulled him close and forced Luke into a headlock. Held the machine to the throbbing veins in his neck.

Fuck he smells good.

"Let me down," Marcus ordered. His eyes grew heavier still, but the adrenaline and the pain kept him going. "I won't ask again."

Dave nodded, hands up in surrender. Climbed to the table and worked at the knots holding Marcus's feet in the air. The rope came undone and Marcus dropped to the table with a thud, his shoulder throbbing in pain from the force. Despite the searing wound, he refused to loosen his hold on Luke.

Natalie and Dave stood on either side of the table, Bob clapping his hands in joy at the unfolding scene. Luke's chest heaved up and down as Marcus tightened his stranglehold, forcing Luke to follow him to the edge of the table.

"Marcus,"—Dave was too calm—"we can talk about this."

"What if I kill *him*? You can all have a meal and let me go," Marcus sneered. "How does that sound?"

But he couldn't do it. As much as he wanted to slice open Luke's throat and guzzle on the blood, he had other things to focus on. Like getting out of the basement.

The Dermatome still pressed against Luke's neck, the vein pulsing up and down just under the skin. Even though the machine wasn't turned on, the pressure against Luke's skin was enough. A thin trickle of blood ran down the machine. Marcus could smell it.

Not now. He begged himself to ignore the fragrant liquid. It was so sweet. Potent. Among the sweat and anxiety and his trembling hands, blood. Fresh. Rich. Dark. He could smell the difference between blood types. How oxygenated it was, how healthy or unhealthy. Luke's smelled like AB negative. Rare. It was the jackpot of blood.

His grip began to soften as the aroma of Luke's red nectar wafted inside his nose. His eyelids fluttered. *Stay focused.*

Dave had noticed. Wrinkled his forehead. The expression said he understood what was happening. Marcus drew his attention back to Luke's neck, to the uncertain position of power he found himself in—and needed to maintain.

The rope he'd been restrained with lay on the cement, next to Dave's feet. Marcus ordered him to pick it up. Tie up his sister. Tight. Then Gwen. Hands behind their backs. Feet, too.

"It's not personal," Dave said to Marcus as he tightened a knot in the rope. Natalie groaned and grimaced at her brother, as he moved on to Gwen. "We have to eat."

"I know about the need to eat," Marcus spat. "But this is…"

Nobody in the basement knew what the next word should be. Looking at the family, Marcus saw it in their eyes. It was so normal for them. So routine.

Gwen didn't struggle against the bonds, but threw Marcus a disappointed look. Whether it was the hunger or the turn of events, Marcus couldn't tell. He didn't much care.

"Now Luke," Marcus said.

Dave sighed. "We're running low on rope, I'm afraid."

"Do it!" Marcus pressed harder against Luke's neck, and Dave moved towards his brother. Dave hadn't been lying. The rope was running short, but there would be enough to tie Luke's hands. Maybe not his feet. But it would be enough.

"What about me and Dad?" Dave asked.

Marcus looked towards the old man. He was weak.

Underfed. Sick with something. He wouldn't be able to get up the stairs either, not in the wheelchair.

"Your dad is fine," Marcus said and edged to the side of the table. "But you—get back there in the corner. As far from me as you can."

Standing up now, he searched for his clothes. Hanging on the back of a chair, his underwear on top of his jeans. His predicament now was whether he wanted a hostage or not. Pushing Luke to the ground, he ran for his clothes. Grabbed at them and raced to the stairs.

"Get him," Bob yelled.

Marcus didn't look back. Didn't have to. Footsteps thudded behind him. Two sets. Luke and Dave. He climbed the stairs two at a time and slammed the door behind him. Searched for a lock.

Nothing.

He had one shot at escape. The front door. If he could find it. Marcus abandoned the door and raced through the house, conscious that Dave and his brother were close. He could hear their breaths. With Luke's hands tied, he wasn't much of a threat. But Dave. The mastermind. He was the real danger.

Marcus pushed through a door. The kitchen. His eyes scanned for an exit. He couldn't remember the way they'd come. Maybe that was the plan, in case of situations like this. Another door on the other side of the kitchen. He raced for it. Grabbed Dave's butcher knife as he passed the island bench.

Slamming through the door, he pressed hard against it with his back. Tried to quieten his heavy breathing. Listened through the wood. Voices. Murmuring in the kitchen. He pulled his jeans on while he had the chance, the zipper sounding louder than anything in his whole life as he thrust it upward.

"Untie my hands."

Marcus heard Luke and Dave fumbling through drawers for something to cut the rope. Looking through the room, shelves of books from floor to ceiling. A library. A fireplace on the left-hand wall. A door on the right. He tried to draw a map of the house in his mind, but he was disoriented.

Through the kitchen to the library. What sense does that make? This place is a fucking maze.

It didn't matter. He moved to the door, his hand hovered over the handle. Feet shuffled behind it. A shadow under the door. Marcus gulped and readied the butcher knife in front of him.

He thrust the door open and jumped through to the other side. Empty. His pounding heart the only sound. He was sure he'd seen movement only moments before. He was in the lobby by the front entrance. It was too easy. Dave and Luke had been right behind him and they knew the house much better than he did.

Approaching the front door, Marcus held up the knife. Ready to strike. Ready to kill. It was two feet away. His car not far on the other side. He was going to make it. Another step forwards and he felt a sharp pain in his left leg.

Looking down with a stifled scream, a steel poker from the fireplace stuck through his upper thigh. Marcus fell to the ground despite his best effort to take another step. He looked up to see Dave standing over him, shaking his head.

"Why did you run?" His confusion seemed genuine. "Now look what you made me do."

Marcus swiped at him with the butcher knife, but he backed away out of reach. He pulled at the poker, speared through his leg, but gave up when it didn't move. Instead, he crawled towards the front door. It was right there, inches away.

The door handle just above his shoulders.

Dave crouched a safe distance away and took a breath. "I saw your face earlier."

"My face? What—"

"When you smelled my brothers blood," Dave continued. "You're like us."

Marcus shook his head, reaching for the handle. His fingers wrapped around it, but they were sweaty. His grip was weak.

"You are," Dave said. "You need to feed. You said so yourself."

"No, I'm not like you. You're sick." Marcus's voice was weak. He rested against the front door, hand dangling from the handle. Energy gone. He lifted the butcher knife, but both men knew it was a final show of defiance.

Dave smirked. Moved to the door handle. His hand on top of Marcus's was warm. He helped Marcus twist and the door opened. The night outside was still. The driveway lit with garden lights, casting a yellow glow against the pine trees.

"One last look at the world," Dave whispered. "Then you know what has to happen."

"It doesn't have to be this way," Marcus begged. "I thought we had something."

Dave paused for a moment. Massaged the back of Marcus's hand with his thumb. "We do." He sighed. "But people like us don't get happily ever afters."

They stayed like that for a moment, contemplating in silence. Even after the kidnapping and the torture, Dave's hand felt like home. It was comfortable. He looked up to see Dave looking down at him, a sad smile across his face.

"We could." Marcus offered with a shallow breath.

"We could?" Dave asked.

"Mum and Nat are all sorted. Dad's pissed. And hungry." Luke chuckled, entering the room. He stopped at the sight before him. "What happened here?"

Dave silenced his brother with a wave and shut the front door. "Time to go." He frowned and took the butcher knife from Marcus.

His leg throbbed as Dave and Luke dragged Marcus across the floor by his feet, leaving a trail of blood. He'd never enjoyed his own, though he'd tried it once or twice. Someone else's was always better. Now, as it flowed out of him, Marcus wished he could have one last taste of the juice. Even if it was his own.

Despite the blood loss, the strength started to ebb back into him. Maybe the adrenaline, who knew. But with each moment being dragged through the lobby towards his own funeral, the energy that had disappeared found new life.

And he intended to use it.

He struggled with his right foot, pulling and jolting to get free. Luke held tight and continued dragging him. Marcus tried again. His foot came free and he kicked at Luke's groin. The only sure-fire way to get him down and out.

"We got a live one!" Luke laughed and grabbed at the foot.

Dave ignored him and tried to get hold of the appendage. His own grip loosened and Marcus slipped free, grunting at the pain in his leg. Pain was good, he reminded himself. It gave him hope. It was part of the plan.

Marcus kicked again, relishing in the "Oof" as he made contact with Luke's balls. The idea was to make him angry and it looked to be working. Luke recovered fast and pushed Marcus's right leg to the side. Dave grabbed at it, too, telling Marcus to give up and accept his fate. The sadness in his voice trumped the anger.

His feet dropped, his left leg stuck in the air, held up from the poker, grating at his skin. Luke bent forward, hands opened towards Marcus's throat. This was it. Marcus reached up.

Grabbed Luke's arm and plunged him down. The poker impaled the young man with a wet sound, tearing through the lungs.

Marcus smiled.

Pushed him further onto the poker. Dave screamed and raced to his brother's side. It was too late. He coughed and choked and swallowed his own blood.

"I'm not dying tonight." Marcus heaved Luke off him and gripped the poker with both hands.

"What have you done?" Dave wept. "We could have…"

Marcus took a few deep breaths and pulled at the poker, screaming with each millimetre the metal slid through his bone. But he didn't stop. Couldn't stop. This poker was his way out.

It came free and Marcus fell back to the floor, his fingers tight around the bloodied, jagged metal. He laughed through the pain and looked at Dave, a pile on the floor. Sobbing for his murderous brother.

"We just need to eat." Dave repeated through his tears. "We just need to eat."

"Yeah?" Marcus struggled to his feet. Used the poker to steady himself. "So do I. And boy am I hungry."

He stumbled towards the basement door, paused by Dave's side. Thought about offering a hand on the shoulder, but remembered what Dave had done to his own. The Dermatome, slicing him away, inch by inch.

Ignoring the impulse to stab Dave through the heart, Marcus whispered, "I'm sorry," and continued to the basement steps. Swung the door shut, locked it. Let the dim light wash through him. He took a deep breath, taking in the stench of sweat and blood wafting from the dining table. From Dave's family.

Started down the stairs, grumble in his belly, poker in his hand.

Dave banged on the door from the other side, desperate to stop the coming onslaught. Marcus grimaced at the sound, a deep sense of regret washing over him. He didn't want to kill these people, but at this point, it was him or them. And it *couldn't* be him.

Stepping into the grim light of the basement, the cold concrete under his bare feet, Marcus gripped the poker tight. The dinner table, where he'd almost been the main meal, was empty. The family gone.

"I know you're down here," Marcus said. His voice caught in his throat, the menacing tone not quite getting there.

Behind him, up the stairs, the banging continued. Dave pleaded for the lives of his parents, repeating the mantra, "We just need to eat." Marcus knew all about that. His stomach was on fire with his own need. Like the organ had a mind of its own, propelling him forward.

Despite the silence in the basement, the lack of movement and the absence of the family, Marcus could smell them. Each with their own distinct flavour.

The dried blood on Bob's bandages.

The scar tissue on Gwen's face.

Natalie's tears.

It made the hunger worse. Fed his need.

"It didn't need to be this way. We could have been friends. We're the same, after all."

A gasp.

Somewhere beyond the dining table. Where the light couldn't reach.

Natalie.

He made his way over, holding the poker before him like a spear. His own blood dripping to the concrete. With each step, the pain surging through his damaged leg, Marcus fought the urge to turn back. To drop the weapon and leave this place. Forget he ever met Dave and this family.

But his pounding heart spurred him on. And the knowledge that these people would never leave him alone. Not now he knew their secret. And they knew his. So he walked, sniffing at the salt and sweet iron in the air.

He'd been here before. Not this basement, but it might as well have been. A man hid from him, disgusted and terrified of Marcus. The monster. He'd torn flesh from body that night. Skull from spine. Sucked down the intestines like spaghetti.

He pushed the memories back, they wouldn't help him now. He wasn't here for that. Not tonight. This was about survival, he told himself. Not hunger.

It's always about the hunger. There is nothing else.

Marcus shook his head. Convinced himself he was wrong. There was more to life than feeding. There was love.

And Dave… But…

The squeak of a wheel broke Marcus from his thoughts. Bob. The wheelchair. He scanned the basement, searching the shadows for movement. Another squeak. Behind him. He twisted to face the sound. Not fast enough.

A shovel swung to the side of his face. Marcus tried to

dodge, but it was too late. He was down, breathing in concrete dust as his ears rang from the force. He felt for the poker. It was gone. He hadn't even noticed it slip from his hands.

He tried to stand. The shove came down again. On his back. His shoulder, seeping white fluid in an effort to heal. Marcus managed to look up. Gwen stood over him, her thin lips stretched into a smile. The crevices on her damaged face a history of their endless hunger. Their will to survive.

Bob's wheelchair sat beside Marcus. The man learned forward, grabbed Marcus by the hair on the back of his head and pulled him up. Marcus complied, unable to do much else as the pain pulsing through his body forced him to surrender.

"You think this is our first time?" Bob spat against Marcus's ear.

Marcus laughed, the sound more like a choke than anything else. He laughed again as Bob dropped him to the ground.

"Why's he laughing?" Natalie asked, her voice low and shaken.

"I'm laughing," Marcus said through heavy breaths, "because I killed Luke."

Gwen wailed at the words, a gut wrenching, inhuman sound. Thick strands of saliva fell from her mouth as she howled and blubbered about her dead son.

"My baby, my baby." The words echoed through the basement.

Marcus smiled again. Her pain fed him. This fight wasn't over. He managed to hoist himself up to his elbows, watched Gwen collapse to the ground, holding her stomach. Her son's origin. Natalie raced to her side, caressing the old woman's hair with a soothing, "Shhh".

A motion to the side caught Marcus's attention. It came

again—a shovel. Marcus blocked it with his forearm, grunting at the whack against his skin. He reached up to Bob, gripped the man's throat, and pried the shovel away from him. It clanged to the ground and he kicked it across the basement.

Bob gurgled under the pressure of Marcus's fingers around his throat, punching at Marcus and grabbing at his arm. Dave looked like his father. The nose and cheekbones were strong. Or had once been. They had the same eye colour.

Marcus leaned forwards to the old man, spat in his face, and pushed the chair backward. A tear came to his eye at the knowledge he'd regret letting Bob live. But Dave. He and Dave. They could have something. Far away from this house and from these people.

"Let me leave." Marcus searched for the poker—his weapon of choice—but couldn't see it. He eyed the shovel instead. It wasn't sharp, but it would do. "Let me leave and you'll never see me again."

Bob stared into Marcus's eyes, the hatred pouring into the basement around them. Marcus knew he wasn't leaving. Not without a fight. He just hoped Dave wouldn't lose any more family members. The banging at the basement door was intermittent now, and weak. Dave had used his energy and rage to no avail.

As Bob continued to stare and the wailing and sobbing from Gwen quietened, Marcus made his way to the shovel. Lifting it, the wood was old and heavy. Marcus clenched his fingers around the handle, Bob watching him the whole time. He wheeled to the base of the stairs, Marcus's only way out. Blocked the entrance.

"Out of my way old man," Marcus said. "Don't make me hurt you."

Bob smirked. "Look at me. You think you can do worse

than I've done to myself?"

Marcus shrugged, eyeing the old man's severed legs. The gaping wounds and rotting flesh of his upper calves were bandaged in haste and bleeding through. Gazing at the limbs now, the hunger came back.

It was fierce. It was always fierce. But it was a rare day that he couldn't control it, suppress it. Push his hunger away with handfuls of raw meat. But now, looking at Bob's chopped-up legs, his stomach raged inside him. The flesh had maybe a few more days before it would be inedible. He could smell the use-by date approaching. The flies could smell it, too, buzzing around the wounds in a frenzy.

Leave him.

The sensation was strong, but Marcus pushed it down. Squeezed the handle of the shovel tighter. The wounds seemed to call to him and the old man's heartbeat thumped through Marcus's ears.

No. No. No.

Natalie and Gwen—curled in the corner in a mess of tears and sorrow—smelled rich, too. He heard their hearts, the veins pumping blood. Gushing like a river around their bodies.

The hunger was coming.

Just leave. Just leave.

Bob wheeled towards Marcus, arms outstretched. His eyes flicked to the side and Marcus turned just in time to see Natalie crash towards him with the poker. He dodged and Natalie fell past him, plunging to the floor with a groan.

Gwen, still motionless on the floor, wept for her dead son. Marcus counted her out of the game and lunged on top of Natalie. Planting his knee in the middle of back, she was stuck, reaching for the poker.

Grabbing it from her, Marcus held it against her throat. "I

don't want to hurt you."

"Fuck you," she spat.

In the seconds that followed, Marcus pressed the poker harder against Natalie's throat, closing his eyes as Bob pleaded him to let her free. The love in his cracked and tormented voice was clear. Marcus wished his own family had been so kind to him. Rather than disowning him, throwing him to the street, calling him a monster.

And that was before he started eating people.

An explosion of sound and wood blasted into the basement from the door upstairs. Marcus looked over to see Dave race down the stairs. Shotgun in hand, finger on the trigger. He raised it towards Marcus and fired.

Using Natalie's weight against his own, Marcus pulled her in front of him, forcing himself back to the concrete below. She saw her own death careening out of the shotgun barrel towards her and closed her eyes. Marcus heard her heartbeat, bouncing heavy and quick inside her chest. And then, nothing.

Her body went limp and Marcus pushed her away. She thudded against the ground, an empty sack of blood and wasted organs. The remaining family rushed to Natalie's body, scooping up her blood as though it would save her.

"What have you done?" Bob shouted, diving out of his wheelchair to lie beside his daughter. Caressing her hair and crying into her face, he repeated the words again and again. Gwen held hands over her face, praying this was all a nightmare.

Dave kneeled next to his sister, tears streaming down his cheeks. Shotgun at his side. For the moment, they were grieving. This was Marcus's chance. And he would take it.

Gripping the poker once more, he used it as a crutch to get to his feet. Dave looked up at him, eyes pleading for answers.

Maybe mercy. Marcus shook his head—no mercy here—and thrust the poker through the back of Bob's skull.

"I didn't want this." Marcus ripped the poker from Bob's head and looked down at Dave.

The shotgun was an inch from his fingers, but he didn't move. Just rocked back and forth on his haunches at the loss of his family. He whispered something between sobs, and as Marcus walked towards the man he knew he could have loved, the words became clear.

"We could have had something."

Over and over, like a mantra.

"We could have," Marcus said. "But now…" He paused, looking down at the fresh and rotting meat sacks of Natalie and Bob. "Now, I'm hungry."

Dave lifted the shotgun. Marcus stabbed fast. The poker glided through the skin on Dave's stomach, pierced the organs beneath. A ripping sound told Marcus the poker had cleared the other side. He gazed down at Dave—*The one that got away*—and shed a tear.

For the love he imagined them sharing and which now could never be.

For the hunger rising in his blood.

For what he knew he was going to do to the family.

Dave coughed up blood, the sweet, thick, red juice that kept Marcus alive. The thing he'd been fighting against for so long, but now had no reason to avoid. Marcus pulled the poker out of Dave and it clanged against the floor. He picked up the shotgun and stepped away from the man with a great sense of pity.

He might eat the family. But not Dave. Maybe then they'd still have a chance.

Hands still over her eyes, Gwen begged for her family's

return. Begged to whom, Marcus didn't know. Didn't care. He stumbled towards her and kneeled in front of the woman.

"It's okay," Marcus whispered.

And shot her in the chest. He didn't like the lungs, anyway.

Her moans stopped in an instant. No chugging or suffering or final breaths. Her life was gone and Marcus reached into her chest, feeling for the heart. His fingers touched the silent muscle and he ripped it free. It would be insensitive to eat it here, with Dave groaning in pain three feet away.

Fuck it.

His teeth sank into the muscle, firm and raw. Uncooked, hearts were tough. But once the outer layer of muscle was breached, the force of his teeth would do the rest. He ripped at the heart, blood smearing his face, and swallowed chunks of the muscle. It was the most satisfying moment in the last five years. Since the last time he'd gotten carried away in a basement.

The acid in his stomach came alive at the muscle splashing around down there. Digesting and eating away at it. Marcus burped and stood up again, sated. He knew it wouldn't last, but perhaps it was enough for now. Enough to help him leave without devouring the rest of Dave's family.

But the air was rich with death and the promise of a feast. Marcus moved towards the basement steps, ignoring the gurgling and choking from Dave. It was fading, his breaths shallower with each passing second.

I can't leave him.

Despite his own wounds, the sliced skin and the hole in his leg, despite Gwen's blood stained across his mouth and lips, despite everything, he wanted nothing more than to run to Dave's side. To hold him. Kiss him. Tell him it would all be okay.

But his foot hit the first step and Marcus began to climb.
"Please," Dave gurgled. "Don't go."

We could have something. Maybe without his family, we could be together. Maybe.

"Marcus," Dave called. "Please. Help me."

He continued up the steps. His heart told him what his head wouldn't. It was too late. Not after everything that had happened tonight. After all, Gwen's heart was still fresh in his digestive system.

But as the morning light streamed through the shattered basement door, Marcus stopped. Dave's groans and pleas rung in his ears. The stench of the family's blood, wafted towards him. Beckoned him back down. He took a deep breath and headed back into the basement.

He kneeled beside Dave, who clutched at his injury. "I can help you." Marcus wiped a tear as Dave stared into his eyes.

"I still..." Dave let the sentence hang. "I... We could..."

Marcus nodded and pressed a finger to Dave's lips. "Let me help you."

He leaned down, their breath hot on each other's faces, and Marcus kissed him. Then helped him the best way he knew how. His teeth ripped into Dave's neck, severing the carotid artery. He cried through the gush of blood pouring over him, mixing with the remnants of Gwen's.

Dave struggled for a moment, then his body—like the rest of the family—went limp. And Marcus let go of his fears. His hesitations. Gave in to his hunger.

And fed.

His tongue was immersed in Dave's throat, suckling on a vein—*Nothing like taking it straight from the tap*—when he heard a creak from over his shoulder.

"What have you done to my family?"

Marcus lifted his face. A stranger stood before him, butcher knife tight in her hands. "Who are you?" he wondered, dizzy from the feast. He remembered the shadow from earlier, someone running past the windows.

Another family member.

"I came for desert," she said, and lunged towards Marcus.

He raised his hands, but they were too wet with red. The woman forced the blade to his throat and sliced him open, left to right. He reached for his neck to hold the wound shut, but it was no use.

His own life force spilled out of him and as his eyes closed, the old woman sat on top of him, and smiled. She leaned forwards and drank, pried her fingers into his neck.

"The throat is my favourite part." As his trachea came out of him, Marcus reached for Dave's hand. Squeezed it with as much energy as he had left. The woman feasted on him, but he didn't care. It was for the best.

Maybe he and Dave could be together.

Somewhere.

Without the need to feed.

PART II

SUPERNATURAL

QUIETUS

Terry woke with a jolt, cold sweat dripping from his naked body. Hot, thick air burned his lungs. Something had happened; he felt it inside him. The memory lurked in the shadows of his foggy mind. On the outskirts of his brain, just out of reach. But his body knew. His heaving chest, the panicked hairs on his arms. The pit of his stomach ached, burning to tell him that something was wrong. An intense, heavy force pressed against him from the inside.

He wiped sleep from his eyes and sat up, conscious his manhood flapped against sweaty thighs as he moved. His head throbbed, ripping at the seams, ready to explode. He looked around with blurry vision, unable to decipher his surroundings. The sense of dread rose as he took in the space around him. The memory of what brought him here still evaded him, and his heart pounded against his ribs. A warning that this place—a room, he could tell that much—was the last he'd ever see.

The room was empty. The walls a deep, intense red. He

touched the hard surface, smooth and cold. Like concrete but more organic, with a steady glow. The walls hummed, shallow breaths matching the panic he felt. He tried to adjust, rubbing his eyes as though the action would diminish the overpowering light. The glow seemed to intensify, and with it, a stale heat hit him in waves. The heat and the light and his throbbing head gave way to nausea, his insides churning. Before he could stop, he heaved, splattering the red floor with dark green and brown chunks.

He wiped his mouth, residue of bile a smear on the back of his hand. Vomiting left him breathless, but he knew he had to stand. To make sense of the situation. The walls began to dim, softening the room into a shadowy quietness. The heat dissipated without warning. The low hum almost inaudible, coming from outside the room.

Beyond the red walls.

Holding his pounding head, he tried to ignore the dread— the surge of panic, the desperate need to scream. He had to focus.

Where am I, why am I here, how did I get here? Was I kidnapped? Why me?

He thought of his mother, the soldier, using her memory to balance his mind. Her strength always calmed him. The last thing he remembered was tucking his daughter in for the night, and then—

Oh, Jesus, Alice! Did someone take her, too?

His seven-year-old daughter had clung to him while they'd said goodnight, a brief peck on the cheek, a token of a parent's love for their child. He'd switched the light off and paused at the door to watch Alice fluff her pillow and sink low into the bed with her stuffed octopus, Mr Tentacles. Everything had been so normal, so routine.

Then someone rang the doorbell. He probed his brain for answers, pushed himself to see a face, but nothing came. Now he was here, wherever 'here' was, encased in a tomb of red. Desperation welled inside him, his hands shaking at the thought of Alice in danger.

Stay calm. What would Mum do?

Her military training would tell her to search the area. Find a weak spot, a way out. In one of the walls, he saw a thin outline of what could have been a door, but no handle was visible. His stomach churned again. An organic, instinctual warning.

The outline faded in and out as though his recovering eyes were playing tricks. He ran his fingers along one of the walls hoping to find something. Anything. He sensed something beyond the wall. Movement, maybe. The low hum and the stench of his stomach contents his only companions.

He called out, his voice hoarse and dry. The walls reverberated his weak efforts, and panic rose once more. Everything within him that was rational and calm disappeared in an instant, and his frantic hands searched the cold surface, pleading for an exit, for any crevice or crack he could exploit.

Nothing.

Remember, his mother had told him, *that you never give up. No matter how hopeless something seems, you dig deep and you fight til the end.*

He bashed against the wall where a door ought to have been, but the faint outline had disappeared. He scratched at the wall to no avail, begging for his release. No matter how deep he dug, he couldn't shake the feeling that these walls would be the last thing he'd ever see. The feeling that he'd never see Alice again.

Thrashing again at the wall, he slipped on the puddle of

vomit and crashed to the floor, scraping the skin on his thighs and feet. For the first time, he looked down at his naked body and curled in a foetal position to hide himself. Terry wept into the chamber around him, distorted and weak. The nudity left him more vulnerable than he cared to admit, even worse than his ignorance of who had taken him or where he was. Every curve and exposed back hair reinforced his powerlessness.

Naked, scared, and alone, he stood up and drew once more on the strength of his mother. He thought of all the letters she sent him. It was what he always did when he was scared, even now, well into his thirties.

Dig deep. For Alice.

The last time he'd seen his mother, she'd been crouching in front of him at the airport. Her arms tight around him, faint traces of a coconut aroma in her hair. It had comforted him, along with her reassurance she'd see him soon for his tenth birthday. When most mothers whispered their love before disappearing into some far-away war, his whispered strategy and tactics.

He needed that now more than ever before, but in that moment the whispered strategies were static in his mind. Her words sounded like a record spinning in reverse and his breath caught in his throat. He forced himself to breathe. In through the nose, out through the mouth. Slow, steady. The fog surrounding his mind refused to lift.

Despite her efforts to instill him with a sense of bravery, he was only ever brave when he imagined her beside him. Maybe it was because she mothered him from a distance, dispensing advice across windswept deserts in remote corners of the Earth. She had tried to teach him not to let fear consume him for more than five seconds, something he couldn't do without the sense of her presence. He knew her advice was needed now if he was going to find Alice. He reached through time and space to see the words she'd left him in her final letter.

Feel your fear as much as you can feel anything. Know the fear, know what it means to you to be alive.

Her words echoed in his mind, and his breathing calmed. He knew what it meant to be alive. Alice was his whole life. She was his reason for being. Renewed, he continued his search for an exit. Alice was out there somewhere, and like his mother had ordered him all those years earlier, he had to dig deep.

Rising to his feet, ignoring the shameful urge to cover his exposed groin, something shimmered in the corner of his eye. From the ceiling, a liquid seeped through the walls. He walked towards the site, anxious, and inspected the liquid as it crept down the wall. One thick stream, spreading like veins, waiting to expose something much larger.

What is that?

Looking beyond the liquid into its origins, he saw no holes or cracks or anything that might suggest a way out, and his chest started pounding again. The liquid continued to seep into the room, its descent matching the rhythmic pulse of his heart. A second stream bled from the walls, pulsating towards him. Thicker this time. Slower in its descent. A transparent ooze that seemed to follow him around the room. He looked closer at the gushing muck, noticing a slight yellow tinge. It reminded him of the splash when his ex-wife's waters broke, ushering Alice into the world.

Alice.

He pressed himself against the opposite wall as the thick, gooey liquid continued towards him. He was petrified of turning his back on the menacing stuff. He remembered his mother's advice. The five seconds was up. The time for fear was over. Fear wasn't the path to finding Alice. Pushing it down to the depths of his stomach and wiping sweat from his eyes, he searched for something, anything, that would set him free. He headed back to where the door ought to have been. He scratched and clawed at the concrete, begging the red surface to open. A fingernail snapped. He ignored the pain and scratched harder.

"Let me out!" He pounded the wall as the ooze approached, slowly pulsing. He looked back to where it seeped from the ceiling. Defying gravity, it ran across the wall in his direction, reaching along the wall. Tentacles searching for its prey. It was after him; it *wanted* him; its slow approach taunted him. Dripping to the floor, the ooze paused for a moment to suckle on the puddle of his vomit, absorbing the stomach contents into its opaque form.

The wall stood firm against his bleeding fists. He barged the wall, embracing the searing pain in his shoulder as he stumbled backwards. The muck shimmered and snaked towards him, its yellowish opaque surface reflecting his own distorted image like a dirty funhouse mirror. The floor and walls were covered now, the ooze closing in on him. He screamed and begged and cried for Alice.

It lapped at his feet, encircling him, tasting him.

"No, no, no! Please, leave me alone!"

The malevolent fluid continued its approach and he dug deep to find his mother's strength.

She wouldn't accept this. She'd be brave. She'd fight!

With no other options and escape seeming impossible, he turned to the offensive. All he could do was kick at it the way a child does with waves at the beach. He kicked and punched with all his might. It didn't react, but his attacks had nevertheless ruptured a semi-hard surface to reveal a thinner, pinkish liquid within. He kicked again and again, droplets of the gunk remaining on his toes. He tried to wipe them away, clawed at them, but the defiant liquid absorbed into his skin.

Before he could react, the ooze wrapped around his feet, biting at his skin like hundreds of bee stings coming all at once, pulling him into submission on the floor. His mother's advice vanished, sucked into the quicksand abyss just like his legs and torso. He clawed at his feet, tore at his arms and legs, watched in horror he was consumed to his chest and arms. His efforts helped its spread as his body drowned.

It crawled across his neck and face and he sensed its pulsating hatred. It despised him. Thrived on his fear. It took pleasure journeying across his skin. Enveloped now, he was blind. Couldn't breathe, couldn't move as the liquid scalded his skin. Suffocating him in an ocean of boiling water. The world stood still for the longest time. His lungs burned and heaved, desperate for air as the liquid swam up his nostrils and down his throat. Knowing he was going to pass out any second, he tried once more to pull the monstrous ooze from him.

The more he fought, the more it tightened around him, squeezing his body like a snake torturing a mouse. His bones snapped under the pressure. Thousands of tiny sharp teeth gnawing at every nerve inside him.

His empty lungs stopped gasping for breath. The squeezing eased and the muck began to disappear into him, sinking through his skin. He fought to keep his eyes open, but knew it was no use. Even though the squeezing had stopped, his nerves still screamed in pain, ordering his body into shutdown.

Alice's face was the last thing he saw before his brain switched off. Her round green eyes, jewels glowing from the centre of her pale skin. Her flowing blonde hair. He saw her brush it away from her face as she so often did, and smile at him. He saw her at the beach, running from the cold water as it crashed against the shore. Smiling. Laughing. Full of life.

In the next moment, her face disappeared.

Alice was gone.

Terry woke coughing and wheezing. His lungs devoured the air, sucking it in like an addict desperate for one last hit. Clutching at his chest, he calmed into a steady pant and scanned the room. The ooze was gone, his body free. It hadn't left any traces. No marks or streaks the way water did while it dried out. He checked every inch of his body, scraping and poking at his flesh. He expected his skin to burst like a pimple overfilling with puss.

Nothing.

If not for the fact that he was surrounded by those red walls, he might have thought this whole thing was a bad dream. The room was real, but there was no evidence of a liquid of any kind. It was almost like the vicious liquid had never existed. His head was woozy and his body felt heavy, the way bones do when forced awake from a deep sleep.

He knew, though, that the liquid hadn't been a terrifying dream. The room was real, the ooze had been, too. And that meant Alice was still out there, waiting for him. He hoped his little girl hadn't succumbed to the malevolent stuff. He knew he wouldn't cope with that.

Dig deep.

His mother's strength grounded him for a moment, allowing him to focus. He was still trapped in the red room.

The low hum from earlier was more noticeable now, vibrating under his naked buttocks.

Before he could consider his next move, a beam of white light emanated into the room. He looked towards the source. Part of the wall was rising, gliding towards the ceiling. It was a door, right where that outline had been. Freedom beckoned him, but He shook his head. It was too easy, too convenient.

Alice.

The beam grew brighter, dulling the intensity of the red walls. The door was open now. It unnerved him that all he heard from outside was that low, steady hum. He peered through the glowing white light to the other side, making out nothing but a strange humanoid shape. Tall, thin. Obscured by the intensity of the white light, he saw another one and reached out to them.

"Help me."

Ignoring the vibrations coursing through his body, he stood. The exit was so close, a metre or so away. He would leave the room and find Alice, and everything would be okay. He walked towards the door, slow at first, considerate in his movements. Remnants of his mother's training took hold.

After a few steps, he felt a pang. A dull ache at first, pressing against his internal organs. Another step. The ache intensified. Every inch of him pulsated and he doubled over, holding his stomach in the fear it would burst open.

Alice needs me.

He knew he had to keep going. The figures outside the room didn't notice him as he reached for their help once more.

"Please, my daughter—"

Something was in his stomach, shifting and moving, scratching at his insides.

He stepped towards the door, his stomach throbbing

hard against his arms. The part of him that was eager to walk through was overpowered by the other half. The half frozen by fear.

Five seconds.

Pushing through the pain in his abdomen, he drew on every inch of strength he could muster. The pain spread to his chest, suffocating him, squeezing his heart. Fighting for breath, he caught a glimpse of his mother. In the corner of his eye, the hallucination of her spirit urged him along. With her memory by his side and knowing Alice was counting on him, he moved across the cold, hard surface. A lightning bolt of pain jolted through his legs and he collapsed to his knees, struggling to keep conscious. His legs throbbed, the skin splitting around his thigh and calf muscles.

Survive. His mother's voice rang in his ears.

The pain jolted through him like volts of electricity, but Terry stood once more, determined to reach the exit and find Alice.

You will not fall again. Orders from beyond the grave.

He watched the skin on his feet and legs continue to split open with each step. His torn flesh fell to the side, releasing a thick black gunk. It seeped from him with each step, like tar from a smoker's lung. The veins on his ankles and lower legs turned black, poisoned by the stuff leaking from his wounds. He slipped on his pieces of his own skin and fell back to his knees, unable to bear the pain as the blackness reached his thighs.

Unable to heed his mother's orders.

He was halfway to the door now, kneeling on his calves, now a mess of torn flesh and black gunk. The pain drove him into stillness, his body refusing to move any further, and just like that, the searing pain coursing through him vanished. He braced himself, waiting for the next onslaught, but it didn't come. A sense of relief followed. Relief that he was gifted this moment without pain. A moment where his skin wasn't splitting, where his bones weren't crumbling into dust. But in his frozen state, he stared towards the open door.

Towards freedom.

Towards Alice.

He remembered how the ooze had reacted to his movements earlier, tracking him across the room. Through the pained fog in his mind, he guessed whatever was inside him now operated in the same way. Any time he moved, the gunk inside him grew stronger. It was he himself who brought the fluid to life. But the exit was right there, and he knew Alice was close.

Too weak to stand, he dragged himself along the concrete floor, the skin on his face scraping away. He hoped upon hope that safety lay half a metre away and forced himself to keep going. What was left of his feet and legs flaked away into ash, filling the air like pollen. He choked on his own remains as pieces of his decomposing skin settled on the red floor around him. The trail of thick, black gunk lay behind him, mixing with his remains.

His body disintegrated into ash with each movement, but he was so close to the door. So close to finding Alice. He heard his elbows crack and split apart with the rest of his arm. His blackened fingers reached for the glowing white light, searching for its comforting heat, hoping it somehow held the key to his survival. Yet he knew it was too late. He looked back to see a trail of remains, clumps of organs still decomposing amidst the sticky gunk that bled from him.

He lay there, unwilling to let this defeat him, crying for Alice.

"Daddy!" Her voice was small, almost an echo.

It was her, there was no doubt. His darling daughter was just outside, waiting for him, calling for him. She needed him.

"Alice, I'm coming!"

Half his body gone, the other half seconds from ruin, he gripped the floor with his remaining strength. Alice was somewhere beyond that door and he'd get to her if it took his last breath. The pain shot through the remnants of his body while behind him the trail of ruins began to stir.

The black ruins, a mixture of ashes and decomposed organs, started to take form. Rising from the floor, an arm with misshapen fingers reached to the ceiling. The grotesque being like wet clay fighting to hold its shape. An elbow formed and the ruined arm began to push against the red floor, pulling a contorted head from the ashes. Its mouth was open, releasing an inaudible gasp as the creature found life.

He clawed with all his might, unable to cry or scream. His lungs began to disintegrate into ash, ready to join the creature growing from his remains. Somehow his heart continued to beat. He reached the door, his fingers crumbling to the floor beneath him reaching for something to grip, something to help pull him along.

His chest rattled, his mouth searching for oxygen that wouldn't come. He looked down to see the creature continue to rise. Faceless and bloody, it wheezed into life.

"Daddy, help me!"

He wanted to call to her, to tell her he loved her. He wanted to hug her and play with her and do everything fathers are supposed to do. But his tongue had fallen away with the rest of his muscles. He would never get that chance now. This was it.

The creature was almost complete now, standing on shaky

legs. It would finish growing once his own corrosion had ended. The pain was gone now, with no nerves left to feel. In a way, it was a blessing. He could no longer feel the skin on his face split apart or the thick gunk bleed from his eyes and mouth. He didn't feel his lungs dissipate into ash or his heart begin to blacken. He watched through blurry vision as the creature came towards him.

He watched it stretch and take a step.

He watched hair start to form and pigment appear in the skin.

He watched the creature turn into him, a mirror-image of the man he had been yesterday.

The last thing Terry ever saw was the creature grow his face, before the last of him succumbed and broke apart.

I look at the mess of my birth, remnants of the man scattered through the dusty air. The remains before me nothing but a pile of ash and leftovers of my primordial fluid. Kneeling before what had been his head, I scoop his ashes into my mouth, letting the particles absorb into me. The brain matter was important. Eating the memories would assist the integration. Help to complete me.

Terry. My new name.

Memories start to flood my mind. I have a sense of who this man was, and I curl my newly formed lips.

Pathetic.

I step out of the room, unsteady on my new legs at first, but adapting. I look back at Terry's remains and smile. He hadn't realised it, but he was one of the lucky ones. The others weren't being reborn in a greater image than their own. They were simply going to die.

An endless corridor stretches in both directions, filled with birthing suites like mine. Some of the others are already there, waiting for me. I take my place in a queue of people just like me. Born minutes ago, from the same ancient liquid coursing through my fresh veins.

My family.

A young girl stands in front me, her back to me. She turns, smiling, and I recognise her flowing blond hair. Those green eyes. He has memories of her. At the beach. A tentacled toy. He has lots of memories of this person. They are my memories now.

"Daddy!" she embraces me.

"Alice." The name is familiar on my new tongue.

"Will we kill them all, Daddy?" she looks at me with those big round eyes, hopeful. Moons at the centre of my universe.

I give a single nod and squeeze her hand, anxious to get started.

THE

WELL

NOW

The wooden spiral stairs of the lighthouse creak as I hold onto the railing and climb. Through clouded vision, I look at my feet and wonder how far I'll get before the stairs shudder and collapse under my weight forever. I can't think about that now. I can't worry myself with the blisters or the splinters digging into my raw skin or the open wounds all over my body. I can't think about the black oil seeping from me where blood used to be.

I have a job to do.

"You can't stop me!" My voice echoes through the stairwell. "I will end you!"

The silence that follows is broken only by my breaths and the adrenaline of my heart thumping through my skull.

Gasoline is slick on the wood, the stench consuming my nostrils. I'm satisfied I've poured enough and choke on the thick vapours filling my lungs. The gasoline splashes around my toes as I climb another stair.

I hear the whisper through the pounding of my heart. That terrible sound carries on a wind that doesn't exist. Audible only to me.

Miiiichaeeeel. The slow drawl of my name grates like nails on a chalkboard. Like a hand wrapped around my soul.

I shrink at the sound, and with each step, the presence grows stronger, whispering my name again. The invisible hand squeezing tighter. The blackness inside me bubbles to the surface, frothing at my lips and splashing against the gasoline.

"Is that the best you can do?" I hurl again and scream into the empty lighthouse.

I slip in the black muck from my stomach and grip the railing again, ignoring the squish as my foot sinks through the liquid. It doesn't matter. None of it matters, not the oil seeping from my eyes or the weight pressing my soul into nothingness. None of it.

I just have to get there.

To the Watch Room.

I'm almost there. Right where this started. Right where it'll end. The door at the landing is open, swinging on its hinges. Beckoning me into the darkness beyond.

Miiiichaeeeel.

I fumble through my pants pocket for the lighter and hold it in front of my face. The presence sneers as the orange flame pierces the darkness.

I smile and close my eyes.

Drop the lighter and laugh.

THREE MONTHS AGO

When I first inquired about the lighthouse, the realtor used the word "derelict." The emails said the place had burned down eighty years earlier, and its original use as a lighthouse had been abandoned long before that. The realtor, Shelley, seemed reluctant, muttering about a sordid history. In the end, she agreed to take me out to see it.

"I must warn you, though," she said in a hushed whisper down the phone. "The place is worthless. Any price will be too much."

"Sounds perfect," I said and hung up, lighting a cigarette. Puffing with a deep sigh.

My phone vibrated in my hand to tell me I had four missed calls from Ted. He was a bear of a man, rugged and thickset with a manicured beard. Yet he acted more like a terrified cat, clinging to me for dear life. I wasn't surprised at the missed calls. Or the texts.

I sighed and pocketed the phone. He wanted space, fine. He wanted me to move out, okay. I told myself I'd do whatever he needed to keep our marriage alive. It was the phone calls, though. The incessant phone calls and the stream-of-consciousness text messages that relayed his every thought about everything at any given time. I just couldn't take it.

I promised myself I'd call him after the inspection. He wouldn't want me living in a burned-out old lighthouse, but he didn't have a say in that. Not now. Not anymore.

The lighthouse was right near the beach—an obvious statement but worth mentioning, though, is that this particular beach was also abandoned. Huge signs advising people to stay off the sand and the obscure "Falling Rocks" warnings had been plastered around the place. It was abandoned, alright.

I stood outside the lighthouse, taking in its shape and the visible burn marks discolouring the once-white tower. According to the listing, the lighthouse was 101 metres tall, the same as the tallest lighthouse in Yokohama. It was situated 300 hundred metres above sea level, overlooking the Pacific, with glimpses of the aurora when the light was just right. It was no surprise that the slightest breeze felt like a hurricane.

Alex would have hated it.

I smiled.

Shelley appeared flustered as she approached the lighthouse, juggling keys, a folder, and her phone while trying not to slip out of her high heels. Brushing hair out of her face, she greeted me with a smile. Forever professional.

"Professor Myers?" She called over the wind.

We shook hands for a brief moment until the delicate balance of folder, phone and keys started to slip. Shelley was jittery and looked uncomfortable. She ushered me to a building around the back, almost invisible from the road leading to the lighthouse.

It turned out to be the living quarters, a quaint little two-bedroom cabin like you might see in an Italian or Spanish seaside town. Unlike the lighthouse, the living quarters had not been burned down. They hadn't been maintained by any stretch, but at least there were no piles of charred wood lying around. Shelley mentioned the boathouse a few hundred metres away.

"So, as you can see…" Shelley started the tour of the living quarters. Despite myself, I tuned her out. There was nothing Shelley could say to me that I couldn't already see. The stained-glass windows filtering blocks of colour onto the wooden floors. The gas stove and cooktop from the early 1900s, never updated. The exposed brick interior and the families of spiders nesting in the wooden beams streaming across the ceiling.

It was perfect.

I tuned back in at the mention of the government fence and the history of disappearances in the area.

"It's quite infamous, I'm surprised Council listed it," Shelley said.

"Infamous?" I raised my eyebrows.

"The caretaker and his whole family—wife and three kids, even the dog—just vanished one night. Gone, like they never even existed."

"That's a bit disturbing," I said with a frown. Still, something about the place spoke to me.

Shelley nodded. "Very disturbing. The next fellow, a real loner according to all sources, also disappeared, but not before shutting the lighthouse lamp down in the middle of a storm. A ship carrying families from England smashed right into the cliff face. Everybody drowned."

"What happened to that caretaker?"

Shelley shrugged. "He was never seen again, either."

I opened my mouth and closed it again, shushing as the story continued.

"That was in 1912. Since then, two other caretakers vanished. The lighthouse was abandoned in 1940 when the last caretaker set fire to the place. Newspapers at the time said he was found wandering across the beach with first-degree burns, muttering about a well. He died a few hours later in hospital."

"Spooky." I laughed.

"It's been a historical site ever since. Closed to the public. That's why I'm surprised Council would list it. But here we are."

"What's your best price?" I asked.

"Professor, uh,"—Shelley paused to look over the folder in her hands—"Michael, is it?"

I nodded.

"Michael, there is no price that would be fair. The lighthouse must be maintained as part of the sale, and as you can see…" She pointed out the window and let the evidence speak for itself.

"Well, whatever the price," I said, a thin smile spreading across my lips, "I'll take it."

Shelley protested as much as someone who didn't want to lose commission would. That being said, I was in her office thirty minutes later, organising the paperwork for a purchase.

Walking to my car, I felt my phone buzzing in my pocket again and swiped to answer.

"Ah, he picks up," Alex said, with *that* tone.

"I was busy, I just bought a property." I swallowed my frustration and lit a cigarette.

"A property?" Alex asked and fell silent.

I sighed. "Alex, this is what you wanted. You asked me to move out, so I'm going."

No response, just a whisper of sharp breaths.

"Look, Alex, I have to go."

The phone, along with my excitement, went dead.

As I drove towards the motel, my home until the property was settled, I found myself gazing at the lighthouse—a beacon in the distance, my new home.

Somewhere beneath the hum of the engine, a voice whispered my name.

MOVING DAY

Alex had promised to help with the move and, unsurprisingly, developed a cough at the last moment. Yet, somehow, I was the one with communication problems. I had told him it was fine and helped the movers with some of the lighter boxes as he watched from the kitchen, sipping herbal tea. Moments like that made the move feel like the right thing to do. Other moments, the ones where his arms were wrapped around me, and his lips caressed mine… The move didn't feel so right, then.

I thought about that as the truck was emptied into my new home and as Jason, the removalist, pushed some papers under my nose and asked for a signature, peering out the window towards the lighthouse.

"Place gives me the creeps," he muttered as I scrawled my name and waved on his way out. "Make sure you review us on Yelp."

I nodded, knowing full well I was never going to leave a review.

Alex tried to phone again, and I silenced the call, letting the screen dim into black. I knew that unpacking would be the only surefire way to push him from my thoughts, so I got to work.

Tearing packing tape from the closest box and throwing it to the messy ground around me, a shiver ran down my spine.

Michael.

A whisper like the one I'd heard that day in my car. Just audible in the silence. Low enough to be my imagination. My tingling spine told me my mind was not playing tricks.

My ears pricked up as the voice came again. Just behind my shoulder. I spun around. The room was empty. I listened to my body, to the crawling of my skin, the knot in my stomach, and walked outside. It was as though a rope was tied to my heart, leading me through the property grounds.

To the lighthouse.

The whisper echoed around the vacant land. It came from inside the lighthouse, somewhere near the lantern at the top.

The door was just a charred plank, a feeble barrier between the inside and the outside. I reached for the brass handle, somehow unscathed in the fire long ago, and pushed the door open with a long, steady creak.

Thin strips of light filtered through cracks in the walls, illuminating the mess inside. The floors were black with ash and what looked to be some kind of dried black gunk—coated and gelatinous, all these years later.

I kneeled and touched the goo, rubbing it between my thumb and forefinger. It reminded me of mouldy custard. Wiping my hands on my jeans, I stood up and looked around. Beams of wood had crashed to the ground, the winding staircase lining the walls missing a few steps here and there. The brass railing, like the door handle, untouched. I could smell smoke and felt it stinging my eyes as I moved through the lighthouse towards the staircase. There was something familiar about the stairs. They reminded me of something. Of some*where* I'd been before.

The walls were rotted, littered with holes, like wounds half-eaten by rats and other vermin.

Michael.

'The whisper rose again, twisting down the staircase towards me. The breath hit my face, washing over me like the detritus of a dead animal. Whoever was calling for me was just upstairs in the Watch Room.

The railing buckled under my grip as I climbed the stairs. I felt the rope again, tightening around my heart, willing me to follow its desire. It pulled me to a place I'd never been to, yet so familiar.

Like home.

The Watch Room was dusty, and patches of mould spread across the crevices in the corners of the ceiling. The fire had reached the door but not the room, which was untouched save for the dust and the mould. I noticed some canisters of gasoline sitting in one of the corners, undisturbed and waiting for eighty years.

Behind the gasoline, an old white sheet hung over something, hiding in the corner. The rope around my heart squeezed again, and I went towards it. I pulled the sheet away to reveal what lay beneath.

A painting. A faded golden frame made the interior seem even darker, casting light away from the image in the painting. I stared into it, wishing the gold away until I could no longer see it. All that remained was the painting. Fumes of the oil still strong, after years of abandonment.

It was a well. Large, grey cement bricks of different sizes and shapes. Jagged edges spiked at my eyes as I took in the well. It sat within a patch of brown, dead grass. Inside the well was nothingness—a deep, inky blackness leading into the depths of the ground. As I looked upon the painting, absorbing each brick in the well, staring into the abyss within, the ashen staircase began to heal, restoring to a former glory nobody had seen for two generations.

Miiiichaeeeel. The whisper turned into a sneer, closer than before.

It came from the well.

Every inch of me wanted to turn and run, but the force around my heart gripped me and pulled me to my knees. I stared into the well, unable to speak, breathe, or blink, unable to move. All I could do was listen.

Something in the well spoke to me in muffled whispers, nonsensical sounds that formed ancient knowledge—words I'd never heard but somehow knew. Penetrating my ears with a message.

My mind sank into the well until everything around me vanished. Everything, save the whispers, the message entering me, filling me with words I didn't understand. Words I didn't want to hear.

The darkness surrounded me. Immersed me in an abyss of nothingness. I tried to breathe. My lungs moved, though only because it was their nature to do so. No air came in, none escaped. It didn't matter. I didn't need to breathe in this space, this eternal black. I didn't need to see or think or fee—the abyss did it all for me.

My skin broke out in goosebumps, shivering up my arms first, then down the back of my neck, caressing the tiny hairs on my upper back. The cold nothingness sunk into my bones, stabbed into my heart and brain, and seized my mind.

I reached through the freezing emptiness, unable to see my fingertips. It called again, the whisper groaning in a language I'd only heard once before. In the lighthouse. Groaning through the depths of the abyss, each syllable like an ice pick jabbing at my brain.

The darkness closed in around me. I opened my mouth to scream—the sound was stolen from me, captured by the darkness. The silence felt heavy, like a presence drawing closer. I couldn't shut my mouth. I couldn't do anything.

The cold black sunk into my open mouth, reaching into me like a bony hand scraping at my insides. It explored my body, twisting through my organs. As the blackness spread through me, I knew I belonged to it and disappeared into the abyss.

In the next moment, the whispers were gone. I was alone in silence, and the grip around my heart was gone. I clutched my chest, drew in deep breaths, and fell to my backside. After my breathing settled, I rose to my feet and reached for the painting.

It needed light. It needed me.

I headed back down the stairs, only just noticing the holes in the walls were gone. The staircase renewed. I moved through the lighthouse towards the charred front door, painting tucked under my arm. I paused to take in the sight of the ash rising into the air, healing the burns and the scars and the rot of the last eighty years. Rubbing my face in disbelief, I felt the same gunk from the floor leak from my eyes and ran back to my new home.

I awoke the next morning, scrambling for air as I fell out of my unmade bed. My lungs burned, my head heavy with sharp pains. On my hands and knees, I retched, coughing and choking on a black oil that drizzled out of my throat. I heaved again, trying to urge the thick liquid out of my body. It crept along my oesophagus for a moment before sliding back down to my stomach. I shoved my fingers down there to force a reaction, to expunge the black bile. Nothing came up. It had settled in me now.

Clutching my stomach, I somehow knew the blackness was inside of me. A life force pulsating around my body. Sharing my oxygen and blood and cells. Taking what it needed.

Across the room, the painting of the well lay dormant, uncovered, facing me. The blackness in the well comforted me. It made me feel something. It made me feel at home.

I ran to it and pressed my face against the oil painting, my head surrounded by the opening of the well. As I leaked tears onto the canvas, the sick feeling dissipated. My headache vanished at the almost inaudible whispering like soft rhythms of my favourite song.

In the days that passed, the lighthouse continued to heal itself. The land, too, had begun to prosper. The grass a bright green, the sand on the beach below a crisp gold unlike anything I had seen before. I had unpacked most of the house, and my new painting took centre stage in the living room. In any other house, I would put the television in the room. Here, though, the sight of The Well gave me a sense of peace.

On the fifth day, as the sun drowned into the horizon and I gazed through the burned oranges and golden yellows from the top of the lighthouse, waves crashed against the shore below. The salty water bubbled and fizzed as it was absorbed back into the ocean. Losing myself in the moment, I forgot about Alex and why I lived here.

A figure moved on the sand. The small entity, a man, ran across the shore with a surfboard, leaving faint footprints as he rushed towards the ocean. The waves crashed around him as he pushed his board further into the water, past the break line. My serenity dissipated with each of his paddles. His hands fishing through the water were like punches to my skin.

He was on my beach.

Bring him to me. The whispering rose from within me as black ooze leaked from my ears.

I made my descent through the lighthouse. The pores in my skin felt heavy with coagulated oil, and I wondered how long before I started to split open. I dragged my fingertips along the walls as I shuffled through the building, feeling the warmth of its energy. The subtle vibrations from the wind outside are like soft heartbeats.

The bleeding sunset fell into shades of black as I waited by the fence at the beach's entrance. With the light fading away, the surfer made his approach back to dry land, shaking water from his long, wavy hair. He threw his board over the fence and climbed the mesh cage with impressive skill.

"Hey." He waved at me and extended a hand.

I shook his hand and smiled because he was damn handsome. "The beach is closed, isn't it?"

The surfer lifted his eyebrows up and down with an excited, childish glee. He stifled a laugh. "Yeah."

"You come here often?" I asked, releasing the man's hand.

He frowned in contemplation and tilted his head. "A few times a week. Are you from around here?"

I thumbed over my shoulder towards the lighthouse. "Just moved in a few days ago."

The surfer gave a confused smile as he looked at the lighthouse. "I've always wanted to go in there, but Council never let me," he said. "You did all that in a few days?"

I nodded and pretended to wipe sweat from my brow. "You should come and have a look. Feel like a coffee or maybe a beer?"

"Absolutely," he said, following me past the lighthouse to the living quarters. "I'm a historian, so this is like all of my Christmases coming at once. I don't care how terrible the history."

I ushered him inside and closed the door behind me; the surfer settled on the lounge, glancing around at the outdated features.

As I headed to the kitchen to get the beer, unsure of what I was supposed to do next, the surfer called out, "You an art collector or something?"

"Professor of Engineering, although I am taking some time off," I called back. "Why?"

I handed him the beer, wiped bottle-sweat on my jeans, and sat next to him. He motioned towards the painting displayed on the wall.

"That painting is rare," he said. At my silence, he continued. "As I said, I'm an historian. I specialise in rare or collectable art and jewellery.

"Good timing that you showed up just after I moved in," I said, suspicion clear in my tone.

The art historian surfer adopted a sheepish grin. "I must confess, I saw you moving in. I was going to come knocking in the next day or so, anyway." He pointed to the painting. "Most people think it was lost in a shipwreck, but I've seen old photos of the Watch Room, and lo and behold, there it was, hanging on the wall. The main reason I've been dying to get inside the lighthouse."

I remembered the realtor, Shelley, telling me about a ship that sank just off the coast and asked the surfer if there was any connection.

He took a swig from the bottle and nodded. "That ship carried more than families. It had a bunch of possessions from some wealthy Spanish family. Jewels, furniture, art. All lost in the shipwreck, of course."

"Except for this," I said.

"Except for this," the surfer agreed. "This painting is one of a kind. 'The Well'. Artist unknown."

We sat in silence for a moment, him sculling down more fermented yeast, me contemplating the origins of the painting.

"Do you mind?" he asked, interrupting my thoughts. He pointed to the painting. "Can I have a closer look?"

"Of course." I smiled and watched him approach the painting.

The surfer wiped strands of damp hair from his face and stood in front of The Well, hands clasped behind his back as though afraid to touch. He muttered amazement under his breath and paused a few times to tell me he thought it was genuine. Asked where I found it. I told him it came from the Watch Room in the lighthouse.

"Another beer?" I asked.

The art historian surfer wasn't listening. He stared into the well as if in a trance. The whispering began again, though I sensed it was not for me. Not this time. The surfer stepped closer to the painting, held out a hand to touch it. His finger seemed to penetrate the canvas, sinking into the oily abyss of the well.

He pulled back, stunned, and wiped oil from his finger. He looked at me for an explanation. I shrugged and pointed back to the painting. Black oil overflowed from the well, dripping from the bottom of the painting.

"What is that?" The surfer stumbled backward.

As if compelled, I caught him. Held him close to the painting as the oil seeped into the carpet and snaked towards us. The blackness inside me stirred in unison with the oil. Now shaped like a hand with thin fingers stretching towards the surfer as he screamed.

The oil crawled across his skin, clutching at his limbs, dragging him towards the canvas. My muscles disobeyed my desire to help the man. My efforts to pull him away from the painting were all but non-existent, and I found my hands pushing the surfer further towards The Well.

He begged as the oil reached from the depths of the well, wrapping around his face and flowing down his throat. His head disappeared into the canvas, his choked screams echoing in the darkness against the jagged grey bricks of the well. His body melted into the canvas, swallowed by the oil as whispers of gratitude sank into me.

The surfer was gone, dragged somewhere into the abyss of The Well, as though he'd never existed. My stomach lurched, though the blackness inside me refused to surface, and I fell to the ground, cursing my weakness. Consciousness felt impossible, and I closed my eyes to the sounds of chewing and slurping coming from the well.

Something at the bottom was hungry, and I had provided its first meal. Through the grinding of teeth against bone was the greedy hiss of one word.

More.

LAST WEEK

The following two weeks were a blur of oil and black gunk and the sounds of an unseen entity feasting on the surfer. And the others. So many others. I didn't even recognise myself, the way I flirted and kissed and invited people back to my lighthouse. Men, women, whatever—what did I care what was between their legs? They were all for The Well anyway.

I woke up the morning after the initial incident with an itch all over my body, to find the painting gone. A patch of black oil in the carpet was the only evidence of its presence in my house. The only way to get rid of the itch was to feed the painting—send someone down the well, kicking and screaming.

My skin crawled as though ants had found a home under the surface. Thin and papery, the skin tore as I scratched, revealing a slow leak of a thick black substance.

The painting was inside me, and despite my surprise that it no longer hung in the living room, I knew without a doubt it had taken itself home.

The Watch Room.

I had tried to move it back, to be close to it, but each morning, the painting was gone. Back in the Watch Room, in the dark, hanging on the wall facing the door, I scratched the skin on my left forearm, clumps of skin melting beneath my blackened fingernails.

The Well called to me as the oily bile seeped onto my hand. The surfer and the others had kept it at bay, but whatever it was that lived at the bottom of the well was hungry again. I had helped it feed, and now it was counting on me.

More. Its orders were relentless.

"I can't." I sobbed, tasting the thick black ooze as it rolled from my tear sockets into my mouth.

I sobbed harder as my legs buckled, giving in to an overwhelming urge to scour the streets for meat. The darkness thrashed inside me, willing me to the door. I punched at my legs until I fell, bringing my knees to my chin, and wrapped myself into a ball. I rocked back and forth, scratching at the unending itching in my limbs.

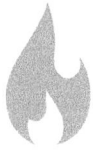

EARLIER TODAY

With the intensity of recent events and the burning desire to bring food to The Well, I hadn't called Alex for weeks. I couldn't endanger him. He, as usual, called every hour or so, and by the time I picked up my phone, there were dozens of voicemails clogging up my digital cloud. The first few were filled with undertones of annoyance and upset and, by the fifth, had progressed to a combination of anger and remorse in typical Alex fashion.

That had been my mistake—giving in to my selfish desire to hear from my husband. The Well sensed the weakness and leapt at its chance.

My fingers dialled his number, automated extremities disobeying my will.

Don't pick up, Alex, please don't pick up.

"Hello." Alex sounded distant, moody.

"Hi," I said. "I missed a bunch of calls." I wanted to scream at him, tell him to stay away. I didn't want him to see the wounds on my arms and legs or the dark rings under my eyes from crying thick black liquid all the time.

I said nothing.

Alex scoffed under his breath, still loud enough for me to hear. I told myself not to react, to let it slide. "You could say that," he said. I imagined him biting his lower lip in frustration. "How's the new place?"

The blackness swelled inside me again. Pushed words

from my mouth. "You should come over. It would be nice to see you. To talk."

No!

"Really?" The note of excitement in his voice was charming. "When?"

No, Alex, stay away.

"Now." I hung up and clasped a hand over my mouth.

He arrived fifteen minutes later, fiddling with his shirt collar as he approached the lighthouse. Alex's nerves always appeared as fiddles or a bouncing knee. I watched from the front door, now no longer charred at all, restored to a beautiful brown oak. He breathed into a cupped hand and smiled, unaware of The Well's plans for him.

We hugged at the door, and I buried my head in his chest. The beat of his heart felt like home. I felt the strength of the darkness inside me falter. I tried to tell him to leave. To never look back. My lips didn't move. I wasn't strong enough.

I kissed him on the cheek, letting his stubble scratch my lips. I ushered him inside with a firm hand on the back, telling him we'd have plenty of time to chat after he asked about my bruises and wounds.

"I want to show you something very special." I smiled, scratching my forearm.

I lit a cigarette and pushed the lighter into my pants pocket. Alex followed me to the Watch Room, saying something about the place looking brand new. I couldn't hear him over the whispering, the snide voice taunting me for being weak, luring my husband to an eternity inside the canvas.

As I reached the door, I managed to grip the frame, using all my energy. Splinters of wood fell to the ground. The stairs behind us creaked as I strained harder against the doorframe, unwilling to let Alex fall victim to the eternal abyss. The splinters disintegrated into ash.

The lighthouse, I thought. *Hurt the lighthouse, hurt the painting. That's it's weakness.*

I remembered Shelley's warnings, the stories about the fire and the other caretakers. The last one, burned beyond repair, walking around the beach. He'd known, too.

Alex put a soft hand on my shoulder. "What is it?"

His touch sent warm energy through my clothes. These were the moments when I knew moving here was wrong, that I needed to be with him at home—our home.

I have to get him out of here.

I tried to turn around, tried to face him and explain, but The Well squeezed around my heart again.

The jolt of pain made my grip loosen, and I spilled through into the Watch Room. The Well greeted us, the dusty gold frame grabbing Alex's attention.

"Alex!" I cried, unable to move from the floor. "Don't look at it!"

It was too late. He glided towards the painting, mesmerised by the darkness inside the well. The whispering grew into laughter. Alex lifted his hand to touch the canvas.

"No!" I cried and strained with all my might to get up from the ground. The black gunk inside me like stones weighing me down, drowning me.

I was up on my feet. That's what mattered.

I reached for Alex and pulled his arm towards me. He lost his balance, slipping back into my arms.

"Alex?" I caressed his cheek. He was still entranced. To the painting, I yelled, "Let him go! You can't have him!"

The laughter pierced my ears once more, the painting spewing the word "Hungry" again and again in an ancient language. As I dragged Alex towards the door, my stomach heaved black bile, the evil inside me splattering across Alex's shirt and the wooden floor. As I was emptied, it spread across the room with a will of its own. It raced to the door behind me, building itself into a barricade.

I felt lighter as the black goo left my body, though I sensed it wasn't all gone. My veins still pumped remnants of the evil into my heart.

Hungry. The voice spat again.

In the corner of my eye, the canisters of gasoline gleaned through the dark. I rushed towards them. Pouring the clear liquid across the room and over the barricade, I begged for Alex to wake up.

As the gasoline splashed against the wooden floor, the laughter stopped. The Well had a weakness, and I'd found it. With that knowledge, I smiled, tipping gasoline onto the gooey barricade. It melted away as the liquid rushed down its surface, revealing the exit once more.

Dragging Alex through the doorway, I looked at the painting, the oil dripping as before. The well overflowed. I felt the evil, now, pouring through the Watch Room towards us.

"Come on, Alex," I yelled at him, eyes unblinking.

I stepped backwards, towards the stairs, pulling his body with me, slipping over the gunk encircling us.

It crept up Alex's legs and torso, bony fingers clawing at his clothes and skin. I pulled as hard as I could, but the liquid was stronger. Alex began to wake, confused yet alert, and struggled against the strength of The Well.

It was no use.

It dragged him towards the canvas, his feet disappearing into the midnight black of the well. I begged it to let him go and told it I would find ten others in his place, but The Well had tasted him now.

"Michael?" Alex looked at me, his upper body sinking into nothingness. His eyes, those beautiful brown eyes, pleaded with me through their terror and confusion.

I rushed to him, grabbed at him.

He was gone.

Through my screams, The Well purred with satisfaction, grinding Alex's flesh and bones in its teeth.

Black bile snaked towards me. The Well knew its control over me had ended.

"I have nothing now," I said to the evil surrounding me.

Grabbing the remaining canisters of gasoline, I began to pour. I tossed the gasoline in every direction, heading towards the stairs. No inch of the lighthouse could be spared. The last drops of gasoline splashed onto the ground of the first floor.

The last of the evil substance leaked from my eyes as I made my way through the lighthouse, which groaned and creaked in anger with each step I took up the staircase.

In defiance, I shouted, "This is how you die."

NOW

The flames lick at my body, melting skin from bone. I tear The Well from the wall and clutch it against my chest as the fire envelops us. I cry as we're devoured by the fire, oil leaking from the frame once more. Painful screams fill the lighthouse from the depths of the well as the fire burns the building from existence once more.

A tear escapes my body. In the heat and pain, I am glad it

is salty water. I close my eyes, letting the fire devour me as the oil melts into my skin. Merges me to the painting.

Takes me to my new home.

Inside The Well.

DARK

"They're haunted," Clementine said. "The Hellfire Caves."

She recounted stories as far back as the 1700s. Of Satan prowling the caves, searching for souls to devour. And last year, a family of five—one of them a baby—disappeared. The father had been seen running through the surrounding forest, covered in blood, and carrying the baby, screaming about demons in the dark. Neither had been seen since.

Matt swallowed as he peered at the mouth of the cave. A deep darkness emanated from it, sucking him in. Calling to him. The thought of going inside made him want to vomit, yet he continued forward. He wasn't about to let a few ghost stories scare him off. Even if he was afraid of the dark. And tight spaces.

"You good?"

He turned to Clementine and nodded.

Clementine was the smartest person he'd ever met, and funny. Their friendship started nine years earlier at a party. Matt had been leaning against a wall, holding a red plastic cup full of water to pretend to be drinking, when he'd heard her voice.

"Is it just me, or is it solipsistic in here?" Her eyebrows were raised as if to say, "Get it?" He'd laughed so hard that water spilled over the top of the cup. They'd been inseparable ever since. Even after he met Paul.

His thoughts were interrupted as the cave entrance beckoned him with a quiet, harsh whisper. Clementine was a few steps behind, spouting facts in that relentless way she did.

"It goes about a quarter of a mile underground," she said, "which isn't that far if you think about it. But you'd be surprised how the light just disappears."

Matt didn't reply, hiding his fear of the dark with a small smile. As she continued her encyclopaedic knowledge of the caves, her words were dulled by a throbbing in his ears. The whispering grew louder. A soft chanting. He focused on the words, though they were unclear.

"They're named after the Hellfire Club, a secret society," Clementine continued. "They get up to all sorts. Devil worship, human sacrifice, ritualistic killings. But anyway, the site was opened to the public in the nineteen-fifties. You're going to love it."

He nodded, letting himself get dragged along, and wondered why he'd come. The soft chanting grew louder with each step.

They descended into the cave, their backs to the bright, warm midday sun. Matt thought about turning back; maybe he could explain to Clementine that he wasn't brave like her.

That he'd wanted them to stay home with Paul. Cuddle up with popcorn and chocolate and watch gay rom-coms about coming out. As usual, he didn't say a word.

"Turn your headlamp on," Clementine instructed.

Matt did as he was told, thankful for small mercies. She'd bought helmets from somewhere—one of those camping places he'd never set foot in—so the batteries were new. He was safe. He was with his best friend.

"Do you think the Hellfire Club is real?" Matt asked as the natural light vanished and the cave met them. The sound of water trickling down the cave walls. The stench of dirt and earth. Thin strips of yellow shone through the dark, allaying Matt's fears for a moment.

"Oh yeah," Clementine said, not missing a beat. "There are hundreds of disappearances here every year. Unexplained. No bodies, no nothing. People just vanish."

"Those stories were just a joke, right?" Matt did stop this time. Dug his heel into the loose dirt beneath him.

Clementine looked at him, her face half-hidden in shadow. "Sure. Just trying to freak you out." She turned away before he could read the truth in her eyes. Or the deceit. "I heard there are some really cool carvings in here." She continued into the darkness.

Matt kept his headlamp trained on her as he half-stumbled, half-walked, not knowing where he was going. The cave mouth shrunk behind him, the last of the daylight disappearing. The chanting sounded again, a hundred voices echoing from the cave walls.

"Do you hear that?" Matt squeaked.

Clementine went to his side and perked her ears to listen. Shrugging, she told him she didn't hear anything. Matt gulped, searching the darkness for the sound. As he looked towards the cave roof, he tripped on a loose rock and tumbled forward. Clementine's face lit up with excitement. She put a hand to her mouth to hide her laughter. When Matt stayed on the ground, nursing his wound, she kneeled next to him.

"You want to go home, don't you?" she asked, shining her headlamp on the elbow. "Let Paul nurse you back to health?"

Matt nodded. His ego was more bruised than anything else.

Clementine pursed her lips, annoyed, and looked around the cave. Her deep sigh made it clear she was disappointed and wanted to go deeper. "Can we just see the carvings?"

He thought about it for a few seconds, his elbow throbbing in mild pain. "Fine." The pit of his stomach warned him of the dangers ahead, but he would push through.

She helped him up and put a hand around his shoulder. "Thank you."

Matt looked back to where the cave mouth should have been. The headlamp hit a wall. They hadn't walked very far or made any turns. The mouth should have been right there. As he stared at the wall, he felt the darkness close in, pushing against him as though it were alive.

You're okay, you're okay, you're okay.

The mantra helped him take a few more steps. As the cave folded in around them, his ears pounded with the voices of the chanting. A deep, visceral groaning.

"What is that chanting?" He scanned the darkness.

Clementine squeezed his hand to reassure him. "Hearing things is part of the experience."

Through the chanting, Clementine whispered about the carvings. They weren't far, thank god. He'd have a look, let her recite some nonsense history about them, and then they could leave. Go back to reality. To Paul. To the light.

Matt stopped breathing when his headlamp flickered for a moment. That second of darkness consumed him, enveloping his entire existence into nothingness. When the headlamp flickered back on, Clementine was a few feet away, seemingly in a trance as her fingers stroked the stone.

Matt approached, trying to stay focused on breathing, and kept his eyes on the thin strip of yellow.

A flash of white behind him.

He spun around, tripping over his feet. The white flashed again like two piercing eyes blinking at him.

Stalking them. Hunting.

"Clementine!" Matt crawled backward.

She hadn't noticed him trip or heard him calling to her. Maybe she didn't want to hear. Matt felt her legs behind his back and looked up. She was looking down at him, her headlamp bright in his face.

He looked away, back to the darkness. The eyes were gone.

"I saw something." He was breathless as Clementine helped him up.

"Something weird is going on here," she said. "I know the dark plays tricks on people, but..."

"But what?"

"It's the carvings." Her voice was urgent, and she spun Matt to face the cave wall.

Shining his headlamp on the surface, the carvings were clear as day. It didn't make sense. They were old, carved into the rock, and faded from years of darkness. Yet his own face stared back at him.

"What is this?" he gasped.

It was like looking in a mirror. The shape of Matt's nose, the crow's feet, the mole on his jaw.

"There's one of me, too," Clementine whispered.

He extended a hand to touch the carving. He traced a finger over the cheek and felt something on his face—a gentle caress, just as he was doing to the image on the cave wall. He withdrew his hand quickly, and the feeling on his face disappeared.

"Clementine, we have to leave." He grabbed at her.

She fought him off. "Matt—" her resistance was interrupted by her headlamp flickering again. She slapped at her helmet, and the light disappeared. Matt held his breath as his own headlamp dimmed to nothingness.

In the pitch black, he heard Clementine—he hoped it was her—fumbling around with her backpack. She would have a spare torch. Clementine would be prepared; she was always prepared.

With little choice but to wait for Clementine to find the spare torch, Matt listened. The darkness surrounded him, groaning with the familiar chanting. Speaking to him. It was heavy, pressing into his body, and he felt the abyss fall onto him.

Into him. Into his lungs and eyes and the pores on his face. As though he *was* the darkness. There was no end to his body, no beginning to the nothingness around him. The chanting thumped inside his heart, and he forgot what lay beyond the cave for a split second. His boyfriend. Their apartment. Their run-down car. He was sure he had all those things, though they felt distant. Not real.

A burst of light brought his memories back, and Clementine held a torch on him. She clasped his hand and pulled him in close to her.

"I'm sorry." Her voice cracked. "We should have left when you said."

He couldn't speak, his chest heaving into the darkness. His

heart beat in unison with the chanting. Clementine picked up her backpack and headed back the way they'd come. The torch flashed to the carvings again, and she stopped. Matt, still unable to speak, followed her eyes.

The carvings were still there, glistening under a trickle of water flowing down the cave wall. Like the cave was weeping.

"I can feel it on me," Clementine whispered.

Matt tried to keep breathing. He wanted to tell her it was a hallucination, that it wasn't real. The darkness was eating at their sanity. The torch flickered again, and Clementine bashed it against the cave wall, muttering about new batteries. Muttering how this was impossible.

The cave wants us.

The light returned, a faint glimmer—just enough to see a silhouetted face—and then it was gone. The chanting drummed through his brain again, constant and steady, and the words began to emerge.

Tu es in domum suam.

"The chanting." Clementine looked at Matt, her eyes wide. "I can hear it."

"It's some kind of Latin." Matt recognised the words, though he didn't know how. Or why.

The torch's light flickered to life. Clementine pointed it back to the carvings, and then the trickling water.

She jumped and twisted herself around to face the inside of the cave. "Did you see that?" she asked, grabbing at Matt's arm.

Matt nodded. "I told you I saw eyes. Someone is in here with us."

The eyes shifted towards them, an animal stalking its prey. The outline of the face, a deeper black than the emptiness, closed in. The eyes blinked again, and the shape disappeared, reclaimed by the dark.

Clementine flashed her torch while she still could. While the light remained. Afraid they'd be surrendered to the darkness again any second. She searched for the cave mouth, frantic as she raced to where it ought to have been. The cave had sealed over. Folded in around them. There was no way out. Thrashing fists at the wall, she screamed into the darkness and dropped the torch.

Matt moved towards it, greedy for the thread of light keeping him safe. Cradled the torch in his arms. He watched his friend attack the wall with fists and feet, begging it to open.

"We have to find another way out," Clementine spat through heavy breaths and snatched the torch.

"You want to go deeper?" He shook his head.

She ignored him and he walked with her, knowing there was no choice. They moved through the cave, stalactites like knives stabbing down at them from the cave ceiling. The ceiling felt so close, folding in on him as the chanting ground those words into his mind.

Tu es in domum suam.

They walked for hours, leaving the carvings in the nothingness behind them, their only company the dull chanting. Clementine stopped in front of him, the torch flickering away again. Matt felt a gentle caress against his face. Clementine felt it, too.

Someone is touching the carving.

He looked back, searching the darkness. There was no way out—not the way they were going or the way they came from. It didn't matter what they tried or where they went. The chanting resounded again, making his hands tingle.

Lifting them to his face, he saw his hands disappearing, erased into the abyss like pencil marks from paper. The darkness flowed inside him, taking him for a moment. He heard a stifled groan and squinted to see his friend. Clementine made the sound again, and an unfathomable darkness pulsated from the wall towards her, smothering her.

Matt rushed to her. She pushed him away. Her eyes were frantic. Her body was transparent, disappearing. The darkness ate at her skin, erasing her. She smacked at what remained of her body, trying to keep her torso from vanishing. The chanting echoed through the cave, drumming through their bodies.

"Clementine!" Matt screamed.

He stepped towards her again and wrapped his arms around her. She latched on to him with what was left of her body, face buried in his chest. Begging the darkness to stop. To leave them be. Her weight in his arms comforted him. Told him he was alive. That he still existed. The chanting and her heavy breaths were the only sounds in the darkness.

Her breaths became low and shallow, and Matt squeezed her tighter. As the darkness ate at his hands, Matt closed his eyes. Clementine wasn't so heavy anymore. Had she moved away? He felt her shirt in his arms but nothing else.

The torch switched back on, drowning Matt in a yellow glow. It faced him from the cave floor, flecks of dust twirling in the air.

His hands returned, gifted into existence by the feeble light. He rubbed his face to prove he was real and tried to understand why he was still there.

The light.

"Clementine, I—"

She was gone. Matt twisted about, searching the cave for her. Her backpack. Her upturned helmet. Her shirt limp in his grasp. Remnants of what once was.

"Clementine?" Matt's voice cracked. He moved to the

torch and picked it up, the glow highlighting her empty clothes and underwear.

The dark took her.

He called again. Knew she wouldn't reply. She was gone. Wiped from existence. And it would happen to him, he had no doubt. It closed in on him, squashing into his body. He felt himself becoming part of the abyss.

I exist.

Something splattered onto his helmet, the hollow clink of liquid against plastic. Matt looked up, shone the torch to the ceiling. Just water.

The water dripped again, landing on his face. Smelled like iron. Like the water ran through the cave like blood. It was just water. Nothing made sense in this place. He dried his fingers on his jeans. Caught a flash of movement. Shone the torch in the direction.

In the shadows beyond the beam of light. Eyes.

"What do you want?" Matt screamed.

The eyes moved closer. The silhouette of a face. A deep darkness that Matt didn't think could exist. The figure made no sound as it floated towards him.

Tu es in domum suam.

The chanting dulled again and moved to the background like the low thump of his heart. "Please." His voice cracked, tears spilling down his face. "I just want to go home."

The eyes grew wider.

The torch went out again.

Matt smacked the plastic casing, but the torch remained dark. After a few seconds, it slipped through his fingers to the dirt. His fingers, once solid and tangible, disappeared into nothingness.

The eyes drew nearer. The chanting thumped into his brain.

Matt ran, grabbing at the cave wall to guide him. Grabbing with fingers and hands that were almost mere memories. He hoped the walls would lead to a path home. The eyes followed him, the deep voices of the chanting growing louder and louder.

Tu es in domum suam.

A rush of air hit his face. A breeze. Coming from outside. What did the outside look like? It was as though the dark moved inside him, tearing at the synapses in his brain. Stealing his memories. He thought of Paul. Their cat. Its name was...

"Its name..." It was gone.

Faces flashed in his mind—*Are they of my parents?*—and he clung to the images until they were ripped away. Matt tried to shake the fogginess from his brain and pull himself back from the brink.

Another flash. Paul.

"No, no, no." He sobbed. "This is all in my head."

Clementine—where did he remember her from?—had rattled off the consequences of caving on the drive in. Paranoia, claustrophobia, panic, hallucinations. More he couldn't think about. The eyes were tricks of the mind. The chanting was just his deep-rooted fear of the dark. That's all it was.

The breeze. Washing over his face. He could still feel his face. The fresh air. That was his way out. A small tunnel in the cave wall. Quite common, according to Clementine. Maybe she'd found it, too. She was waiting for him outside. A glimmer of light came from the tunnel. Even though the day was fading, it gave him hope. A chance.

Tu es in domum suam.

"I exist!" he screamed, crawling in the tunnel headfirst. "I exist!"

The walls pressed against him. Squeezed the air from his

lungs. He pulled himself forwards with fingers that clung to existence. Focused on the light ahead. He could almost feel the warmth of the sun.

A hand grabbed his ankle.

He shook it free. It grabbed again. The bones in his ankle cracked under its grip. Matt clawed at the cave wall, desperate to grab onto something. A loose tree root, anything. Daylight was right there. The fading sun was on his face. The breeze, the soft air. He sucked it into his lungs, hoping it would give him strength.

The hand pulled him backward. Nails scraped against rock, and he screamed as freedom disappeared. He was back. Surrounded by the emptiness. Matt searched for whatever had grabbed him. His ankle throbbed. He couldn't stand.

Tu es in domum suam.

The chanting shouted at him until his ears wept with blood. He screamed again to tell himself and whoever was listening that he was still alive. His voice was enveloped by the darkness.

The eyes were above him when the silhouette appeared. A deep, unfathomable blackness, like the emptiness itself, was alive. It was near-human, standing before him in a hooded cloak. The face was blank, save for the eyes and three vertical slits where the mouth should have been as though its skin had been sliced open.

"What do you want?" Tears streamed down his face. "Where's Clementine?"

It raised a hand from under the cloak and pointed towards a wall in the distance. To the carvings.

"I don't understand." He wept.

The figure pointed again.

Tu es in domum suam.

Its finger, hanging in the air, laid a path for Matt. His ankle continued to throb, and he sensed the figure needed him to go to the wall—to those carvings.

To myself.

The thought slipped away when water dripped to the ground around him. Each drip thumped in the dark, ringing in his mind. Flashes of friends and co-workers ran behind his eyes, melting from him. His cat. What was its name? Paul. His beautiful Paul with deep brown eyes. That smile. He missed that smile. He clung to his memory. He could lose everything else, just not him. Not Paul.

With each drip of water, more of his life flowed out of him, into the dark. Everything that made him was being erased; the more he clung to himself, the more he lost.

Some things remained.

Paul. Clementine.

He turned back to the tunnel, hoping with all his might that they were outside, waiting for him. Staring into the dim light drifting through the tunnel, he heard Clementine's voice. She was laughing. As he moved towards the sound, the laughter disappeared.

The figure was torturing him.

"Alright," he muttered through his tears. "I'll go."

Crawling to the carvings, the cave wall grew darker. That deep darkness that felt so alive—a beacon devoid of light beckoning him towards it, calling him home. All he wanted was to go home. The darkness washed over him. It felt warm, comfortable, and familiar.

He reached the wall and pulled himself to his feet. A shooting pain in his ankle a stark reminder he was still alive.

Clementine's picture was faded. The water had washed her features away.

Erasing her.

Matt looked back towards the figure. It was gone. The darkness began to dissipate, descending him once more into emptiness, and a whisper floated through the empty cave towards him.

Tu es in domum suam.

The words penetrated him, and he understood. Something ancient lived here, deep inside the earth, and it wanted him. It was all he knew for certain. Grabbing at remnants of his life was useless. It was gone. Paul was gone. But the darkness kept him safe. He couldn't tell where he ended and the emptiness began. Extending a hand towards the wall, he felt the carving of himself. Felt his hands on the rock, and also on his face. As he had before.

Tu es in domum suam.

The words came to him as the gentle caress on his face disappeared. Stolen by the water. The image of himself grew faint, just as Clementine's had. And the tingling started again, all through his body. The tips of his fingers, his nose, his eyeballs.

Falling to his knees, Matt screamed to the cave ceiling, trying with all his might to fight his own erasure. To fight for his existence. It didn't matter how safe or familiar the unfathomable darkness had felt. His boyfriend, the love they shared. That was his real home. And he would get back there. Forget about this cave.

The darkness melted around him, and he fought to remember. His parents. His cat.

Paul.

The outside. There was an outside; he knew it.

The tunnel.

He tried to feel his legs with his hands, but his jeans were empty. His upper body remained—only just—and he pulled himself towards the tunnel. A dim light just out of reach. A breeze, cool on his face. He could make it. He pulled himself again as his fingers disappeared. Abandoned to the dark.

"You can't do this to me. I exist!" He pleaded with the darkness to recognise his presence. It pushed against him harder, folding in on him. Erasing him.

He knew he existed—he could feel what remained of his body. He had thoughts. Desires. Fears. He didn't know who he was anymore. He didn't know where he was. The darkness had taken that from him. He'd come here with someone. A girl? She was gone. He caught a glimpse of her face. Words echoed through his mind.

Is it just me, or is it solipsistic in here?

He opened his mouth to scream again, to beg and plead. Nothing came out. The darkness entered him. Rushed into his mouth and lungs, filling him until there was no air left. His eyes were gone, and he couldn't remember his own face. He reached for the carving again to feel himself. He hoped if he could touch the drawing and feel something, it would prove that the dark couldn't take him. That he could win.

That he existed.

But the carving was gone, as though it had never been there at all—his hands, too. He tried to raise his arms, fading into non-existence, and threw what remained of himself at the wall. The water splashed against his face for a moment, then disappeared.

I exist.

His face melted away, and only remnants of consciousness remained—distant memories struggling for existence—Paul's face—that smile he loved so much. The image blurred, yet he clung to it. It was all he had.

Tu es in domum suam.

His mind went dark.

Paul. I can't forget him. The face was gone.

I...

Tu es in domum suam, the figure whispered as Matt disappeared. *You are home.*

PART III
CREATURES

SOMETHING
IN THE
WATER

The orange light flashed on the dashboard. Mitch sighed and bit his lip. Gazing into the deserted road ahead, he struggled to remember the last sign he'd seen. Or when he'd seen it. It had been when the sun was still up, long since melted into the skyline. The engine started to chug. The old Dodge Challenger's warning that it needed to drink. No sign of a gas station, just an empty strip of road lined with ashen trees and plains of dead grass. Bushfires had ravaged the land earlier in the year—arson—and the land was just now starting to heal.

Mitch had hoped leaving the Blue Mountains behind them would also leave the devastation of the fires, of their lives. He realised he was wrong as the road stretched into infinity before him.

"Ryan." Mitch shook his husband's shoulder.

The man was hunched in his seat, head hanging low on his chest like a man awaiting the guillotine. Yawning to life, Ryan pushed his glasses up his nose and squinted to his left. "Huh?"

"We're almost out of petrol," Mitch whispered.

The silence that followed was familiar. Too familiar. Moments like this were the reason for the drive in the first place. Mitch kept that thought to himself and waited for Ryan to speak. He had something to say. He always did.

"Well," he groaned, sitting up in the passenger seat, "what would you like *me* to do about this?"

A bolt of lightning tore across the sky, illuminating the bleak landscape.

Noticing a herd of cows running into the distance— *Cows can run?*—Mitch wiped at his face. To brush away the exhaustion and a burst of anger. "Who said I wanted you to do anything?"

Ryan ignored him and switched on the radio. He liked talkback. Mitch despised it. Turning it on at this moment was a power play. When Ryan didn't care, he had to let the whole world know it. And the world, in this case, was the five-seater '78 Challenger Mitch inherited from his late father, decades of cigar smoke embedded into the fabric. His dad had imported it from America years earlier and restored it. He loved that car, and Mitch sometimes wondered if he loved it more than him. Driving it now, Mitch felt a bittersweet closeness to his father—more than when he'd been alive.

"We're not going to get much further on what we have. We need to find petrol." Mitch continued over the late-night banter of someone called Woolly and his enigmatic co-host, Socks.

What kind of names… He refused to finish the thought. *Don't let this get under your skin.*

Mitch continued driving while Ryan glared at the radio, as if it made a difference in the sound quality. It might have, because Mitch reverted to silence.

Horses galloped beside the car, shaking their manes of the rain and neighing. Mitch smiled for a moment until the neighs became strange. Like the horses were afraid. As another bolt of electricity thundered through the clouds, they turned away from the road and followed the direction of the cows.

Where are they going? Mitch frowned. He didn't know much about animals, yet something about the behaviour seemed strange. He strained his eyes to watch them disappear through the plains, into the trees, as though searching for shelter. And the world outside went silent.

Except for the rain.

As the radio hosts yammered on about the weather— *Get your umbrellas, folks!*—something moved in the corner of Mitch's eye. On the other side of the road. Probably just another horse.

After a few minutes with Woolly and Socks, Mitch was grateful for the rain. Falling right from the heavens to pummel against the car and the windshield. Drowning out whatever useless thoughts the radio hosts were laughing about now.

"That rain is really coming down," Ryan muttered. He enjoyed stating the obvious. He pushed his glasses up his nose again. Chewed another nail. The gnawing was like a razor to Mitch's wrists. Ryan knew it, too. Another mind game to see how long it would take to break.

Mitch summoned his father's knack for diffusing anger with kindness.

"Yeah." He nodded and turned off the radio. Ryan glared

at him, and Mitch smiled. "Can't hear them over this rain, anyway."

It was true and one more reason to be grateful. The rain grew heavier, gushing against the windshield like waves. Mitch held his breath, straining to see through the water. The world beyond the car was distorted, the road almost invisible.

Movement again. Closer now. A strange shape emerged through the rain. Mitch swallowed hard and turned the wheel.

"You're *not* pulling over." Ryan chewed his nail again.

"I can't see," Mitch snapped. "You want to drive? Oh wait, that's right…"

Ryan scoffed and peered out the window. "Really? You want to mention that now?"

"Besides, we're finished." Mitch pointed at the dashboard.

They both sighed, tired from the fighting and the drive and the uncertainty. Maybe a weekend away wouldn't change anything. Maybe they both knew it already.

The rain smashed against the roof, and both men sat in silence, absorbing the sound. There was nothing left to say, anyway. The truth had been shouting at them for over a year.

Mitch didn't want to think about it anymore. Or the man he'd found Ryan fucking in their marital bed. He'd spilled enough tears; now the rain could do it for him. He switched the engine off, the dangling keys clanging against each other. Ryan yawned again—an exaggerated imitation of a yawn— and leaned against the window, pulling his jacket tight to stay warm.

Despite the seven-hour trip and the bickering over where to stop, what to eat, how many coffees was too many, and how much weight Mitch had or hadn't put on, Mitch couldn't sleep. Couldn't even think about it. He knew he'd be transported right back to *that* moment as soon as he closed his eyes.

All the moments that followed, too. The blame and the guilt and the endless fucking talks and Ryan pointing fingers and how Mitch wasn't the man he used to be and what else did he expect when he'd put on weight and lost his job. Thoughts and arguments spiralled through his brain until they were louder than the rain bashing against the car windows.

Knowing sleep would never come, he stared into the countryside and the rain, thin spikes stabbing into the earth. Goosebumps scattered across his body, the damp and the cold sinking into his skin. His hand hovered at the keys in the ignition, tempted to turn the heating on. Glimpsing across to Ryan, his breathing growing heavier and heavier, he put his hand down.

Ryan didn't deserve heating.

Neither do I.

Between the spikes of rain, Mitch saw something outside. Just a flash. The strange shape. Following them. His heart skipped a beat at the thought of being stalked by something in the middle of the night. In the middle of nowhere. In a storm.

He reminded himself he'd seen too many movies and heard too many true crime podcasts and started to breathe again.

But the flash returned. Something moved between the rain. *Inside* the rain. Mitch rubbed his eyes again and yawned. He'd been driving a long time and hadn't eaten since they'd had an early dinner at some awful roadside café. The same place Ryan had refused to fill up the tank because it was too expensive. Mitch knew better than to point that particular finger.

I need a coffee. Ryan would love *that.*

Mitch leaned against the headrest and closed his eyes. Just for a second. Until the memories forced themselves in again.

The empty bottles. The fist in the wall. The fist in his face. Opening his eyes, he gazed into the storm, the water now like bullets crashing against the car.

The temperature had dropped again, and Ryan pulled his jacket tighter still. If that were even possible. Mitch shivered and rubbed his arms. Moved to turn the heating on. And he hated himself for it.

Both men knew he was the weaker one. His will power. His muscle power. His emotions. Ryan had said it on more than one occasion and Mitch hadn't argued. He was weak.

The heater didn't work, and Mitch smiled, his breath visible through the cold. As his body shivered to generate heat, Mitch gazed at his husband. Quiet snores just audible over the storm. He shook his head. Only Ryan could fall asleep on the side of the road without a care in the world.

Turning back to the road, Mitch stared into the sky. Nothing, save a deep, black cloud. It rumbled above him, lightning shooting horizontally amid the formation. The cloud lit up, glowing like a torch shining through closed fingers.

In the briefest of moments, the world lit up, too. And Mitch peered through the darkness. Through the rain. The flash of movement came again. Between pellets of water.

Inside the rain. Mitch smirked at the ridiculousness of his own thoughts.

Lightning flashed.

The shape. At his window. A face with no eyes.

Mitch jumped and grabbed Ryan's arm. Instinct.

The light disappeared, the figure along with it. Ryan shrugged Mitch's hand away and continued to snore.

Mitch, wide-eyed, stared out the window. The figure was real. The flashes of movement. He wasn't crazy, despite what Ryan told people. It wasn't his exhausted brain playing tricks.

He knew better than that.

In short, jagged breaths, Mitch watched, trying to ignore the tightness in his chest. Something was out there. He'd seen its face. Slits where the nose should be. Thin, wide lips. Black, like thick mud. And no eyes. Yet somehow, it stared right into him.

"Ryan." Mitch reached across to the sleeping man. "Please wake up."

He stretched, boring those angry eyes into Mitch. "What's wrong now?"

Mitch clutched at Ryan's hand. Fought to clasp his fingers. Ryan made no move to stop him. No move to let him, either. "There's something out there," he whispered.

"It's probably just Leatherface." He took off his glasses and breathed on them. Wiped them against the inside of his jacket.

"Who?" Mitch's short breaths got shorter.

Ryan rolled his eyes. "Never mind."

Another thing I don't understand. Mitch squeezed Ryan's hand and looked out the window again. "I'm serious. It was… I don't know."

"Can you let go of me, please?" Ryan's voice was low and empty.

Mitch did, though couldn't look away from the rain outside. "It's in the rain. Maybe… it *is* the rain. I… Ryan, I…"

Ryan creased his forehead and chewed his nail again. Took a deep breath. "Look," he said, "if this is some kind of play, to make me protect you or something, it's not—"

A thunderous lightning strike cut him off. It crashed right in front of the car. Bits of road flew into the air, a chunk smashing against the hood.

"Holy shit." Ryan gave a nervous laugh.

Mitch clutched at the steering wheel, his lungs seizing for

a second. His eyes frantic. Searching.

"You're serious, aren't you?" Ryan tilted his head to catch Mitch's eyes. "You really did see something?"

All Mitch could do was nod. Squinting into the storm, he saw it again. Flicked on the high beams. The creature stumbled towards them, the yellow light revealing its disfigured body. Like still-forming clay, thin torso attached to elongated arms and legs. Fingers like tree roots emerging from the eight-foot body. It had eyes now.

Empty circles in its face. Staring at Mitch.

"What is that?" Ryan whispered.

The rain grew heavier as the creature approached. Tree-stump feet stomped across to the car. Mitch felt the ground tremble under its weight. His breath caught, and his chest tightened. It was as though his lungs hated him, stopping the air from getting out. Or in. As the creature neared the car—three metres away—his lungs sealed up.

It was the wheezing that caught Ryan's attention. "Oh, shit," he said and flipped the glovebox open. "You have to do this now?" A red inhaler was hidden between the service book and Ryan's beanie. He grabbed the inhaler and thrust it into Mitch's hand.

Mitch shook the canister a few times and then sucked in the Ventolin. The creature's muddy hands touched the hood and its vacant black eyes stared into Mitch. He focused on breathing and sucked another puff of the medication.

"You good? Because I kind of need you right now." Ryan didn't take his eyes from the creature as it crawled up the hood. The metal crushed under its weight, the rough wooden fingers scratching at the windshield.

"What do we do?" Mitch sputtered through his renewed lungs.

"Your dad kept a tire iron in the boot, right?" Ryan spoke fast.

Mitch nodded.

The creature slapped at the windshield, sending cracks through the glass.

Ryan swung his door open and disappeared into the rain without a word. Mitch held his breath and clutched the inhaler tight. He knew he'd need it again soon. The door swung in the storm and water crept into the car.

Like it's thinking.

The creature punched at the windshield again and Mitch pushed his own door open. He fell from the car, hitting the wet road as the creature reached for him. He crawled away on his hands and knees, the water drenching him.

As he got to his feet, the creature flashed a smile. Its thin lips opened, the bottom half of its face becoming jagged, sharp teeth. It tilted its head as if to sniff something and leaped from the car.

Mitch cowered behind his raised arms and closed his eyes. He slammed down, smacking his head hard. Ryan was on top of him, tire iron swinging at the creature.

The creature grabbed at the metal, swiping it from Ryan's hands. And bashed him. Ryan went down. Face down on the road, puddles of water pooled near his mouth. Mitch ran to his side, rolled him over and cried for help. Help he knew wasn't coming. They were alone with that *thing*.

He turned to the creature. "Please," he begged on his knees. "If you can understand me, please don't hurt us."

At that moment, he felt weaker than ever before. Weaker than when he took Ryan back for the third time. Begging this monster, its sandpaper tongue licking sharp teeth. Not comprehending his plea. Not caring. The creature pounced at them, and he ducked, aware Ryan was right behind him. As he dodged the creature's fingers, he looked up to Ryan and screamed. The creature's gaping mouth snapped closed over the top of Ryan's head.

Mitch heard the cracking of bone as the teeth tore through. Blood spattered down.

The creature picked Ryan up. Through the gaps in its teeth, Mitch saw Ryan's eyes, still staring. Wide in shock. Dead.

Spinning to Mitch as it devoured his husband's head, the creature tore Ryan's arms from his body, blood gushing across the road like a river. Shoved them whole down its throat with one arm, holding the remaining corpse in the other.

Mitch scurried back to the car, sucking on his inhaler and wheezing as the creature shoved its tree-root fingers down Ryan's neck. Searching like a child digging through a bag of candy.

Climbing back into the car, Mitch landed on shards of the smashed windshield. Slammed the door shut and watched through blurred, teary vision. The creature ripped Ryan's organs free. First, the heart and lungs. Chewing on the squishy things like marshmallow. He reached again and squashed the stomach between its fingers, relishing in the acid that gushed free. Ryan's body fell to the ground as the intestines were snapped free, noodles sucked down the creature's throat. Blood and guts garnishing its meal.

Slapping a hand across his mouth to silence his screams, Mitch rocked back and forth in the driver's seat. The inhaler tight in his grasp. His husband had been torn to shreds in front of him, and all he could do was watch.

Weak, weak, weak.

Through his tears, he saw the creature burp and scratch at Ryan's empty carcass. Something else caught Mitch's eye.

The blood. Ryan's blood. Sinking into the rainwater and the puddles.

Moving.

As though it tasted the blood. As though it wanted more. Puddles of water began to draw together like a jigsaw making itself. Forming a hand. And through the crashing of the storm around him, Mitch watched as watery fingers reached from the road, swirling fingertips in Ryan's blood. The water seemed to be tasting the blood, like a child playing with its food.

Ryan's carcass began to move, sliding around the road like a boat in a rough harbour. His feet began to sink into the road, disappearing into the water as the creature, too, watched on. Almost in stasis, waiting for its master to feed before finding the next meal.

As Ryan's shins sank into the water, Mitch hated himself. He wanted to run out there, pull his husband free. Dead or otherwise. He deserved a burial. A funeral with his loved ones. Mitch wanted to do something, to save what was left of him.

He was stiff. Frozen. He could do nothing. Not even breathe. He sucked deep on the inhaler again, watching as the water swallowed Ryan from existence. The blood began to disintegrate, too, vanishing into the puddles forming along the road. Puddles that seemed to tremble and vibrate.

Coming to life.

The last of Ryan's body was sucked down, like waste down a drain. Mitch sobbed, saying a silent goodbye. The goodbye he wished he could have said with a hug. Or with a fight. Anything but this.

Formations grew in the puddles outside, all along the road. Mouths. Hundreds of hungry mouths rising out of the water. Gaping in muffled groans as they swallowed Ryan. Mouths reached for the sky, the water-creatures dripping away and forming again.

A groan came from behind him.

Mitch spun. Water bubbled in the passenger footwell, a water-logged face fighting for existence. Like someone floating just at the surface of a bath.

"Run." Water spilled from the mouth as the word choked out. "Run."

Just as Mitch began to recognise a face he hadn't seen for months, stomping from the road drew his attention.

He turned.

The mud-creature raced at him—wooden fingers extended in anticipation. The mouth ordered him to run again, and Mitch scrambled to the passenger door. Flung it open with his shoulder and jumped to the wet earth.

Mud covered his elbows as he landed, metal crashing behind him. He crawled on his hands and knees to the tree line, stealing a glance over his shoulder. The car was launched into the air like a paper plane. It smashed back to the road a few metres away, struck by a fork of lightning.

The car, a box of light and electricity, was a beacon to Mitch at that moment. Beyond the wreckage: a road sign. He hadn't noticed it earlier. A petrol station, two kilometres ahead.

Safety.

As the creature stomped towards him, teeth dripping with blood and saliva and bits of Ryan's intestines, Mitch got to his feet. And ran to the trees.

The trees seemed to bend around him, branches clawing at him, leaves scratching his arms. He pushed ahead, the creature moving through the trees like it belonged to them. He heard it pouncing from behind, its muddy body melting around Mitch as wooden fingers tore at his back.

He dragged himself forward, unable to do much else, and screamed for mercy. Against the pounding rain and thunder, his voice was meek and low. The creature heard him.

It understood.

The claws deep in Mitch's back came free and the creature sniffed at the wounds. Mitch cried and pleaded "Please" over and over. He didn't want to become a flesh sack of food for this monster. More than anything, he wanted to live.

His mouth couldn't stop begging and he couldn't stop hearing Ryan's words, echoing like a familiar mantra.

Weak, weak, weak.

Lying in the mud of the trees, the mud-creature sniffing at the open wounds on his back, Mitch knew it was true. He was weak. He couldn't fight, had never even tried. He'd cowered before and it got Ryan killed. He'd ran away and it would be the end of him. And he couldn't breathe again. Wheezing air from his lungs, Mitch clutched at the inhaler and then let it go.

Maybe I deserve to die.

The creature recoiled as though it sensed his thoughts. Sneezed as if to clear its nostrils from a foul stench and turned away. Mitch heard the rustling of leaves and twigs underfoot as the creature vanished into the forest.

He lay there for a few moments before picking up the inhaler. Sucked Ventolin and let the rain wash his back. Unsure if he could go on. Unsure if he wanted to. Yet he looked up at the trees around him. The leaves were green. The trees a deep brown, rather than ashen as they had been earlier.

With the creature long gone, Mitch stumbled to his feet. Leaned a shoulder against a tree and considered his options. There was only one option, though. The petrol station. Two kilometres on foot in the rain with a shredded back.

His shoes squished in the mud as Mitch made his way back to the road. It wouldn't be far—the creature had caught him fast. Too fast. Why, he wondered, had it let him go when it could have torn him up in seconds? Why had it had taken Ryan and not him?

And where the hell was the paved road? He could see the tire tracks from where he'd pulled over. His dad's Dodge crumpled and burned ahead. The road was now just a stretch of mud in both directions.

He thought back to the green and fresh leaves. Whatever was happening out here, the water was alive, conscious. So was the Earth itself—the creature made of mud, twigs, and tree roots, the puddles of faces, Ryan disintegrating into the water.

The water. It's eating. It's taking Earth back.

Mitch stumbled to the Dodge, hoping something in their overnight bags could be useful. Maybe some antiseptic cream. Like that would be enough to stop an infection. He wanted to try. Had to try.

The Dodge was upside down, the trunk open. Their stuff scattered like junk on the water-logged ground, some sinking into new puddles forming around him. Mitch fell to his knees at his overnight bag and tugged at the zipper. His spare inhaler would be in there. Pain medication. He couldn't recall what else.

Grabbing at the spare inhaler like a lifeline, Mitch thrust it into his pocket. Popped some painkillers into his mouth and tipped his head back to use the rain to swallow them down. His back would ache for a while yet. He hoped the pills would help, even if just a little.

Among the other pieces of luggage, Mitch saw a small metal box sinking into the dirt. He didn't recognise it. A key dangled from the box's lock. Before it sunk into the puddles,

Mitch plucked it from the ground and twisted the key.

A gun.

"What the...?"

Ryan didn't own a gun, and Mitch sure as hell hadn't ever touched one, let alone purchased one. But his father, despite the kindness and the everlasting smile, had always talked about being responsible for your own protection.

"Thanks, Dad." Mitch took the gun from the box and kissed it. A cardboard box of bullets lay unopened next to it, so Mitch grabbed those, too. Fiddled with the weapon until he figured out how to load the thing. It was a revolver of some sort. Six bullets at a time. Holding the gun away from him, Mitch filled the cartridge with bullets, hoping he'd be able to use it if—*No, when*—the time came.

Taking a long, deep breath, Mitch readied himself and got back to his feet. The gas station wasn't getting any closer and with his adrenaline petering out, he was starting to feel cold.

Mitch walked. He stumbled at first, then found strength somewhere inside him to walk with purpose. Gazing at the sky, still night—*How long have I been here?*—the rain gave no sign of easing. He continued to the petrol station, determined to get somewhere dry and call for help. Despite his determination, he noticed the trees lining the mud road. He noticed how healthy they looked. He didn't notice how each drop of blood hitting the water disintegrated on impact.

Or the watery faces and fingers following him.

The gun was heavy in his hand, and he trembled at the

thought of needing to use it. Keeping his eyes peeled at the trees, he searched for the creature. It felt odd there was only one, though he remembered how its face had still been forming. The eyes that developed from nothing into empty holes.

More will come.

His skin tingled with fear, and he felt eyes devouring him. Mitch spun around, pointing the gun into the darkness and squinting through the rain and the trees. He was alone—just him and the rain and the mud. The night sky wasn't getting any brighter, and dark clouds loomed low above him. It felt as though he could touch them. Bursts of lightning travelled across the sky, and for the first time, Mitch noticed how low the clouds were.

It felt as though he'd been walking for hours, yet darkness clung to the skyline. The petrol station was a kilometre ahead, and Mitch sighed a breath of relief, even though he had no idea what he'd do when he arrived.

His wounds felt distant, a dull throb once in a while. The painkillers couldn't do that, he knew. He didn't have time to think about what else might be happening. To him. To the trees.

As he approached the petrol station, Mitch started to feel stronger. He'd made it. He wasn't weak like Ryan told him. He wasn't useless or crazy or anything else his husband had said. He'd survived.

His thoughts were broken by his feet. They wouldn't move, stuck in place with a heavy squelch. He looked down. Water had started climbing up his feet, sucking him into the earth. Tiny mouths coalesced at the sides of his shoes, watery teeth munching into the material.

Mitch pulled hard, and his left foot began to rise. The

water felt thick, like mucus or string. It snapped against the strength of Mitch's muscles, the mouths splashing back into the puddles below. His moment of freedom was cut short as the water rushed up again. Mitch aimed the gun to the ground and fired.

The water recoiled. A roar in the distance motivated Mitch to run.

With as much strength as he could muster, Mitch freed his right foot and splashed through the puddles towards the petrol station. Mouths and fingers clutched at him, and Mitch kicked them away, firing the gun once more to scare the water back into itself.

The roar came again.

It was close. He could almost feel the spittle on his neck. Had to remind himself it was the rain. Hoped it was *just* rain. The mouths sucking at his feet told him it was something else. The rain wasn't rain. Not anymore.

For the first time, he wondered how far-reaching this phenomenon was. Where did the storm end, if at all? With the petrol station just up ahead, the rain still gave no sign of stopping.

The ground was mud, and Mitch slipped across the wet, brown earth past the petrol bowsers. A vacant car, the engine still running, sat with a nozzle hanging from the tank. He moved to it, and just as he opened the driver's door, he noticed the tires. Sinking in the mud. Halfway down already. The water was hungry again. Mitch couldn't see a pattern to what it ate. Human skin and bones, rubber tires. Would it eat the whole car?

The station's entrance, a cracked and dirty glass door, beckoned Mitch, and he left the car to idle in the rain.

Pushing on the door as the sign indicated, it didn't budge.

He pushed harder, conscious that the mouths in the mud were circling behind him. The roar following him grew closer now, too, and Mitch barged the door with his shoulder.

Reeling in pain from the wounds on his back, Mitch forced himself to barge again. He let out a cry and tried a third time, ignoring the stabbing pain in his shoulder. He thrust the gun into the already-cracked glass and gave a sigh of relief as it smashed.

The roar again. Close.

Too close.

Mitch fed his hand through the hole in the glass. Felt around for a lock.

"Who's there?" a soft voice called from inside.

Mitch stopped and pulled his hand back. "My name is Mitch. I just need some shelter. Please let me in."

He heard more than one person whispering before the voice came again. "We can't. You have to go."

"Please." Mitch leaned his head against the doorframe, breathing hard. "There's something out here… and I'm hurt."

The whispers again. Mitch knew the answer. Whoever was inside wanted the place to themselves. Wanted the safety it offered. The roar sounded again, and Mitch saw the creature in the reflection of the glass. His lungs began to seize.

Twisting to face the creature, Mitch pointed the gun and fired. The creature jolted backward, just for a moment, before coming at him again. Faster. The bullet did nothing. Mitch fired again.

That's four. He banged an elbow against the door. "Open the fucking door!" he called to the people inside the station.

Behind him, shuffling and rattling.

The door swung open, and hands pulled him inside. The creature leaped at the door. Mitch fired again, fighting to open his lungs. Someone—a woman—slammed the door shut and dragged an oil drum to block the entrance.

Mitch reached for his inhaler and puffed. "It's not going… to hold," he sputtered. "It's too strong."

"It's afraid of oil," the woman whispered, brushing sweaty hair from her eyes. "We don't know why." More oil had been splashed around the internal perimeter of the station. A barricade. A way to fight back.

Looking around, Mitch saw two others. A man with a rifle and a backwards camo hat. Dog tags shining out from his chest. And a younger woman, wide-eyed. Maybe his daughter. Mitch didn't care. He was just grateful for the shelter. For somewhere to dry off. To hide.

"Thanks for letting me in." Mitch's lungs started to recover.

The woman looked to the man before holding out her hand. Covered in grime and sweat. "Natalie."

Mitch nodded hello and introduced himself to the others. Cleveland and Mary. A family. They owned the car out front and had escaped a creature of their own just as their fourth member, Cleveland's brother, was ripped to shreds in front of them.

"A military man." Cleveland sniffed away a tear. "Served his whole adult life."

The creature prowled outside, growling at the doors and windows, retreating at the stench of oil. Like it feared the black gunk. Cleveland led Mitch and the others to the "Staff Only" area, containing a lunchroom with a small table and a fridge. His stomach lurched at the thought of food and despite all he'd seen—and flashes of Ryan's guts being chewed and swallowed—he needed to eat.

"We found a radio," Cleveland said as Mitch chewed on a stale sandwich. Meat of some kind, though the flavour was long gone. "I've been trying to get a signal."

Mitch nodded, appreciative of the food, the company, and the possibility of staying dry until the storm passed. It was almost enough to give him the illusion of safety. Almost.

A sound crackled through the lunchroom, and all sets of eyes stared. "Oh, shit!" Cleveland clapped his hands. "I got something."

They each took a seat at the table and listened through the static. A voice, distant and incoherent at first. Cleveland fiddled with the tuner and the signal became stronger.

"… faces of our family… people as fertiliser…" The voice faded in and out through static. "… only the strong… renew… earth… revenge…"

And the voice disappeared.

"What do you think it means?" Mary, maybe fifteen, asked.

Natalie and Cleveland exchanged glances. It was clear to them all, that Mary just didn't want to believe it. Whoever was on the other end of that radio had verbalised what Mitch hadn't even wanted to consider.

"It's eating us," Mitch whispered. "The rain is eating us and anything else it can use."

"Use? For what?" Mary gulped and looked to her father. Her mascara ran down her cheeks, her pleading eyes unblinking. Her father stared back, his own eyes demanding her silence.

Mitch knew the look. The same one Ryan used to give him. He didn't want to remember Ryan that way, though the truth was the truth. Instead, he contemplated Mary's question.

He remembered the trees. Ashen and brown. Dead from the bushfires. The leaves had become so green and vibrant after the rain had taken Ryan. He remembered how Ryan's blood and body had disintegrated under the water, cells broken down and rearranged.

Like fertiliser.

"For what?" Mary asked again into the silent room.

"With all the damage we've done to the planet"—Natalie put a hand on her daughter's shoulder—"it's using us to fix itself."

And Mitch knew it was true. The rain was ushering in a new dawn. A human-free dawn.

It didn't make sense. The creature had the chance to destroy him, to send him into the rain, into those sucking mouths. And it didn't. It ran off instead. Why did it let him go?

Weak.

He finished his sandwich and leaned back in his chair. His inhaler and the gun were on the table in front of him. Mitch looked across the table at his company. Mary sobbed into her mum's chest. Natalie, too, had tears streaming down her face. Cleveland clutched at his rifle, knuckles white from the grip.

"Hush up," Cleveland spat at them.

They tried. Mitch could tell by the way they shrank from his voice. When he wanted something, he got it. All too familiar.

Weak.

The radio crackled to life again with a high-pitched whirring sound. The signal was stronger now. "…like hellhounds, the earth come to life. As far as I can tell, they're afraid of oil. Can't digest it. But it's *only* a deterrent. They will find a way to hunt you. That's what they do. You have to run. Keep running. You cannot—*cannot*—wait them out. If anyone is out there, if anyone can hear me, the rain is not going to stop. The weather satellites show the storm keeps building…"

"We can't stay here." Mitch switched the radio off.

The family looked at him, and their eyes gave Mitch all he

needed to know. Why they were all still alive. Why he was still alive. The fear and terror and inaction.

Weak. Weak. Weak.

Picking up the gun, Mitch looked at the family and said, "It doesn't want us because we're weak. Too afraid to fight back, even to save our loved ones. Or ourselves." He pressed the gun to his chest and closed his eyes. "I don't want to be weak." Moving to the edge of the lunchroom, Mitch said over his shoulder, "You don't have to be either, Natalie."

Leaving the family to stare back at him, Mitch left the room. Headed back to the front door. Only one shot remained in the gun. The petrol station wouldn't sell bullets, so he'd have to make it count.

The creature stomped around outside the station, and Mitch peered through the front door at its still-forming body. It's elongated arms and legs had grown solid, yet the face was still changing. It grew ears, forming like soft clay. Two horns sprouted on its forehead, and the jagged teeth looked sharper.

Looking at the creature, Mitch felt his lungs close again, only for an instant. Instead of reaching for his inhaler, he closed his fist and dared his lungs to inhale, exhale. The wheezing never came. Mitch tossed the inhaler to the ground and with it, the power Ryan had held over him.

I am not weak.

As the thought left his mind, the creature stopped. Turned. Its hollow eyes, now a tinge of dirty yellow, stared at him.

"Come get me," he shouted.

The creature obeyed, wooden fingers digging into the mud as it tore towards the building. Mitch remembered the voice on the radio—*only a deterrent*—and readied himself for what came next.

He moved backwards, aiming the gun at the creature. It

reached the door, and Mitch fired. The bullet hit the drum, and oil leaked to the ground. The creature roared in anger; Mitch ran.

Crashing through the door, the creature tipped the oil drum over with a thud and scrambled to Mitch. He reached the service counter and launched over to the other side. Smashed into a shelf of cigarettes. He scanned the rest of the shelves, searching for something that could help him.

Chewing gum, lighters, lollies.

Fuck.

The creature's thundering feet cascaded against the floor. Mitch forced himself to stand. If he was going to die, he'd face it on his feet. No more cowering.

Convulsing, the creature fell to the side, and Mitch turned to see Cleveland emptying his rifle into the creature's torso. The rapid fire kept it down, though Mitch knew it was a temporary measure. Cleveland would run out of bullets soon.

And then what?

Its body, still thick wet mud, enveloped the bullets. The wounds healed without a trace as if nothing had ever penetrated the skin. If that's what it even was. And the creature bared its teeth, yellow saliva dripping to the floor.

"I'm out," Cleveland screamed. His eyes shifted between the rifle and the creature, unsure what this meant for him. For all of them.

Mitch raced around the counter as the creature launched through the air towards Cleveland. Mitch reached him first and tackled him to the ground. The creature went past them, its claws scraping against Mitch's wounded back.

"Get up," Mitch yelled at Cleveland, who was paralysed with fear. "Come on." Mitch pulled the man to his feet. "Get the *fuck* up!"

As he pushed Cleveland to the "Staff Only" door, a lightning strike crashed against the station roof outside, and the creature turned around. Swiped at Cleveland with a mucky paw. Mud and blood sprayed against the walls and the man went down. His face scraped away by the tree-root fingers.

Mitch fell backwards and watched as Cleveland's face hit the floor with a wet slap. His body in the clutches of the creature. It growled in satisfaction as its teeth and jaw devoured the man's brain.

Holding back the urge to vomit, Mitch's eyes were drawn to Natalie and Mary, staring agape at their loved one's insides being ripped out through the neck. Just as Ryan's had been.

Lightning struck again and the wind outside howled like a wolf. The storm raged and it struck Mitch that it seemed connected to the creature. To its hunger.

Natalie noticed, too, her eyes drawn to the roof. A small leak seeped through.

The station wasn't safe anymore. Mitch motioned for the mother and daughter to come to him while the creature devoured Cleveland's kidneys. Their heads trembled and shook. Mitch knew it was then or never. His eyes pleaded again, and Natalie gripped her daughter's hand. The creature didn't notice anything other than the fleshy insides it sucked down.

Natalie and Mary crept around the creature, their footsteps inaudible against the rain outside. A drop of water fell onto Natalie's head as they passed Cleveland's discarded face. The leak in the roof was dripping right onto it. Disintegrating the flesh.

Fertiliser.

Natalie was fine, though, as Cleveland's body, devoid of organs, was thrown to the ground. She was unharmed by the water somehow. So was he, now that he thought about it, having walked kilometres through the wet to get to the station.

But if we're fertiliser....

The creature, now sated, hibernated once more. Water was drawn to the meat sack, pooling around his corpse like flies. Mitch saw the mouths again and a face forming amid the liquid.

It was kind. He could tell, despite the lack of features. Just as it had earlier, in his car. And just as it had then, the face turned to him. "You're not weak," it said. The voice, gravelly and hoarse, like a man who'd smoked too many cigars.

"Dad?" Mitch held a hand to his heart. The face of his father, now one with the earth, rose from the rain.

"It's not taking the *strong*," his father told him. "It's taking the corrupt. That's why the rain doesn't hurt you—any of you. It's washing away the damage on this planet. Human and otherwise."

"But..." Mitch looked at Natalie. At Mary.

The face slushed around beneath him. A shake of disagreement. "Ryan was weak. Not you. Don't confuse forgiveness for weakness."

With that, the face re-joined the pool and a thousand tiny mouths sucked Cleveland down. The station floor was eroded, too, sending the site back to its original form of dirt and mud. Of earth.

Thunder came again, lightning crashing against the renewed planet outside. Mitch looked out the window. The petrol bowsers were gone. The car, too. Eaten by the rain. A patch of grass was forming in their places.

Mitch thought back to the creature, how it attacked him in the forest.

No, not attacked, he thought. *It caught me. To judge me.*

The rain came harder still, and the station roof began to groan. Mitch held out a hand to Natalie and Mary.

"We have to go," he said. "This place is falling apart."

They went with him outside, letting the rain wash over them. It seemed different now. The petrol station door clanged behind them, and they walked to where the road had been. Now a strip of grass.

Mitch looked over his shoulder. The creature stepped into the rain; its eyes fully formed now. The mud-body dry, despite the water rolling off its back. And Mitch knew. This creature was part of the new world. It wasn't going away.

And neither was he.

"What do we do now?" Mary asked, looking at her mother.

"Now," Natalie said, smiling at the new world, "we start again."

They walked to the strip of grass, the creature joining by their side. As the last drop of rain splashed against the earth, and the sun greeted them, Mitch smiled.

That's right. We start again.

And he walked.

THE

RAVEN

"Put the knife down."

Ted tried to stay calm in situations where most people would panic. Ava held a knife to his throat, and his world collapsed. He couldn't show his emotion. Not now. Not with the blade pressed against his jugular.

The girl just turned sixteen and after five days in a new school in a new town, Ted was beginning to think the change was too much. His new job was at the high school of Ravensfield, an all but dead town in the middle of nothing. Miles around their new house were farms and crops and horses that were too hot and bothered to do much of anything.

Even so, Ava had seemed excited to start a new adventure, compiling lists of things to talk about with her new teachers, and strategies to make new friends. Having same-sex parents was a go-to these days, so the internet had said. Even if one of them was dead. It wasn't taboo anymore, and so, top of the list: "My dads".

After the first day, she'd rushed through the front door and stomped to her room, bypassing Ted's anxious smiles. Since she'd been told she was adopted and that neither father was a biological relative, Ava seemed distant.

Now, day five, and she had a knife to his throat. To keep him from doing anything stupid, she'd said. He was on the floor, his daughter kneeling over him, animal eyes prowling around the room like she expected company. A gold chain dangled from her neck, swinging above Ted's eyes. He didn't recognise it.

Ted put his hands up, palms out in defeat, and repeated his earlier plea. "Put the knife down, honey." His voice was quiet.

Drops of sweat pooled around his hairline and he knew she could see it. Her eyes flicked to his trembling hands, and she shook her head in defiance.

"Don't make me go back there," Ava said, teeth gritted. "I won't go back to that school."

Ted knew something was wrong at school, but Ava wouldn't talk about it. None of the kids would. Just mumbled about the Raven.

"What happened?" Ted asked. "Is this about the missing kids?"

Ava's face flashed with sadness and fear. Her grip on the knife loosened and she looked at the blood. Looked down at her father.

"Oh, Daddy," she cried. "What have I done?"

Ted took the opportunity and pulled himself from Ava's grasp. Grabbed the knife and tossed it across the living room. It clanged against the tiled floor as he wrapped Ava in his arms.

"Talk to me, sweetie," Ted managed through a gush of tears.

"It's the Raven," Ava cried into Ted's chest. "It's evil."

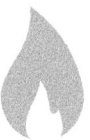

With Ava sedated on sleeping pills, Ted felt okay about leaving her on her own. Something was happening at the school that had terrified his daughter, and he intended to find out what. He hoped the principal would have some answers. She'd been open to an after-hours meeting that same day, and Ted was still counting his lucky stars when he pulled up to the parking lot at seven pm. Heading to the principal's office, he felt eyes on the back of his neck and was conscious that the shadows were morphing into strange shapes.

"Dr Cutter?" His hand was poised at the door when the voice broke. Ted pushed through the door and smiled.

"Please, just call me Ted."

Principal Wuornos shook his hand. They'd met last month over a digital interview and again a few days earlier when he started as the school counsellor. "Call me Laura."

Ted took a seat in the office. A small tabletop lamp provided dim light for the meeting. A ceiling fan blew warm air around the room.

"My daughter, Ava," he said, lifting one knee over the other, "has raised some concerns about this raven of yours. With those kids going missing recently, I had to say something."

Laura squirmed at the mention of the mascot and held back a frown. The edges of her lips betrayed her, though Ted suspected the untrained eye would have missed it. His training was second nature now.

"Is Ava okay?" Laura swallowed. She watched Ted for a few moments as he recounted the attack earlier that evening. She seemed to be sizing him up. Her eyes moved between him and the door, which had been left ajar. She leaned across the desk, their eyes now fixed on each other, and took a long, slow breath.

"Ted, I'm sorry," she whispered. "Something strange is going on in this school." Her eyes shifted to the door again. "It's the kids…"

Waiting for more, Ted found himself on the edge of the seat. Laura opened her mouth to continue, tucked her auburn hair behind her ears, and flashed a look at the door again. Like she was waiting for someone to come in.

"What did Ava tell you?"

Before he could speak, the lamp flickered and went out. The whoosh of the fan stopped, and they both looked to the ceiling. Laura gulped as the two sat in silence in the dying light.

The door swung shut behind them and Laura jumped, a hand to her heart. She went to the door, peered through the glass pane with her name on it, and turned back to Ted. Her eyes wide, she slid down the door and put a finger to her lips.

"Get down," she hissed.

A shadow appeared behind the door and Ted dove under Laura's desk, his own heart pounding. The figure stopped by the door, raised a hand to the glass, and scratched at Laura's nameplate. Ted watched the shadow as it moved along the hallway outside, Laura's eyes blaring into him, begging him to signal it was safe.

He nodded.

She moved to her knees, gripped the windowsill, and

peered through. Ted waited, though he didn't know for what, and held his breath until Laura exhaled.

"Did you see it?" she asked him.

Ted shook his head. Laura moved back around her desk, pulled open a drawer, and lifted out a gun. Her eyes glided over the silver weapon as it shone through the bleak light.

"What the hell is that for?" Ted stepped back.

"I'm going to level with you." Laura held the gun firm by her side and put a hand palm-down on the desk. "There's something wrong with our mascot. At first, I thought… With the missing kids… But it's something else."

Ted stared at her, unsure what to make of this. "I'm calling the police." He reached for his phone. The screen was dark. He tapped it. Dead. Like the lamp and the fan. He raised his eyes to Laura, who didn't look surprised.

"It started about three months ago, over break. You know girls have been going missing,"—Laura didn't blink, the words coming from her like she'd had this conversation a hundred times before—"but the boys, they're getting violent. And I think it's got something to do with Daryl, our mascot."

The Raven stalked the hallways, dripping muck and blood with each step. Its feathers melted to its body, still forming. The change almost complete. Clawed feet tapped at the linoleum flooring as it walked. Back to its hideout. The girl was inside, waiting. Sobbing. Begging to a god that wasn't watching. A god that didn't care. A god that gave up on the town of Ravensfield.

It's beak, razor-sharp, pushed the door open with a creak. Alerting the child chained in the basement that it was feeding time. The crying and moaning excited the bird. It stepped down the concrete stairs, wings dragging along the walls, leaving a trail of muck to drip to the floor.

"I want my mummy," the girl begged.

The Raven tilted its head, hollow eyes staring at the tender flesh, and lunged towards her.

Ava woke in a cold sweat, sucking air into her lungs with greedy deep breaths and sharp exhales. She was nauseous and her stomach ached. Hair matted to her face, sweat like glue, she tried to push the nightmare from her brain. The Raven, tearing skin from bone. The child screaming in the dark.

Another one.

Wiping strands of wet hair from her eyes and mouth, Ava sat up in bed, trembling, head throbbing. Her entire body was slick with sweat, skin crawling with goosebumps. The pain in her stomach came again, and she breathed through it. Clutched at the gold chain around her neck.

Dim light flowed into her room between cracks in the shutters. Remnants of the dream clung to the inside of her eyelids, and she shook the imagery away. The Raven's blood-soaked beak pulling at veins and tearing through muscle. With a gasp, she remembered what she'd done that afternoon. The violent impulses were bubbling under the surface, even now, though they were outweighed by the shame she felt. Her dad was a beautiful man, she loved him more than anything.

The Raven could not take that away from her.

He'd said he was going to see the principal tonight. Ava lifted the bedsheets and twisted to the side, knowing she had to get to the school. Her stomach lurched, her vision swirling into nothing but static. The impulses started again. The rage that led her to hold a knife to her father's throat. They started in her stomach, as though her life force was turning on her.

A sharp pain up the back of her neck, her veins filled with anger. She tried to fight, to remember love and happiness. The pain pulsated through her body. All that remained was despair. Hatred. A deep cold washed over her. Everything inside her wanted to stab someone's eyes out.

An offering for the Raven.

Her throat tightened, her chest convulsed, and Ava opened her mouth to vomit. She tilted her head to the side and let the liquid soak into the sheets and the mattress. The static in her eyes cleared—just a little—and she saw the vomit was black. Muck. And that's when she remembered what happened on her first day of school. Remembered the janitor.

Choking back a scream, Ava lay in the vomit, the stench somehow familiar, and fell back to sleep. The impulse to kill thumped in her stomach.

Nobody knew much about Daryl. Laura recounted his interview a few months earlier, and how the requisite police checks all turned up nothing. As far as his personal life, she drew a blank. All she had were vague, contradictory details. Like how he'd said he was from the south during the interview, and then in subsequent conversations had shrugged and told her he moved around a lot. All she knew for sure, she told Ted, was that he worked in an old bookstore before applying for a janitorial position at the school. The school mascot gig came later—a bonus payment to help make ends meet. That was when the kids started disappearing. Laura had her suspicions from the start, though they were no more than a gut feeling.

As they tip-toed down the hallways, towards the exit, hissing back and forth about Daryl, Ted heard a sharp sound behind him. He spun around.

The Raven.

Arms lined with large feathers, as though transforming into wings. The creature still had the hands of a man. A human neck, but black, hollow raven eyes, and a razor-sharp beak. Like a knife, ready to cut into flesh. Its chest was puffed out like a bird with the school logo front and centre, and the legs bent backwards at the knees, thinning out to clawed feet.

It was wet with some kind of muck dripping from the suit. In the fading daylight, Ted thought he saw real feathers underneath the slick surface. As though it wasn't a suit at all. The Raven stepped towards them. Laura fumbled with her gun as the clawed feet scraped against the floor.

"Stay away," Laura begged. Her voice cracked, but her arm was steady, outstretched with the gun aimed at the Raven.

Ted looked closer. The muck was mixed with blood, glistening with spots of red. The drops were heavy, splatting to the ground with a wet squish.

"I don't think that's Daryl," Ted muttered and turned to flee.

The Raven rushed towards them, wings outstretched, and sent a soulless cry through the hallways. Laura pulled the trigger, the bullet sinking into the Raven's chest. It didn't flinch. She tried again.

"Come on!" Ted pulled on her arm. The third bullet missed, and Laura followed after Ted. The school's front entrance was chained, and as Ted pushed hard against the doors, he saw thick rain careening to the earth, lightning stirring in the clouds.

Laura was down around the corner, high heels clicking into the distance, and Ted ran to follow. The Raven snatched at his shirt from behind and Ted felt the muck on his neck. It burned a little and he fought to pick up the pace.

The Raven's hands were on him, pulling him to the ground. His face smacked against the floor, head ringing from the force, and the Raven jumped onto his back.

A gunshot tore through the hallway and the Raven, poised to tear into Ted's neck, stopped.

THREE MONTHS EARLIER

He'd never been serious about the occult or demons or whatever. It was just a hobby. A while back he'd been so deep in a search engine rabbit hole looking through books on the occult for the store. That's when he saw it. Sometimes things spoke to him without words. He heard it loud and clear, felt it like a compulsion. Like his whole body wanted him to hear the unspoken words. This had been one of those times.

Hala.

An old leather-bound book with Slavic inscriptions. It was fate. It had to be. His father and his father's father were Slavic. He caressed the computer screen, feeling the static biting at his fingertip, and knew he had to have it.

When it arrived, his hobby changed. He didn't know why or how, but the book was telling him to do things. To move to a town called Ravensfield. As much as he tried to ignore the demands, something inside him knew he'd like it. Knew he'd enjoy the taste.

The first girl, Isabelle, was an outcast like him. The book chose her. When she was down in his basement, tied up and screaming through the sock stuffed in her mouth, it didn't feel right. He wasn't a murderer. As he'd moved to untie the girl, to apologise and beg for forgiveness, the book flipped open.

The ritual.

Seven sacrifices and a vessel. Isabelle would be the first, and despite his rational mind urging him against it, he lunged at her and sunk his teeth into her neck.

From the girl's blood, an object began to form. It was soft and shapeless, like unformed clay. As he burped the last of the girl away, her organs absorbed into him, changed him. He knew what needed to be done. Six more and the object would be complete. Then he'd find the vessel. First, he needed recruits. More like him. And he knew just where to go to get them.

Heading for the stairs, back to the world of the living, the book whispered to him again. He looked at the mascot suit—the raven—and pulled it on.

Yes, he thought as the bird head slipped over his human facade. *This is what I am now.*

Laura stepped closer, flashing the gun in the dying light. Ted couldn't hear her words—the sharpness in her tone was enough. The strength in her voice. The gunfire. The Raven fell off him, hissing at the principal as it collided with the floor. It's clawed feet ripped at Ted's flesh, the pain searing through him. He got to his feet in a daze of confusion, letting Laura pull him away from the mascot.

"In here." Laura pushed through a door. The words "Staff Only" glimmered in the night. The door slammed behind them, Laura flicking a feeble lock, and they piled down a staircase into a basement.

A light hung from the ceiling and Ted pulled the cord. A dim yellow glow revealed an unmade bed in a dank corner of the room. Sheets sprawled in a mess, sweat and urine wafting from the fabric. Cleaning supplies and an open bottle of bleach by a shower that hadn't been maintained for some time. The stench of mould was almost too much, but the bleach cut through it, stinging Ted's eyes.

Someone lived down here.

Through the discomfort, he scanned the room, stopping at the brick wall painted in blood, still wet, dripping to the floor. A shrine of severed heads, tips of the spines jutting out, decorated the floor in a circle. A thick leather-bound book sat open in the middle, the eyes of the Raven's victims staring into the writing.

Half-melted candles lined a home-made shelf, an inscription carved into the bricks. Further along the wall, a blood-portrait of a half-human, half-bird monster. Ted brought a hand to his heart and let out a shocked gasp as thunder and lightning rolled outside. A blue glow flashed through the basement, coming from a small window, level with the ground outside.

Laura vomited despite herself, holding a hand over her mouth to stop the flow. It streamed through the gaps in her fingers. She stepped towards the wall, and breathing hard, choked out, "What the fuck is this?"

Reaching to the book, he pulled at a fabric bookmark jutting out of the bottom of the pages. Flicked it open and scanned. "The Aloviti."

Thunder crashed just beyond the basement window and rain pummelled at the fragile piece of glass. Ted repeated the words and the thunder sounded closer, as though the storm responded to the name.

"What is that?" Laura asked, brow furrowed, wiping her hand on her trousers, and looking out the window at the storm.

Ted's gaze looked fierce. "A demon. Slave to the Hala. A child-eater."

In spite of what they'd seen, of how the Raven appeared, Ted wasn't ready to believe in demons. He was a man of science. Cannibalism could explain the missing kids, but not this. Not a demon praying on the town's youth. Nonetheless, he continued reading. "It brings extreme changes to the weather. The rain, the dead crops, it's all the Aloviti. It can take many forms. The raven is just one of them. The Aloviti are men who have characteristics of the more common female demon, the Hala. Aloviti don't usually eat children, but it's not unheard of."

Ted scanned a few more pages in horror, devouring passages about the Aloviti recruiting male children to do its bidding. It described a cult, though didn't explain what was happening here. Ted's unconscious mind was shouting at him, begging him to pay attention. He'd seen the truth in these pages and hadn't paid attention. Flipping back, his eyes stopped on an image. A gold necklace. Those same inscriptions from the walls were carved into the surface.

Ava!

The chain was thin, but it held tight to her skin as Ava leaned over the edge of the mattress, heaving. Instinct told her to hold the gold necklace to her heart while chunks of yesterday's dinner spewed to the ground. It felt hot against her beating chest, even through her pyjamas, stinging her skin.

Breathing through another convulsion, Ava laid back, sweat oozing from her body. The pain in her stomach was sharp. Like something was squirming inside her. She lifted her pyjama shirt and drew her eyes downward. Black veins stretched across her torso. Ava pressed a finger to her stomach, felt movement deep within her again.

Despite the stench of vomit and sweat, she focused on the rain drumming against the window. Clutched the necklace tight in both hands. She pleaded for her father to return, to take her away from this place. Prayed into the gold necklace, terrified of what was happening inside her body.

Thunder clapped against the sky outside and a figure appeared in the doorway. "It's going to be okay," it said.

Ava lifted her head as far as she could, squinted through the bleak room. The figure entered her room. She didn't recognise the face, although the symbol on his jacket was all too familiar. A football jacket. The Ravensfield Claws. When she'd first heard the name, she'd giggled at the lack of imagination. Now, lying weak and helpless in her own bedroom, the logo made her tremble.

"You're going to be okay, Ava." The voice drew closer.

Others in the football team followed him into the bedroom,

eyes boring into her with a look Ava couldn't identify. Another crash of thunder lit up the room for a moment. The team formed a circle and kneeled around her bed. The first boy— team captain, Jimmy Lowe—stood over her. The team began a low hum, which turned into a chant. Ava didn't recognise the language.

"What are you going to do to me?" Ava asked, her voice hoarse. The necklace began to burn into her skin.

Jimmy frowned. "It isn't what we're going to do to you," he said. "It's what you're going to do for us."

She gripped her necklace again, the heat searing her hands, and wished harder than she had ever before that her dad would burst through the door. Deep down, she knew. Nobody was going to help her.

Jimmy pressed a hand over the girl's mouth and held it there. Too weak to do much of anything, Ava wept hard, almost watching herself from above, as Jimmy and the Claws lifted her from the bed and carried her down the stairs. Out the front door, into the storm. Towards the school.

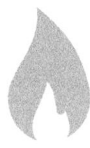

"I have to get home." Ted's voice and body were shaking as he looked upon the image of the necklace. How she'd gotten it was unknown, and the description of the page was undeniable. The Aloviti, the Raven banging on the basement door, was collecting materials—the children's bones, blood, and organs—for the arrival of the Hala.

Seven sacrifices.

The pages depicted the ritual in clear detail. Ted swallowed hard and focused on breathing, afraid to continue reading. The contents were unlike anything he could imagine. Specific ways to dismember the bodies. Certain sections of flesh could not be eaten, and must remain untouched for the ritual to succeed, until the vessel was chosen.

From the remains of the children grew an artefact. The necklace, imbued with the spirit of the demon and an ancient inscription. The artefact chose a vessel. A beating heart to feed on. To steal from. The chosen one must consume the untainted flesh of the sacrifices. To give life to the Hala.

Ted ignored the banging on the basement door and focused on the text. He digested every word, his stomach turning with each description and the knowledge that the mascot had carried out each step to the letter to his baby girl. He searched the text for any indication of what happened to the vessel once the ritual was complete.

He found nothing and feared the worst. "Ava has the necklace," Ted told Laura—her hands clasped around her mouth—"She's the vessel."

The banging stopped. Laura lifted the gun, aimed and waited. The bleak light swinging above them went out. The door burst open, the Raven's inhuman leg crashing through into the darkness. Something had happened to the mascot. It was less human than before, more transformed. The mascot suit was just a shell. A skin the creature was shedding. Chunks of the suit, and the once-human skin dwelling beneath, dropped to the floor in clumps and the Raven stepped towards them.

Laura fired in the darkness. The bullet missed. Her hands shook too much, she couldn't focus. The Raven approached, wings outstretched, beak wide. A row of sharp teeth grew from the beak and its jaw stretched wider than either Ted or Laura imagined.

She fired her weapon again. Her finger pressed against the trigger, and she squeezed once more. Ted pulled at her arm.

"We have to get out of here!" He dragged her to the window as a bolt of lightning crashed outside. It was small, he didn't know if he'd be able to squeeze through. There was no other option.

He torpedoed the book through the brittle glass and lifted Laura up. She cut her hands on shards as she pulled herself through the window. The Raven stalked Ted, a shrill cry reverberating through the basement. Laura crawled out the window, ignoring the pain in her arms and elbows, grabbed at the book and ran into the storm.

Ted jumped, clung to the windowsill, and pulled himself up. He called for Laura, but she was gone. The rain smacked against the concrete outside as Ted shimmied through the small hole.

The Raven gripped Ted's legs with both arms, the heat from the black muck melting through his pants. He cried in pain and begged for Laura to help. As the Raven pulled Ted back inside the dark basement, his fingernails scraped against the wet cement. He grabbed onto the broken glass on the sides of the window, slashing open his forearms and palms, and held on to a shard with all his might. The Raven threw him back to the ground.

He hit the floor hard, his upper body soaked from the rain, and he hid the glass shard behind his back as he sat up. The Raven grinned through the darkness, its yellow teeth like a fluorescent light, the hard beak curling up at the sides. An impossible sight that sent Ted's heart into his throat.

"What do you want?" he screamed at the creature, gripping the shard. It was soaked in red now, slippery from the blood seeping through the slashes on his forearms.

The Raven did not answer. It closed its wings around its body, covering the school logo on its chest, and walked towards him. Tilted its head to one side. It's eyes, black and hollow, looked straight into him. Searched him for something. And Ted felt its presence moving inside him, prying into the depths of his soul.

Closing its eyes, the Raven began to recite a phrase. Though he recalled seeing them in the book, Ted didn't know the words. A passage—what was it about? He couldn't think with the Raven searching him. Seeking to know him. To see if he was worthy of being an Aloviti.

"You might as well kill me," Ted said, struggling to stand. "I will never be like you."

The Raven opened its eyes and lunged at Ted, dragging him back to the ground. Teeth bared, beak pecking at his throat and neck. Shoving his weakening forearm under the Raven's chin, pushing into its neck, he tried to fight it off. His other hand reached for the glass shard. It sliced his fingers as he gripped it, and screamed into the Raven's face, plunging the shard into the creature's eye.

Black muck spewed from the eye like a geyser, pouring into Ted's own eyes and mouth, but he didn't stop. He stabbed again and again, slicing the Raven's face open. The Raven retreated, the shard deep inside its head, and fell to the ground.

Lightning crashed again and Ted saw the window. He leapt towards it, pulled himself through, and crawled like a newborn into the rain gushing from the heavens. His arms were weak, he'd lost so much blood. He managed to stand and stumbled away from the basement, knowing only one thing for certain.

He had to get home to Ava.

Ava dreamed of drowning. Wished the water spilling from the heavens would fill her lungs until she could no longer breathe. Begged for a way out, for this to end. The Claws carried her through the rain, reciting those same words over and over and over. Drilling them into her brain.

She was weak. The gold necklace sunk into her skin. It felt like the object was attached to her heart, moving up and down to the steady beat. Jimmy looked back at her every now and then and smiled. Even in her dazed state, she could tell it was more than confidence. It was a knowing look. He was waiting for something, for *someone*.

They walked through the school parking lot and the Claws put her down on the front steps. Banged on the door and waited. She knew who was coming. Her stomach ached at the memory of chewing down the flesh. The Raven watching her, holding her mouth open and throwing in more. She'd coughed and choked, and when the Raven forced her mouth shut and held her nose, Ava had done the unthinkable. She'd eaten the remains of her classmates.

The memory was distant—a nightmare brought forth by an unknown force. She had woken in the middle of class, screaming, the other students laughing at her and filming the insanity for Instagram and TikTok. The sickness inside her had begun to grow—the hatred, the rage—until her father had asked one too many times what was wrong. Now he was here, at the school, with the Raven.

It's all my fault.

She knew that wasn't true, but it didn't matter. Something

squirmed in her stomach, and the Claws responded with an excited groan. Whatever was going to happen, it would be soon.

Jimmy banged on the door again, impatient. He called out to someone. His voice was silenced by a gunshot tearing through the storm. Ava tried to look and see what was happening but couldn't. The football team surrounded her, as though she were precious cargo.

"Get away from her," a female voice said, "or the next shot won't miss."

Ted staggered through the rain at the sound of gunfire, held onto the brick walls of the school as he went. His vision was fading. He knew he needed to bandage his wounds, or he wouldn't see morning. Turning a corner, he saw the Claws with their hands raised. Laura pointing her gun at them and cradling the book.

"Laura!" Ted called.

She ignored him. "Let her go," she repeated, her voice firm and strong. The boys moved aside, each hesitant step smaller than the last. Through the gaps, Ted saw his daughter lying on the school's front steps.

"Ava!" He limped to her, feet almost numb, and fell to her side. He ran his fingers over her hair and bent down to kiss her forehead.

She gazed up at him, whispered, "Daddy", and then shut her eyes.

"It's too late," one of the footballers said.

Ted recognised him as the team captain and asked him

what he meant. Jimmy shrugged and pointed behind them. Ted followed the boy's finger. Held Ava tight as the Raven appeared in the storm, half its face disguised by black muck.

Moving Ava into a sitting position and wrapping his arms around her, Ted screamed for the Raven to leave them alone. Laura ran to their side, gun still threatening the teenagers. They didn't seem bothered by the weapon anymore. The Raven gave them power.

"Like I said," Jimmy repeated. "It's too late. Look." He nodded towards Ava.

Ted looked down at his daughter, black veins covering her body, and watched a lump forming in her stomach. He lifted her shirt to see and recognised the shape of a hand, pushing out of the skin. Before he could react, the hand moved for Ava's chest. The girl groaned in pain and clutched at her necklace. She opened her mouth to scream, and the hand filled her throat. Silencing her pain.

Ava broke free from Ted's arms, fell to her hands and knees, and convulsed with the Raven and the football team reciting those unknown words. Louder and louder, over the thumping rain.

The hand pushed itself from Ava's mouth, exposing an elbow. Ted and Laura moved to see what was happening. A face appeared inside Ava's throat, slick with black muck, and the exposed arm dragged itself across the concrete to pull the face free. A razor-sharp beak, hollow eyes, just like the Raven. It was not the face of anything human.

"Hala," the Claws murmured, raising their arms to the sky, and screaming the demon's name. "Hala, be thy queen!"

The Raven stepped forward, pushing Ted and Laura aside, and kneeled in front of Ava. It took the hand in its own, caressed the newborn face, and pulled hard. The creature sprung forth from Ava, who collapsed to the ground, unconscious. The demon curled in the foetal position in the Raven's arms, and Ted moved to his daughter's side.

Holding his daughter, her body limp, Ted felt his own eyes grow heavy. Despite the rain, his arms were stained from his wounds, and he knew it was too late. There was no coming back from this. He turned to Laura and whispered, "Get Ava out of here."

The woman's mouth was agape, her eyes red with tears, and she shook her head. The Claws encircled them. Jimmy snatched the gun from Laura and tossed it away. As Ted fought to keep his eyes open, the newborn demon, the Hala, began to take shape. Half-human, half-bird.

A raven.

Its empty eyes scanned the area, sized up the teenage boys, and looked back to the Raven. In a language shared only between the two of them, a decision was made, and both sprung to life. The Claws screamed in confusion as the demons tore their bodies apart, gulping down their flesh. Despite his best efforts, Ted fell into darkness.

Ava woke to silence. The Raven and the Hala stood over her, gentle feathers tracing her cheekbones and chin. Taking her in. Adoring her. She crawled backwards on her hands, kicking out at the creatures before her, until her hands hit something familiar. Looking down, she saw her dad, unmoving and covered in blood.

Tears streamed from her face as she stared at her father's

corpse. She looked away, tried to blink the reality into nothingness, and saw the Claws. The principal. What was left of them. Scattered around the school parking lot, half-eaten.

The necklace didn't burn anymore. It just sat atop Ava's skin as a necklace ought to. The inscriptions were different. She could read them.

The bearer of this chain will bring forth Queen Hala.

The Raven and the Hala moved towards her. A glimmer appeared in their hollow eyes. A light she recognised from the way her father looked at her. Caring. Ava eyed the principal's weapon, still clutched in her dead hands, and moved to reach for it.

Her fingers stopped short. She looked back at the Hala. Something inside her felt warm. The impulses shot through her neck again, and Ava didn't fight it. She liked it. Embraced it the way she'd embraced her fathers. She looked back at her dad. Dead. Both of them dead. Her family.

Family.

The child-eaters helped her up. As rage boiled through her blackened veins, they led her back to Ravensfield. To her home. To eat.

AN
HONEST
WORM

The larvae wriggled and squirmed as Henry poured another bucket of them into the mud. He scrunched his nose to keep the stench at bay, couldn't stop it travelling through his nasal cavities anyway. These creatures didn't smell like death, per se, just something right next to it. His eyes stung and watered as the tiny things worked their way into the bath, taking refuge beneath the surface of the grey mud.

Henry didn't know what these creatures were for, and he didn't much care. Some guy in a white coat had paid him cash—lots of cash—to move what he referred to as "stock" and paid extra for picking up a van load of the stuff and driving it up a mountain. Pouring another bucket into the filthy liquid, he noticed a couple of the wrigglers worming to the surface. Even though they didn't have faces, Henry swore he saw them smiling—revelling in the thick, gooey mud they now called home.

With all the buckets now empty, he headed back to the van, remembering the instructions Dr White Coat had given: take the van back to where you found it and walk away like nothing ever happened. Driving down the mountain, Henry's phone buzzed in his pocket. He fumbled through his jeans, grabbed his phone, and hit the green button.

"It's done?" Dr White Coat.

"Yeah, man, I'm on my way back," Henry answered. "What are those things, anyway?"

Dr White Coat held the silence for a moment too long, leaving Henry to ask if the old guy was still there. Sounded like he was sucking on something, and Henry remembered the older guy was a smoker. Like, full-on chain-smoking, which he thought was weird for a scientist.

"You want a job, Henry?" White Coat asked.

"I got a job," Henry replied. "Flipping burgers at *The Shack*."

"I'll do you one better. Come work for me. Permanently." He paused. "And I'll tell you all about what we're working on here."

"What did you say they were, again?"

"*Olgoi-khorkhoi*," he said. After a moment of silence, he added: "Worms."

Not into superchubs lose some weight ya fat fuck.

The message appeared on my notification screen first thing in the morning. The reply was from Growlr user *BearChaser98*, whose profile read that he was into bears, daddies, and chubs.

I've always been a bear, even when I was a teenager. My facial hair sprouted on my twelfth birthday, by which time I already had patches of hair everywhere except the soles of my feet and my palms. I thought I'd grown into my looks in my thirties, and the gay bear community seemed to agree. For the most part, at least.

At some point, I'd morphed from a cute bear into a superchub. *BearChaser98* wasn't the first to tell me to lose weight, nor the first to send a string of subsequent messages berating me for being obese. I never considered myself fat, though even if I was, what was wrong with that? Everybody is beautiful—it wasn't my problem if these superficial twats couldn't appreciate curves. They would be better off on Tindr than an app designed for men who like larger men.

I swiped the message away and stared at my naked body in the mirror. According to the BMI, I was morbidly obese, but I liked my weight. Whether it was muscle or not, that had always been beside the point to me. That was until messages like those from BearChaser98 started to become more frequent.

My stomach did hang a little, and my pecs looked a bit sad as they drooped down my chest, though guys who chased bears had always liked that. At least until the muscle bears took over. Gym bunnies with body hair, that's all they were. Yet, here I was, being rejected again while some muscle bear was out getting laid.

Sighing, I remembered a commercial I'd seen on television the night prior, spruiking a new weight loss treatment. Since the bear chasers had started to ignore me, I'd tried the shakes, the bars, the pills; I'd been to a gym and did the trainer thing for a while. Nothing worked. I'd given up on losing weight until this commercial the night before: a thin, gorgeous woman with flowing black hair had seduced the viewer with a new treatment hailed as the only treatment you'd ever need: Magic Mud.

If I were straight, I might have been seduced by her, but it was the mud I took an interest in. The details were hazy, though I remembered something about a mountain retreat where you wouldn't be judged and where the crisp air and unity with nature exacerbated the properties of the mud.

Now, as I tried to forget *BearChaser98*, and all the others who had swiped past my picture in the last year or more since joining Growlr, I sat at my laptop and started searching. It was the first result when I typed "magic mud weight loss". A slideshow of before and after photos was convincing. Not like the ones on TV that you can tell are photoshopped, or even different people. These seemed legitimate.

There was one spot available for the weekend. The mouse hovered over "Book Now" while I considered my options. Did I want to be that guy who caved to traditional ideas of beauty? Was I okay with being a self-hating, self-shaming bear?

I clicked the mouse and booked my spot.

Took a deep breath as I read the confirmation email, saddened that I felt the need to do this to myself. I wasn't unhealthy, I just didn't look like a classic model. The curves I had spent so long with, and which I was so comfortable and familiar with—and which I loved—were soon to be features of the past.

The stereotypical trope of "thin equals beautiful" had won. *Goodbye body.*

The first thing I noticed as the Uber driver threw my bags to the kerb and sped off was that the mountain retreat was as advertised. A grandiose manor with bold electric gates and a white sand driveway lined with palm trees. A slice of tropical paradise on a mountain.

I threw a bag over my shoulder, released the handle on my 4-wheel spinner luggage and headed towards the gates. As I approached, a car sputtered up the mountain, the exhaust choking on petrol with a bang. I watched a man push the door open, his thick arms and belly stopping my heart. Manicured beard with specks of grey running through the brown chest hair jutting from beneath his flannel shirt.

The man was a Greek god.

I gulped down my hormones and waited for him to join me at the gates, his eyebrows lifting by way of greeting. Our eyes locked for a bit too long and a surge of energy pulsed through me. I nodded in reply and before either of us could press the button at the gate, a buzz jolted me back to reality.

The gates began to roll apart, and we entered the retreat grounds.

"Ian." The Greek god held out a hand.

I shook it, trying to ignore the bolt of sensation in my groin as our skin connected. His grip was strong, yet his skin was so soft and comforting. I mumbled my name, and we exchanged a few pleasantries as we strolled towards the manor.

As it turned out, neither of us knew what to expect from

the weekend, except that we'd be bathing in this so-called magic mud with instant weight loss results. I was nervous about how much I could expect to lose. A friend of mine had undergone bariatric surgery a few months earlier and was now a beanpole. I didn't like skinny, and I didn't want to be skinny.

A thin, buxom woman—Gretel—greeted us at the door and showed us to our quarters. Ian and I were next-door neighbours for the weekend, and I saw a shy grin hidden in his beard as the woman made a joke about it.

"There's no time like the present," Gretel said, "so your treatments will begin as soon as the other guests arrive. As your confirmation email stated, there's only one treatment, but we encourage you to stay the duration of the weekend so we can monitor the initial results."

Ian and I nodded and watched her disappear down a corridor.

I was about to enter my room when I noticed a sticker on one of his suitcases that read: "Fat is Beautiful". My stomach tightened.

"It is, you know," Ian said, following my gaze.

"So then why are you here?"

"Why are you here?"

I paused. "I'm really not sure."

Ian frowned and disappeared into his room. I winced as the door clicked shut.

I was left alone with my thoughts. *Fat is beautiful,* I thought with a sigh heavy on the irony.

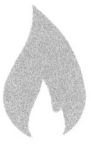

The treatment room reminded me of a bath house. An oversized pool converted into a mud pit. The mud itself was grey, with flecks of brown and black and red visible through the rising steam. I thought I saw something moving in the thick liquid. Some other guests stood with Ian and I, gazing around the room in wonder at the mud and the concrete columns straight from Ancient Greece. Even though the room was impressive, my stomach tightened more and more as the seconds ticked away.

There were seven of us—four women, three men—standing half-naked and exposed in treatment costumes provided for us. The women seemed to know each other, making small talk and pointing out features of the room here and there. The other man said nothing, eyeing the group with uncertainty and covering his pecs with shaking hands.

Ian seemed to be cataloguing things around the room, taking in all the features and details. He stepped towards the pool, filled to the brim with mud. I stood beside him, drawn to his hairy back and the deep growl coming from his lips as he stared into the thick brown liquid.

"What is it?" I asked and moved to dip my toe.

"Don't," he said, and I retreated.

"What's wrong?"

He shook his head. "I know we just met," he said, "but you don't need to do this. None of us do. You're… beautiful."

I saw his cheeks burn bright red, and his eyes avoided mine. "No, I'm not." I paused. "And anyway, if you really believe none of us need this, then why are you here?"

Ian looked around, scanning the room, and leaned close to me. I could feel the warmth of his breath on my shoulder and neck as he whispered, "I'm a journalist. There's something up with this so-called magic mud."

Before either of us could say anything, our eyes locked, Gretel entered the room, holding a small remote. Pressing a button, the room came alive with music. Relaxing, soft tones emanated from unseen speakers, sinking through the air to settle inside us.

"Alright, everyone," she was almost whispering, "disrobe, and let's get started."

One of the women raised a hand and looked sheepish as she realised she was free to speak at any time. "Uh, what do we actually do?"

Gretel smiled, whimsical and carefree. "You just sit in the mud and let the fat melt away."

"How does it work, exactly?" Ian asked, stepping away from the pool.

I looked down at the mud once more, inspecting it for magical properties, as though it would shine or glisten at me. Give a sign it wasn't from this world. It was just mud. Brown, thick, stinky mud.

"There are particles in the mud that sink through your pores. Essentially, they bond to the fat cells and melt them away. After your treatment here, we will retreat to the showers. With our specially formulated body wash, you will complete the process by literally washing the fat out of your body. It is *that* simple." Gretel motioned to the mud pool, and requested we disrobe once more.

As the others did as they were asked, revealing their undergarments, Ian and I exchanged glances. All I could think about was what he'd said to me. About being beautiful. I hadn't heard that for such a long time, and his eyes when he'd said it... I could tell he meant it.

Sensing my hesitation, Gretel placed a cool hand at the centre of my back. "You'll be a new man," she said.

A new man. I don't want to be new.

"I'm going to sit it out," Ian said. "Sorry, I just changed my mind."

Gretel pouted, her lips glossy and thin. "You've already paid, dear. There are no refunds."

"That's okay," Ian replied. "I just can't."

The slosh of mud around ankles and thighs caught my attention, and I gazed across to the pool once more. Watched the others descend into the mud, nervous smiles wide across their faces. They all sat around the edge of the pool, holding on to the sides.

"It's not deep," one of them said. "You can walk around and everything."

"That's right," Gretel said, encouraging them. "We recommend you walk around as much as you can; it stimulates the process. Please, also immerse your whole body in the mud."

"Our *whole* body? Even our faces?" another woman asked.

"Just scoop it up and rub it on your face, Sharon," her friend said.

Sharon did, making sure to also rub the mud around her hair. The lone man in the pool did the same, looking unsure about the entire process.

"Are you sure you won't participate?" Gretel asked Ian. "Seems an awful shame to come all the way here and then... chicken out."

I saw the arch of her eyebrow as she spoke those last words. Baiting him, for whatever reason. He didn't bite, just shook his head. And without consciously being aware of it, I said, "I've changed my mind, too."

Gretel smiled, wide and thin. Her eyes were empty. "I understand."

Without another word, she turned her back to us, and entered the mud pool herself. "We need to stay in here for an hour. Can you believe it, just *one hour* and you can say goodbye to those nasty fat cells forever."

Ian retreated to a bench seat at the side of the pool and leaned back. He patted the seat next to him, inviting me to sit. As I flopped down, he whispered, "I'm glad you changed your mind."

"What paper are you with?" I asked, watching the other guests splash around in the mud like it was a day at the beach. Slops of brown slid down their faces, and they all laughed and cooed like it was the most fun they'd ever had.

"I can feel it working," one of the women said.

"Me too, Cheryl!"

Shaking his head, Ian said, "No paper. I'm a journalist for *Bear Weekly*."

"Are you serious? I fucking love that magazine." I slapped my knee and laughed. "I have every issue."

Ian blushed a little. "I'm actually the co-founder, but I prefer the journalistic stuff to the bureaucratic day-to-day operational crap."

"It's sinking into me," the man said, excited. "I can feel it!"

"That's the particles at work," Gretel replied.

I sighed, half wanting to join them, half wanting the fattiest burger and fries I could find. My stomach grumbled, and Ian put an arm around my shoulders. It felt familiar, as though I'd known him for the longest time.

"Your stomach is right." He smiled across at me. "Shall we find a kitchen in this shit hole?"

Leaning into his grasp a little—his hand caressing my shoulder—I nodded. I really wanted to just stay there forever, feeling his thick meaty arm around me. His chest hair rubbing against my own. But he let go and jumped to his feet, clearing his throat and adjusting his towel.

"Let's get dressed first."

Those two were going to ruin everything. Dr Taylor smacked at the monitor as he watched them wander away from the pool untouched. Every experiment needed variables, he was more aware of that than most, but that's what the control group was for. These two were supposed to be neck-deep in mud by now. He drew out a cigarette and lit it.

"Sir, what do we do?" his assistant, Jamie, asked, adjusting her glasses.

Taylor sighed, stifling his anger, and thought for a moment. Sucked on a cigarette and blew smoke at the monitor. "They said they were going to find some food, right?"

Jamie nodded.

"Well, they don't need to bathe in the mud to have the treatment," Taylor said. "After all, it's not the mud eating their fat, is it?"

Jamie scrunched up her face, and Taylor shot her a look. He knew his assistant was opposed to the program, but they had a rare opportunity here. To change the world. To save lives. To make a fuck load of money. Taylor would not squander that.

Moving to a tank on the other side of the room, where

they watched, recorded, and compiled data, Taylor lifted a lid to stare inside the tank. He used a scooper to lift out some of his squirming babies. "Hello, my precious ones," he whispered and then caught himself before Jamie overheard.

The young woman came to his side and swallowed hard to hide her disgust. "I can't believe they're even alive. Thousands of years frozen like that, and we can just… revive them. Incredible."

"Permafrost is a scientist's best friend." Taylor nodded. "There's more to be discovered in there, I'm sure. But for now, we've got our little worm friends here. And these tiny things are going to make us rich."

Jamie pushed her glasses up her nose. "I'll arrange for these to be cooked into their food, then?"

"Don't be stupid," Taylor snarled. "In their diet shakes. The only drink on the menu, remember?"

"Yes, sir." Jamie scooped the worms into a plastic zip bag and was out the door to the kitchen.

Turning back to the tank, Taylor stared at his babies. Only three months earlier, he'd been on an expedition in Mongolia, excavating through permafrost. He'd found something there, buried under seventy thousand years of ice. Something nobody expected or believed. Yet it was there, stretching fifty yards from head to tail, ready for his gloved hand to caress.

Upon seeing the creature, something shifted in Taylor. He felt alive for the first time—he realised he had been fooled by the world, and nothing was true except for what lay before his eyes.

In the lab, alone and exhausted, but unable to walk away from his discovery, Taylor undertook a revival process and he'd discovered a second marvel. The creature contained eggs. It was a mother.

That made him the father, the only human in existence to know of worms' true secret. The only human to be able to exploit it.

His research revealed the mother possessed teeth, unusual for worms. It had glands that secreted a rare toxin that would digest lipocytes. Others might presume this metabolic function only the means to an end: assisting the creature with breaking down its food.

But he knew the consumption of fat cells led to metamorphosis.

"Soon, gorgeous," he whispered. "Soon."

The café was mundane in décor, and as Ian and I sat across from each other, I made any excuse to find the boring pale green walls interesting. The chairs were a little small for us, our behinds teetering over the edges of the seats.

I adjusted in my chair, let my elbows smack against the plastic tabletop, and sighed. Not only had I wasted my money on this weight loss venture, but now I found myself unable to look at the only person who'd flirted with me in over a year. A lump in my throat refused to be swallowed despite my many attempts, and in the corner of my eyes, I saw Ian smiling.

"Something funny?" I asked.

"Not funny, so much as cute." His smile turned into a grin.

I blushed a little and found the courage to meet his gaze. "You… think I'm cute?"

He nodded and reached his hands across the table to meet mine. His thumb caressed the back of my hands, sending warm spikes up my arms. Straight to my heart. "I think you're fucking sexy," he said, confident and unapologetic.

"We should…get some food." I nodded towards a pimple-faced young man waiting behind a counter.

Without looking away from me, Ian said, "Sure. I could eat."

The warmth filling my heart made its way down my body, landing somewhere around my groin, and I felt a sudden urge to kiss this man. His hands were still caressing me, it was the perfect opportunity. Instead, I stood, pushed my chair back, and headed to the café counter.

Fuck fuck fuck fuck fuck.

Ian was behind me a few paces and stood next to me as I stopped at the counter.

"Hi," I said to the young man.

He stared back with pursed lips—Employee of the Month, he was not. "Sup bro."

"Ah, you got a menu?" I noticed his nametag. *Henry.*

Henry shook his head and sniffed, bored. "Nah, man. Up here, you got the liquid diet. Shakes, that's it. You want?"

Ian and I exchanged glances. I didn't want to tell him I could murder an entire cow, though part of me was sure he could read it in my expression.

"Two shakes," Ian said. "Thanks, Henry." He pulled at my arm and we headed back to the table—our table—to wait for whatever that kid was going to make us.

Staring at the pale green walls again, I sighed. "There's not much to do around here, is there?"

"I can think of a few things." Ian winked.

I swallowed. "You're… very forward."

"You're very shy. It brings out the devil in me."

Henry plonked down two shakes in plain white milkshake

cups. Pink straws. "Enjoy," he said over his shoulder, already on his way back to the counter.

"He's a real delight," Ian said before slowly putting the straw into his mouth.

The way he did it, I was sure it was innuendo. My mind raced—I'd wanted this sort of attention for so long, but now it was here and I didn't know what to do.

"So, you're a journalist, you said." My eyes watched his mouth as it prepared to suck down the shake. "What's the story about this place?"

Ian let the straw fall into the thick liquid and cleared his throat. "This magic mud…" He trailed off for a second, eyes scanning the room to make sure they were alone. "We're the second group to come through this facility. Did you know that?"

I shook my head, fiddled with my straw. The liquid looked almost the same as the mud, and I wasn't sure I wanted it in my mouth.

"I had a friend come through in the last round. He… never came back."

"What? What do you mean?"

Ian shrugged. "I got a text from him. It was weird, jumbled. It didn't make sense. But the words 'it's in the mud' were pretty clear." He sighed and leaned back in his chair. "Something happened here. The police can't do anything because he's an adult, he can technically disappear if he wants to. But it's not like him."

"And you think…"

"I don't know what I think," Ian said. "But he hasn't been home, he hasn't been to work, he's not anywhere."

They were interrupted by Gretel and the other guests, strutting in like empowered barbie dolls. The lonesome Ken of the group fell behind a little, his face pale as he held his stomach.

"Oh. My. God!" Sharon or Cheryl—I couldn't remember who was who—said. "That was *incredible!*"

"I feel like I've lost weight already."

The other two women nodded and said nothing, one of them attending to the ill Ken doll. She got him seated at a large, round table, and the others sat around it, too. Gretel slinked across to the counter, and I watched as the pimples on Henry's face almost fell off in trepidation. The young man straightened, cleared his throat, and fixed his hair.

I feel you, kid. I fixed my own hair, though it was for Ian's benefit.

"You right, mate?" Ian asked, his attention on the Ken doll.

Taking the sick man's form in, I noticed his skin dropping a bit more than it had been earlier. His breast tissue looked like it was deflating, and his cheeks were beginning to hang from his face.

"I... uh... I don't feel good." He coughed, his hands holding his abdomen tight.

Ian stood and headed to the man, whose stomach was visibly shuddering. I followed Ian and he kneeled next to the man. Cheryl and Sharon were too busy talking among themselves, and the other two—the nice ones—were fussing over Ken doll, asking if he was alright, even though he clearly wasn't.

Gretel strolled back to the group with a tray of shakes, looking nonplussed about Ken doll's situation. Putting the tray on the table, she said, "Lunch is served."

I looked at her, a broad grin on her face, and vacant eyes, almost as though she was unaware of her surroundings. As Cheryl and Sharon grabbed a shake each, I turned back to

Ken doll. His cheeks were hanging low now, as though the skin was melting from his face. The skin on his chest was loose, too, and rippling to the floor.

Ian asked the man if he was okay, asked how he felt, asked him to describe the sensation. Ken doll couldn't speak, and the skin around his throat started to expand. Almost like a bubble forming under the skin.

"Shit," Ian said. "He's choking on something!"

Gretel came to his side and ushered us back to give the man some space. "This is *all* part of the *process*."

"This is part of the process? Are you fucking serious?" I pointed to Ken doll's melting body. "Look at him!"

Gretel faced him and smiled again. "He's almost ready."

"Call an ambulance!" Ian called to Henry, who was chewing a nail with great interest. "Now, kid, now!"

I watched as Ken doll started to inflate again. His throat, his chest, his stomach. He looked like a stretched balloon, the skin expanding, but it was thin and almost transparent. His eyes were wide, so wide, and as he choked and sputtered for breath, I could tell he was begging for help.

"What do we do?" I asked Gretel, who kneeled before him.

She raised her hands above her head in a prayer, and began to whisper. I strained to hear her, but Ken doll opened his mouth and gurgled a hollow, scratchy scream. I stepped back as he inflated more and more, the skin stretching farther than I realised possible.

"Fuck," I heard Ian mutter.

Ken doll exploded into a mess of blood and skin and bone. Ian grabbed my hand and pulled me down as flecks of muscle and shredded skin splattered across the café. As Ken stopped screaming—his upper and low jaw on different sides of the room now—the others began.

I stared at the chair where Ken's body used to be, now the remains of his skin suit—like the leftovers of a popped balloon, with a bloodied spine hanging over the back of the chair. Gretel still kneeled before him, her hands raised high, clutching something tight. As she stood, and moved away from Ken's empty skin, I saw it.

Ian saw it, too. "What. The. Fuck."

A reddish-brown worm rose from the chair, flecks of Ken's skin clinging to its coiling body, thick hairs sprouting from it in all directions. What I imagined was its head had sharp black spikes jutting outwards from the flesh—teeth—and a mouth gaping wide, searching. It wormed off the chair, blind but somehow sensing Gretel was nearby.

"This is all part of the process," she repeated with a lazy smile, and brought her hands to her chest. She held Ken's heart tight to her, and squeezed, letting the organ drip blood across her gown.

Through the screaming and the crying, I heard only the sound of my own heart thrashing in my chest. The worm crawled towards Gretel in wavelike motions, its body expanding and contracting as it made its way to her.

She let the worm sniff at her ankles and her thighs, a wet brown tongue snaking forth and wrapping around her.

"Yul," she whispered, "take me, God."

Ian and I slipped in red puddles as we stood and moved to the group of women still shrieking.

"We have to get out of here," Ian told them.

Looking down at the women—Cheryl and Sharon, whichever was which—I saw a familiar sickness drawn across their faces. As Gretel whispered again to her worm god, begging it to take her, I watched as it coiled around her and squeezed, the way a snake would.

The tongue licked at her body, the black spiky teeth nipping at her arms and shoulders. Her vacant eyes filled with lust and desire and hope, and she looked right at me as she said, "Behold His passage."

I blinked, just once, and the worm squeezed hard around her again. She smiled through the pain as the pressure churned her insides to mush, screaming prayers in an ancient language, until the spikes of the worm's mouth stabbed through her head.

Her eyeballs popped and leaked down her face, the worm tongue lapping at the liquid and shuddering with delight at the taste. In one swift motion, the spike-teeth firm through Gretel's skull, it pulled hard and tore her head from her body. Taking her head into its coils, the worm returned for the rest of her.

Ian grabbed at me, telling me to move away—slow, quiet— to head to the counter where Henry yawned and scratched his balls like nothing was amiss at all. As the worm pushed its body inside Gretel's neck, burrowing through her freshly squeezed organs, Ian whispered to me that it was time.

"We have to go. Right fucking now."

The women, looking ill, and wiping vomit from their faces, agreed, and followed us to the counter. Henry smiled at us as we ran past him, searching for an exit somewhere. "It's all part of the process, man," he said. "Nothing to worry about."

I looked back one last time, saw tiny worms oozing from Gretel's flesh, coiling and squirming on the ground, crawling through hers and Ken's blood like it was the freshest soil they'd ever known.

Behind the counter, a door to a storeroom. We raced through, Ian's hand clutched to my own, and searched the room. A small kitchen, but mostly just blenders lining the food prep areas.

"Over there!" Ian pointed to another door—it *had* to be the exit—and we moved to it, me panting and huffing and clutching at my heart.

As Ian fumbled with the door, I leaned against a counter to catch my breath, and saw it was a chest fridge with plastic sliding doors. I slid one open and reached for a white container within. Popped the lid open.

"Holy shit." I dropped it back into the fridge and watched the small worms spill out. "What the hell is happening here?"

Ian came to my side and, looking down at the worms, grimaced. "I don't know, but we have to go."

Kicking the door open, Ian pulled me into the fresh mountain air, and scanned the area. Mentally locating himself. I remembered seeing the café from the front gate earlier, but I couldn't visualise the rest of the place; Ian had distracted me with his beautiful arms and beard, and Gretel—*Fuck, poor Gretel!*—had led us straight to our rooms. Which direction had they been?

"This way," someone else said. Sharon pushed between us, holding her guts and stumbling. She pointed to the right. "We head this way; it'll take us through the grounds and back to the guest rooms."

"How—"

"I'm a city planner, I have good instincts for this shit." She swayed a little, and her face had gone a unique shade of green, and I saw the flesh at her belly quivering.

Ian and I exchanged glances, but we took her by an arm each and steadied her. "Come on," I said. "Lead the way."

Behind us, the door swung open again. Spinning to face the clanking metal sound, I saw it was just Henry. Carrying a hazard bucket, sloshing with dark red liquid at the sides, he poured it out onto the grass. Kicking at a kidney as it slipped from the bucket.

"Grab him," Ian hissed at me.

I didn't know why, but I trusted Ian with my life. Trusted that he had a good reason. I let go of Sharon's arm and lunged at the kid. He turned in surprise, but my arms were around him in a bear hug.

"Help," he screamed. "Help!"

"Who are you calling for?" I asked, squeezing tighter. It reminded me of the worm back there, and I felt a sudden urge to throw up.

Henry cried, "Let me go, poofter!"

Rage bubbled inside me and just as I was about to let go, to punch him in the face and tell him to get fucked, someone else's fist did it for me. One of the other women in Cheryl and Sharon's group. Never did get her name.

"Fuck you." She rubbed at her hand as Henry shook off the shock. She turned her attention to me and said, "My wife runs a kickboxing class at the gym. She taught me a few things." Then she doubled over, and I saw her skin was sagging, too, just like Ken doll back there.

I smiled, impressed, despite the obvious illness spreading through the group and Henry struggling to get free of my grip.

"We have to go." Ian reminded us. "The giant worm…"

As we were jolted to movement, following Sharon's directions through the grounds, Henry laughed—way too hard for someone who'd just been smashed in the face. I pulled him along in my arms, and he laughed harder.

"You're all going to die," he chuckled. "One by one, you'll—"

Another punch in the face and he was out, head dropping to the side.

"Thanks," I said to the kickboxer's wife.

She nodded and helped me carry Henry, even though the skin on her arms was sagging low, like clothes a few sizes too big.

I could see the front gate of the wellness centre, Ian's shitty car on the other side. I swallowed my excitement, knowing we couldn't take anyone else with us—Sharon, Cheryl, the other two, they were all sick.

Infested.

"In here," Ian called, as we reached the guest rooms. He shouldered the door open, still clutching Sharon, even though her arm was three times smaller than it had been. He grabbed mostly loose skin, but he pulled her along, nonetheless.

As we entered the building, a crash of glass and metal and bricks came from behind us. I spun around, watched as the giant worm smashed its way through the café walls. The windows exploded into shards and the bricks shattered, crumbling like sand as the worm coiled its way into the crisp mountain air.

I closed the door to the guest house, realising the futility as I did so, and stared out at the beast. It's giant, black teeth were high in the air, its mouth opening and closing like it was breathing. Then it turned its head in our direction, and I knew. It was sniffing.

And it could smell all of us.

Moving back from the door, I let go of Henry and shouted at the others to run, conscious that half the group was essentially a pile of loose flesh by now. Still, they tried, shuffling and tripping over their own skin like untied shoelaces.

The worm had tasted us in the air, caught our scent, and it was moving fast. The body segments expanded and contracted to give it momentum. As I ran from the door, I could almost feel the glass shattering behind me, the worm roaring like a fucking demon from behind me.

Its teeth scraped at me, and I ignored the pain of tearing flesh as I ran. My weight slowed me down, my belly jiggled up and down as I went, and I pushed my legs harder—as hard as I could—to gain some speed. As horrible as it was, I ran straight past Cheryl and her two friends, crawling along as skeletons surrounded by flat, saggy skin. The treatment was doing what it was supposed to do. It was eating all the fat in their bodies.

The next part was what terrified me. It was too late for them, and as much as I felt like a coward, I knew I couldn't stop for them. There was nothing to be done for them.

Ian and Sharon were ahead of me, but he was stopped at one of the rooms. Sharon rested against a wall, her eyes wide with fear. She pushed her forehead skin out of her face to better see the worm and screamed.

Pushing into the room, Ian disappeared. I caught up to Sharon, puffing as much as I'd ever puffed, and grabbed at her. Guided her into the room behind Ian. He was searching through objects and a bag—*Fat is beautiful*—and I knew what he was after.

Car keys.

I risked a peek around the doorframe, saw Henry lying unharmed at the building's entrance. Saw the worm coiled around Cheryl, and sniffing at one of the other women. The kickboxer's wife. My heart sank and every fibre of my being screamed to go help her. Screamed to run down the hall and do something. But my body didn't move.

Just watched.

The worm nudged at the woman, its head pushing gently against hers as she lay motionless on the ground. Her eyes blinked, and my heart sank further. As I stepped forward, into the hall, Ian pulled me back.

"We *all* want to help her. But we both know it's too late. Look."

Peeking around the frame once more, I saw what I had feared. The women's bodies were beginning to inflate again, just as Ken doll's had.

"I'm going to take a guess here, but we're about to have a few more of those fucking things," Ian hissed.

We stepped back and clicked the door shut.

Sharon sat on the edge of the bed, clutching at a set of car keys attached to a small, metallic keychain coloured like the gay bear flag. I had the same one, and if there wasn't a giant worm outside waiting to devour us, I might have enjoyed the coincidence.

As it was, I heard the screams from beyond the door, imagining the women's bodies inflating with a giant worm. Their skin splitting open as the creatures poked their heads from the remains.

With the images in my head, I panted hard. All the dreams I had for my future had disappeared, replaced by the worm. Replaced by the knowledge there were about to be a few more of them.

My heart hammered and my chest felt tight.

The women screamed outside, their bodies filling with worms.

I gasped for breath, but it was like the room was a vacuum. I couldn't find any oxygen, and tears escaped my eyes.

Ian raced to me, cupped my cheeks in his hands. Through the pounding of my heart and the blood gushing to my ears, I couldn't hear what he was saying to me. His lips moved fast, forming words that were beyond me. But his eyes. They spoke to me without sound.

"Come back to me," I heard him say. "We don't have time for this."

I nodded, letting in a small amount of air. The women screamed again—pained, terrified—and I covered my ears. My chest heaved, but I sucked in through my nose, and all I smelled was blood. I cried a few more tears, and Ian moved me away from the door. Back to Sharon, who had become a sagging lump of flesh on the bed.

"What are we going to do, Ian?" I asked, trying not to collapse in a ball of fear.

He grabbed the car keys from Sharon's hand and thanked her. Her face was all but melted away, but a thin sound escaped her lips. It sounded like "Help."

A *pop-pop* came from beyond the door. Another one.

As the screaming stopped, Ian and I knew.

Waited in the silence.

A high-pitched screech echoed through the hallway, and any hope of getting out alive vanished. Almost as soon as the screech sounded, the walls began to shake. Ian raced to the bedroom window and slid it up, ordering me to go through. The hole wasn't large enough—we both knew it—but there was no other option.

The walls shook again, and the plaster began to crack. I made my way to the window, climbing through until my belly got stuck. Ian pushing at my arse to get me through, and I sucked in as much as I could.

"Come on!" he cried, but I wouldn't budge. "They're right on my arse!"

My arms were through, and I pushed against the outside wall. I felt my belly slide a little and wished I wasn't so big. Maybe the haters were right. Maybe I was disgusting.

Ian yelled, "Almost there!"

I plopped out the window, landing on my arm on the grass with a thud. Ian jumped down as a worm crashed through the glass, its teeth and mouth searching for his flesh.

He pulled me up, I cradled my arm, and we ran. The worms were fast, smashing through the building like it was paper. I felt the teeth at me again, felt them pierce the skin on my back. Ian pulled me along, but I couldn't move on my own. I couldn't feel the ground. Just the spiked teeth sinking deeper into my back as I was lifted into the air.

"No," Ian called from the ground.

I looked down to see him stumbling backward, watching as the worms fought over me. I closed my eyes, my lips trembling as fate clenched down on me. I waited for more teeth to grind me into nothingness in the worm's belly.

A wave of heat came over me, singeing the skin on my face, and I opened my eyes. The worm threw me to the ground and coiled away as a flame came through the air towards it. Crashing to the grass, Ian crawled to my side as the worms screeched and fled.

We looked for the source of the flame: A young woman in a white coat. "Gods or not," she said, "these things hate fire."

"You're saying you found one of these things buried in the ice, and decided it was a good idea to defrost it?" Ian asked.

The young woman, Jamie, nodded. "Well, not *me*, personally. But yes. It was an incredible discovery. The thing was... we didn't realise the Mongolian Death Worm was actually real, we—"

"The what?"

She tended to my arm—a fracture, nothing serious, I was told—and looked at me. I was grateful for the rescue, and for her guiding us to the laboratory where she and her superior had been watching us. I wasn't so grateful to be part of their sick fucking experiment, though.

"It's an ancient worm, never actually proven to exist. Until now." Jamie tightened a bandage over my arm and patted me to signal it was done. "Except, my boss, Dr Taylor, already knew somehow. He knew the legend of the Mongolian Death Worm was actually a story from much, much earlier in human history."

Ian cocked an eyebrow. "What story?"

Sighing, Jamie shook her head and rubbed at her temples. "It's hard for me to grasp it. But those worms out there are… "—she paused to gauge our expressions—"Gods."

I laughed, still cradling my arm, and went to stand next to Ian. I felt safe with him, and he shifted to close the gap between us. It was nice, despite the dire situation.

"Worm gods?" he asked, suspicious. Disbelieving. "That's the stupidest thing I've ever heard."

Jamie agreed and continued. "Once Doctor Taylor figured out what the worm was, he was able to study it. He figured out that it feeds on fat cells. It's not interested in the flesh or whatever. It just wants the fat… He thought he could control it. Use the larvae to stimulate weight loss."

"And make a fortune," I said. "Well, it's not working, is it?"

"That's why I came to get you," Jamie told them. "I don't like what he's doing. What he's asking me to do."

"What did he ask you to do?" Ian asked.

She looked away and tucked hair behind her ear. "You didn't drink the shake," she said. "That's the only reason you're still alive."

I remembered the fridge full of tiny worms. "You put those things in our drinks?"

"Wait." Ian creased his brow. "You mean all of the worms will turn into those giant things out there if they eat enough fat?"

Jamie nodded. "They're the offspring. The children of the worm god."

"How do you know it's a god?" Ian asked. "A giant worm, sure. But a god?"

She didn't answer. Just sighed and met our gazes. Her eyes were filled with terror, like she'd seen something and couldn't form the words. Or didn't want to.

The laboratory door opened, and an older man stepped inside. Hands buried deep in his coat pockets, tired and drawn face staring at them. "Jamie, Jamie, Jamie." He shook his head. "I'm disappointed in you."

Ian and I tensed, unsure what his presence meant for us.

"Sir, I—"

"You betrayed me," he said, his lips curled into an angry frown. "And what's worse, you've destroyed the integrity of the experiment."

"What *is* the experiment?" I asked.

The older man shifted his eyes from Jamie across to me. He stepped forward, took his hands from his pockets. He held something, but I couldn't see what it was. "Why didn't you go into the mud pool?"

"Can we kill those things?" Ian ignored him, and spoke to Jamie.

Dr Taylor snapped his fingers, drawing our attention. "The mud pool. Why did you not go in?"

"Fire hurts them, theoretically it should kill them." Jamie nodded.

The doctor slammed his fists against a table, a microscope and other science equipment bouncing from the force. "I will not be ignored." His voice was calm and steady.

Ian moved to the doctor, his face an inch from the older man, and spat in his face. "Fuck you, and fuck your experiment. I'm going to kill every single one of those *fucking* things."

Wiping spit from his eye, the doctor smirked. His hand flitted up fast, a flash of metal and plastic, and stopped at Ian's neck. A syringe poked from the skin, the doctor's thumb on the plunger, ready to push down.

"Do you know how tiny a worm egg is?" he whispered, his thin lips spreading into a smile. "I push this, and you're infested with a child of God."

Ian stopped, breathing hard. His eyes shot down to the needle in his neck.

"Doctor, please," Jamie pleaded. "The experiment is over. This is out of control."

He shook his head. "No, my dear. This is going *exactly* as intended." His thumb began to depress the plunger.

Ian swiped at the doctor's arm, kicked him in the groin, and lunged forward. The needle stuck out of his neck as he tackled the older man to the laboratory floor. He wrapped his hands around the doctor's neck and squeezed hard.

Jamie and I raced to help him, conscious that one of my arms was of no use. I collapsed onto the doctor's legs to keep him from struggling, and Jamie pulled the syringe from Ian's neck. She thrust it into the doctor's chest and pushed down on the plunger.

"Is this what you intended?" she asked.

Dr Taylor stopped struggling, choking under the pressure of Ian's meaty hands. "What have you done?"

Ian leaned back and let go of the doctor's neck with a deep

sigh. Thanking Jamie, he stood, and helped me up. The doctor, hand to his chest, scrambled to the nearest wall, and stared at Jamie. Drool gushing from his mouth, he choked, *"What have you done?"*

"Sorry, doc." Jamie shrugged. "Enough is enough." Turning to me and Ian, she said, "We have to kill those things."

"How?" I asked.

She nodded towards her flamethrower. "I made this. I'm sure I can make another one. We can hunt those fucking things. Kill them before they find their way down the mountain."

I hadn't even thought about that possibility. My own survival was enough to think about, but Jamie was right. If those things made it back down the mountain—to civilisation—who knew what sort of damage they could do?

Ian and I swallowed hard and agreed. We headed from the laboratory, following Jamie, and leaving the doctor to ponder his fate.

Henry lay still, unwilling to blink or breathe, as the worms coiled towards him. He could smell them, their thick fleshy skin reeking of metallic puss, dripping in blood and guts and skin. Until Gretel had been so callously devoured, he'd thought he was safe. He'd thought they were all safe, the acolytes. He was part of bringing them to life, feeding them and their children.

Now he wasn't sure, but as he lay in the hallway, the giant worms sniffing at him, clawing at him with their blackened teeth, he held his breath.

I'm being tested. My faith.

He opened his eyes.

The worms seemed to notice, bringing their eyeless faces to his. He breathed out, slow and gentle, and stared into them. The worms seemed to stare back, motionless above him. Remnants of one of the guests skin splatted to the floor next to his face, and Henry faltered, grimacing.

One of the worms leaned in closer, emitting a low growl that Henry thought impossible. If this was a test, he was failing. Breathing hard, he sat up, and the worms moved away from him. Not in fear, but out of respect. The way they bowed their heads to him, teeth scraping gently at his body as though they needed him.

In the next instant, their attention was turned to the wall. To the men hiding in the room behind it. And they began their attack, with Henry crying, "Go! Destroy them!" *Yes,* he thought. *I am a true acolyte.*

As the worms plunged their way through the wall to devour the remaining guests, Henry stepped through the rubble of the building's entrance. He had to find Dr White Coat—*Taylor*, he reminded himself. *He deserves respect, after all.*

He had to tell him the news.

Dr Taylor clutched at his neck, cursing his arrogance. The trio had left him there to die, and he wasn't sure they were wrong. Jamie had fucked him over for reasons unknown, and there were minuscule worm eggs floating in his bloodstream.

Searching his memory for notes and clues, sifting through

his research, he stood and raced to a computer. He had to find a way to remove the eggs before they hatched. Before he turned into one of their guests—a fleshy blob on the ground, a host for one of his gods.

There had to be something in his research that could help him. He'd studied these things more than anyone else on the planet. He knew them inside and out. What they loved. What they hated. What they needed to survive.

Rifling through digital files and folders, he found nothing. The entry point on his neck was beginning to itch, and he knew what that meant. The eggs were inside him, floating around, waiting to hatch. They'd find their way through his bloodstream, burrow into his body. And feed.

"Fuck!" He swiped at his desk and sent the computer crashing to the floor. "Jamie, you *fucking bitch!*"

Staring down at his smashed computer, the screen cracked, the monitor beginning to steam, held his neck once more. If he couldn't get the eggs out, he might be able to—

Yes. That's it.

He ran from the laboratory, with one destination in mind.

I felt like Sigourney Weaver's sidekick, watching Ian strap on a makeshift flamethrower. He and Jamie resembled ghostbusters or something, and I cradled my injured arm like the character everyone expects to die. And quick, in the first thirty minutes of film. By the end, nobody would remember me.

Yet, Ian kept looking over at me, asking if I was okay. I told him I was fine, and he threw me the car keys.

"What am I supposed to do with these?" I asked. "I'm not leaving you."

He gave a half-smile and said, "Just in case something happens to me."

Jamie finished strapping herself into her own flamethrower, and cleared her throat. "We know there are five of them out there. I say we head back to the guest house and start there. They'll probably be looking for a food source of some kind." She looked at me with sad eyes.

"The café?" I asked.

She shook her head. "These worms feed on fat," she said. "Remember?"

Ian stepped between me and Jamie, raising the barrel of his flamethrower as a warning. "We're not using bait."

I raised my eyebrows at the realisation. Took a deep breath. "Hey, Ian… it's okay. It's a good way to get them all in one place together."

"No way," Ian said, matter-of-factly. "I'm not letting that happen." He turned to face me, lowered his weapon, and stepped close. "I *just* found you. I'm not losing you."

"I—"

Sweaty lips connected to mine, stopping me. It had been so long I almost didn't recognise what was happening. Ian was soft and gentle, but passionate. Pushing himself against me, and wrapping a meaty hand around the back of my head.

"We can find another way," he whispered, pulling back. Setting me free.

Jamie tapped Ian on the shoulder, drawing his attention. "We have to figure something out."

"We could set a trap," I suggested. "Is there a garden facility here? Fertiliser, that kind of thing?"

Her eyes lit up, following my train of thought. "There is."

"Well, worms like soil. And *I* like fertiliser. I can work with that." Smiling wide, I kissed Ian once more, and said to Jamie, "Show me the way."

We exited into the fading mountain light, Jamie leading us to the garden centre.

"You like fertiliser? What does that even mean?" Ian asked.

"I work in the film industry. Explosives expert."

Ian scoffed and exhaled deeply. "Thank god."

The worms were nowhere in sight, and we scrambled to the garden centre. I was hit with the stench of soil and plants and, my favourite, fertiliser. One of the best, and most accessible, ingredients for an explosive. Looking around the centre, I smiled.

"We're in luck," I said. "There's a ton of it."

"What else do you need?" Ian asked.

I gave them a list, and Jamie seemed to know where the other items would be. Diesel was a key ingredient, and she raced off somewhere to find some. Ian and I got started grabbing bags of fertiliser.

Outside, I heard the rumblings of the worms, scouring for food or fat or whatever it was they wanted. Looking out the window of the garden centre, I saw them coming to us. Fast. Their sense of smell must have been incredible. It didn't help that my armpits were dripping in sweat. Ian's too.

"Where is Jamie with that diesel?" I searched for her, though had no idea where she was coming from.

With the worms coiling along the grass to us—all five of them—I knew we didn't have long.

Come on, Jamie!

Ian stepped to the door of the garden centre, kicked it open, and moved outside. His flamethrower at the ready, he waited. The worms came closer, almost like a coordinated attack, in a semi-circle pattern. There would be no way through, even if that's what we'd intended to do.

While Ian switched on his flamethrower, a small orange fire blazing from the end of the barrel, I kept working on the fertiliser. Just needed Jamie to bring the diesel. Where the fuck was she?

The worms were on us, segments of their bodies curling through the grass towards us, screeching. Ian screamed back at them and pulled the trigger on his weapon. A stream of fire unleashed through the air, and Ian shifted left and right in a slow, steady pattern. The fire licked at the worms, and Ian raced to get closer.

The worms' high-pitched screams were like music to my ears, and I stopped to watch Ian burning the creatures—their tail-ends curling, burning. As he repeated his left-to-right pattern, a worm from the side came at him, knocking him to his feet.

I cried, "Ian!"

Another worm turned towards me, headed for the garden centre, and crashed through the building like it was dirt. Pieces of the roof and the walls flew apart, and I fell backwards into the incomplete fertiliser bomb.

Where the fuck is Jamie?

With Ian down, but still squeezing the trigger and sending flames into the air, I was on my own. The worm lifted its body high in the air, like a snake, and brought its face down to me. Its breath was hot and pus-like, the spike-teeth opening up to eat me.

I screamed and rolled out of the way as it struck. Hitting the fertiliser and shaking its head, the worm searched for me. I was up, on my feet, and running through the garden centre. The worm snaked behind me, and I tipped a shelf of plants to slow it down. The worm moved straight past it, gaining on me fast.

Zipping through an aisle of ferns, I ducked out of sight and double-backed to Ian. We'd be stronger together than separate. I saw him, sitting up, but on the defensive, and wondered how long his flame would last. The tank on his back must have been almost empty by now.

The worms gathered around him, burned and injured, but still very much alive. One of them whipped its tail at Ian and smacked him in the face. He lost his hold on the trigger and the flame vanished.

I raced to him, my own worm right on my arse, and grabbed the barrel and trigger from Ian as he recovered. The worm tail was coiling around him now, and I stamped on it as I squeezed the trigger. "*Fuck you!*" I squeezed again, but the flame was smaller this time, and my fears were now a reality.

Ian tried to stand, but the worms had him now, wrapping around him and lifting him into the air. He shrugged off the flamethrower, letting it hit the earth. One worm bit at another, fighting over who would eat the fat, and I felt a thick, viscous flesh around my own torso.

Looking down, I spun in time to see the worm that had been chasing me now wrapping itself around me. I cursed Jamie for taking so fucking long and pulled the flamethrower to me. Squeezed the trigger once more.

It was small, but it was enough, firing straight into the creature's mouth. The orange flame burned through the worm's head, glowing a pinkish-brown as it did so. It dropped me hard and I landed on my injured arm with a shriek.

I hoped the flamethrower had one more use to it, and as I saw Ian being devoured into a worm's mouth, I ran to the worm in question and squeezed again.

The flame was short, but hot, and it recoiled from the burning sensation. I pressed the barrel to its body, pushed hard, and squeezed again. The worm screeched so loud my ears bled, but it did the job. Ian was on the ground, covered in saliva. His face scratched and bleeding from the worm's teeth.

But he was alive.

"Come on!" I called to him.

He got to his feet as another worm moved to him. He jumped over its body and came to me. Just as he reached me, another worm tail struck us, and sent us through the air. I landed hard on my back, smacking against the cool concrete flooring of the garden centre. Ian was next to me, barely conscious, and bleeding. He'd landed on a broken piece of bamboo, and it jutted through his leg.

"We have to go," I said to him, and helped him up.

The worms were around us now, our only option was to retreat backward.

Ian was on his feet, coughing and spluttering from his injuries. We hobbled as fast as we could, but the worms—as burned as they were—came for us again.

"I got the diesel!" Jamie's voice came through the door. She carried two jerrycans of the stuff, her flamethrower still on her back.

We bumped into her, the jerrycans falling with a loud clang. The worms recoiled at the sound—only for a moment—and lunged at us. I dove out of the way, pulling Ian down with me. Jamie dodged in another direction, scrambling for a jerrycan.

She grabbed it and ran for the fertiliser, ducking and weaving as a worm struck out at her, its tail flicking out like a tongue. She stumbled a little, but kept going, her eyes unmoving from the target.

As though the worms understood what was happening, three of them turned on her, making chase. A sense of relief flowed through me, as selfish as that was, at the thought of the worms leaving me alone.

One was still on us, though, and its mouth came down for my fat. I put a defensive arm up—as useless as I knew it was—and the worm took it down the throat. Suckling on my flesh for a moment, tasting me. Ian, recovered from his earlier fall, bolted away as my arm sank further into the worm. I could feel its teeth closing around me. I pulled hard to try and break free but the suction kept me inside.

"Fucking let go of me!" I yelled, and pulled as hard as I could.

A flash of metal from the corner of my eye.

Ian screaming. Ian thrusting hard into the worm's side.

Its mouth came off me with a high-pitched screech, and I saw Ian ripping garden shears from the worm. He plunged them in again, twisting and pushing hard until globs of red blood oozed down it's body.

Now free, I stood, and wrapped my arms around the creature to steady it as best I could while Ian stabbed again and again and again. The worm struggled against us, but it was getting weaker. Its head bowed, the screeching now a low howl.

"Keep going!" I cried, and Ian obliged.

As the worm's head came down further, it's hot, pussy breath on my face, I wrapped my arms around it, and pulled down.

"Ian!" I grabbed his attention, and he got my meaning.

Tearing the shears from the worm once more, he came to the head, and used the shears like a saw. The metal blade grinded against the rough worm skin, but he broke through with a wet pop. Blood spurted across my face as he sawed, sawed, sawed, the worm struggling and coiling and hissing.

Its head plopped to the floor with a dull splat, and the worm body fell to the ground.

I panted and puffed, and looked at Ian, who stabbed the shears into the worm one more time.

"We just killed a worm god," I huffed.

Ian nodded, and wiped sweat and blood from his eyes. "There are three left. Jamie needs our help."

Scanning the garden centre, I found the other worms easy enough. Coiling and snaking their way towards where I'd laid the fertiliser mix. Jamie just had to add the diesel and then set the fucking thing on fire. We had better not be nearby when it blew.

I spotted Jamie, hiding behind a row of plants, jerrycan heavy in her arms. Our eyes met, she was pleading for help. I didn't know what I could do—maybe create a distraction? I remembered her suggestion earlier, gulped hard at the prospect. It was time.

I'm the bait.

Raising my arms high, I cried out to the worms, "Hey! Big, juicy, fat man here! Come eat me you cunts!" The worms shifted their attention to me, and I immediately regretted my bravery. "Fuck," I whispered, and ran.

With the weight I carried, I couldn't run very fast. The adrenaline helped, and even though I had no idea where I was going, my feet kept moving. Ian was beside me—I didn't have the energy to ask why, but I was glad to not be alone in that moment.

Risking a glance over my shoulder, I saw the worms giving chase. Saw Jamie scramble to the fertiliser mix and pour the diesel.

About fucking time!

We had to find a way to circle back. Get the worms right on the site. Ian threw his arm out to the side, catching my belly, and panted, "This way!"

I followed him, changing direction just as a worm bit down at me. It tasted air, but I'd felt the teeth at my neck. We'd gone down another aisle to double-back, the three worms descending on us fast.

Ian's hand clasped mine, and he pulled me along, faster than I could bare. I stumbled and tripped, bringing Ian down with me. The worms surrounded us, growling and groaning as their mouths came down.

I felt teeth pierce my abdomen, my legs. Felt my body tearing, the skin pulling in all directions. I screamed and screamed, and heard Ian doing the same. I managed a look over at Jamie, whose hands were clasped over her mouth, frozen in fear.

"*Do it!*" I yelled, screaming again as the teeth gnawed further into me.

Jamie gripped her flamethrower, finger pulsing at the trigger.

"I wouldn't do that." A voice came from behind her.

The worms stopped. Ripped their teeth from us. Left us bleeding and torn apart, and faced the voice.

Dr Taylor.

Henry was at his side, both unharmed. But the doctor looked different. Through the haze of the stabbing pains in my body, and the tears gushing from my eyes, I couldn't see him clearly. Just enough to identify a wide smile, yellowing teeth, and piercing eyes.

"Do... it..." Ian repeated my earlier command.

Jamie stared between the doctor, the worms, and us. Her

finger trembled on the trigger.

"Jamie…" I stuttered. "These things… can't… survive."

Dr Taylor approached his assistant, laid a hand on the flamethrower barrel, and encouraged her with his eyes to put it down. Somehow, for some reason, she obeyed. Lowered the barrel, released the trigger.

"That's it, my girl," he said. "That's it."

With the worms distracted—enamoured—by Dr Taylor, moving back towards him, I wiped my eyes a few times and blinked. Had to get a better look. That's when I saw it.

Jamie's trigger finger, shifting back, resting on the metal.

We didn't have long, of that, I was sure.

I managed to heave myself to my stomach. Crawled in the opposite direction like a soldier through the dirt, dragging my legs behind me.

"What are you doing?" Ian whispered.

"Come on!" I hissed back.

He did as I ordered, moaning and groaning from his own injuries. I felt myself growing weak, not just from exhaustion, but also from the blood flooding out of me.

"I have to say," Dr Taylor said to Jamie, "you will make a formidable acolyte. Henry is the first, and he's going to do great things. But you… you will be my right hand."

"*Your* right hand? What does that mean?" Jamie asked. "What's happened to your skin?"

"I must thank you, Jamie," he said. "For jabbing me in the neck like that. It forced me to think creatively."

Jamie stepped back as Ian and I crawled towards the back exit of the garden centre. I glanced back to see the worms coalescing around her—right on the fertiliser bomb. She just had to pull that trigger, and this would all be over.

Why is she waiting?

"I've come to realise something," Dr Taylor said. "Humans are… outdated."

"Outdated?" Jamie asked, confused.

Dr Taylor nodded. "It's time for a change of management."

"And these things"—she motioned a hand towards the worms—"are that change?"

"No, not them." Dr Taylor laughed and waved at the creatures, who were bowing down to him now. "Me."

"What happened to you? Why didn't the worm egg hatch and kill you, like the others?" Jamie asked.

"Like I said,"—Dr Taylor shrugged—"I got creative."

"I won't join you," Jamie said. "I can't."

"Come on, Jamie," Henry said, scratching at a pimple on his nose. "We're bringing in a new world order. Don't you wanna be part of that?"

Ian and I kept crawling, straining to hear their conversation. Praying she'd pull that fucking trigger and end this. We were at the back exit of the garden centre now, but I could feel the energy draining from me fast. A few more feet and I'd be clear of the blast radius, but I didn't know if we could make it.

"No," Jamie replied.

Her finger moved for the trigger, but a worm flicked its tail at her and she lost balance. Fumbling into the centre of the fertiliser, she grabbed for the flamethrower barrel. Dr Taylor raised a hand and the worms stopped. He walked to her and grabbed her by the scruff of her coat.

"I'm giving you a chance," he hissed.

Jamie breathed hard in his face and grabbed at him. "I'm giving *you* one last chance," she spat.

He laughed again and looked up at the worms. They still bowed, motionless, waiting for Dr Taylor's orders. Like he was *their* god, not the other way round. With one glance, they understood what he wanted, and sprang into action.

Lurching forward, their mouths stretched wide, they took Jamie into their mouths. Began ripping her apart.

Her screams echoed through the garden centre, but she didn't let go of Dr Taylor. As their teeth ripped her skin and flesh and bones, searched for organs, and slurped them down, she pulled Dr Taylor in close.

"We could have had it all," he whispered to her.

Through her screams, she felt through his pockets until she found what she needed. With the flamethrower out of arms reach, she had to think fast.

"You'll *never* have it all." She ripped his lighter from his pocket and lit the flame. Dr Taylor's eyes went wide—Henry's too—as she dropped it to the ground, the intense orange flame exploding through the garden centre, drowning out her final scream.

I covered my head with both hands, catching a glimpse of Ian doing the same, as the garden centre exploded behind us. The force of the blast sent us rolling across the grass, debris punching the earth around us. I managed a quick look at the wreck, not seeing any signs of life—worm, or otherwise—before the blood loss became too much.

Succumbing to the weakness, the world went black.

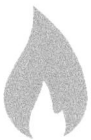

The fire had burned for hours before Arnie got the call. He and his colleagues had been playing cards at the firehouse—running drills, if anybody asked—when the call came in. Some concerned citizen had called it in, a fire up the mountain, they'd said.

They jumped into action, as they always did, and sped like motherfuckers all the way to the top. Arnie had heard about the place before, some weight loss retreat or something. The treatments up there were all hush hush, like they weren't just getting fancy liposuction. It didn't matter, the call had come in, and he and his crew would answer it.

The place was a shit show when they arrived. Cops and paramedics were also on the scene, waiting for them to hose the fire out.

Buildings had been torn to shreds, rubble and debris everywhere. He could tell it wasn't all from a fire, either. Something else had happened here.

When the fire was out, which was easy enough to do, Arnie saw what had caused it. An explosive. His instincts told him there was a real problem here. In all his years as a fireman, he'd seen some fucked up shit. A few bombs in his time, too. This one was elaborate. Designed to kill anything in the area.

Pieces of flesh were scattered about the place, it smelled like a crematorium, with ash and dust swirling in the air. Kneeling down, he picked up a piece of burned flesh, unable to tell what it had once been. It didn't smell human, though. A smell he unfortunately was familiar with.

"Spread out," he commanded his crew. "Help the cops search for survivors."

Arnie searched the area himself, too. They'd need to call in an investigator to find out what happened here, but until they arrived, he could try and find some answers. Rummaging through the rubble, he found a shoe. The foot was still in it.

"Fuck." He dropped it, conscious this was an active scene, and stood, hands on hips.

"Chief!" one of the crew, Johnson, called from beyond

the rear exit. Or, where it should have been. "We've got two survivors!"

Arnie raced through the rubble, seeing the two survivors mangled in the grass. The wounds were pretty deep, they'd both lost a lot of blood. Neither was moving, but he confirmed Johnson's declaration by putting two fingers to their necks.

The pulses were so faint he wasn't sure how much longer they'd last.

"Get them out of here," he called to a paramedic.

They rushed over, gurneys at the ready, and did whatever it was they did to keep people alive. Through the chaos of the scene, he saw a group of people—cops, and some his crew—heading into an untouched building a few yards away. He followed them in, sure there was something crazy in there by the way everyone stood, frozen and staring. He was surprised to see it was just a pool filled with mud.

So, what are they staring at?

Gazing down into the pool, he saw the surface bubbling. As he stepped closer, he was held back by a pair of hands. Looking back, he saw an older man, covered in dirt and blood. Through the mess, Arnie made out an odd pattern on his skin, and his deep black eyes.

"What—"

"Shhhh," the man whispered, and cocked his head. "Watch."

Turning back to the pool, he gasped as a giant creature emerged, globs of mud dripping back to the pool as it roared into the room.

It was a worm, but it had a gaping mouth of folded jaws, black spikes for teeth, two giant red eyes, pinkish-brown flesh. Curled wings sopped with mud began to stretch, dragon-like.

Arnie struggled against the man, his strength deceptive.

"What the hell is this? Who are you?"

The older man laughed, and hissed, "I am a soldier of Yul. The worm god."

"You're fucking crazy, man!" Arnie struggled again, but it was no use. He looked into the worm's eyes, captivated. And he knew. He knew the old man told the truth. This creature wasn't just a worm. It was a god.

His god.

"His children are all dead," the older man said, his voice sullen. "But we can rebuild. It's time to serve your god."

Arnie nodded, and felt himself falling into the mud, heard the splashes of the others as they willingly jumped in.

Dr Taylor needed a new name. He wasn't the same person he was the day before. Jamie's act of betrayal had turned into the greatest gift a human could receive. With the knowledge of the worm egg growing inside him, waiting to hatch, he'd run, desperate and terrified, to Yul, who lay dormant in the mud pool.

The giant worm god needed to recover after seventy thousand years frozen in the permafrost. It had told him what he needed to do, and he'd done it. He'd learned a few days later that the mud was where it laid its eggs, and that the eggs needed a host to thrive.

He was happy to oblige.

And when he'd become infested with one of Yul's children, he remembered what Yul had told him: *I am Yul, the honest worm. I am at the beginning and end of lives.* Yul, the eternally graceful and humble God, had granted a favour. In His infinite wisdom, Yul changed Dr Taylor into a true servant of the Deep. He allowed the egg to harvest inside him without destroying the human shell.

He was now a living host, the first in seven millennia.

Yul had plans, and a human servant would help.

And he was happy to oblige.

The two men had survived—a miracle if he'd ever seen one—and had taken their shallow breaths as a sign. Those two were true warriors, and Yul had a gift for them; he was confident they'd be changed when they woke in the hospital. Perhaps even slimmer. If that's what Yul wanted for them.

With the fireman and the others serving Yul below the surface of the mud, Dr Taylor pondered his new name. He wasn't cocky enough to go all out and call himself Jesus. Even if he was technically the son of a god. The answer came to him like a lightning bolt from somewhere deep inside him. From the worm squirming around his guts.

Xol. The virtuous worm.

Xol. His new name.

He was happy to oblige.

Xol made his way through the ruined mountain retreat and called for help. A young paramedic raced towards him, asking if he was okay and what happened and calling other people over. Xol was put onto a gurney. Rushed to an ambulance.

Yul had given him instructions: *Be there when your brothers—Eir and Akka—wake up. Then we take the world.* He was happy to oblige.

ABOUT THE AUTHOR

David-Jack Fletcher is a gore-hound. He loves body horror and extreme horror, but equally, he is interested in the depths of our fears. These are often driven by isolation, loneliness, paranoia, anxiety, depression, loss, and an array of other factors. A gay man himself, David-Jack writes from the perspective of characters he understands; his experiences of social stigma and discrimination often drive the concepts in his stories. He likes to make visible the enduring intolerance toward—and sometimes *within*—the LGBTQI+ community and enjoys writing characters whose physicality does not meet gay stereotypes. He writes about older men and hairy, burly bears and explores the real-world issues these types of characters might face.

His debut novella, *The Haunting of Harry Peck*, was a 2022 Amazon International Bestseller in several horror categories, and his bestselling sophomore novel, *Raven's Creek*, won the 2023 Bookstagram Award for LGBTQI Novel of the Year. David-Jack also owns and operates the queer horror publisher Slashic Horror Press.

He resides in the Hunter Valley, NSW, Australia, with his burly, hairy bear husband and their two dogs.

ACKNOWLEDGEMENTS

As always, I couldn't have written any of these stories without the encouragement of my husband, Paul. I'd like to also thank all at Lethe Press for their belief in my writing and the weird stories spewing from my brain.

Most of all, I'd like to acknowledge all the enduring hatred and intolerance experienced by my peers in the LGBTQ+ community. Hell really is other people, and I hope my book, as gross as it is, has enabled a short reprieve for you, the reader.

www.ingramcontent.com/pod-product-compliance
Ingram Content Group UK Ltd.
Pitfield, Milton Keynes, MK11 3LW, UK
UKHW040730050525
5762UKWH00032B/314